Lucinda Hare was born ...
years roaming the local woods with her dogs, imagining worlds where wolves, knights and dragons battled in deep forests. She and her husband share their Edinburgh home with an ever-changing number of rescue animals, ranging from cats, dogs, rabbits and guinea pigs to escaped battery hens on the run. She specializes in cruelty cases and animals with behavioural problems, and friends often comment that she can weave magic and talk to the animals – a real life 'whisperer'! Her debut novel, *The Dragon Whisperer*, was shortlisted for the 2010 Royal Mail Scottish Book Awards.

Praise for *The Dragon Whisperer*:

'It made me laugh, cry and remember exactly what's so special about the time when you or your child lived in hope of finding a dragon of your own' Amanda Craig, *Sunday Times*

'In this sweeping novel of fantasy, action, adventure and coming of age, the reader will find beautiful dragons, a feisty heroine, and epic battles . . . This is a world that will immerse its reader in its magnificence and danger – compelling reading'
Write Away

'It's going to be a huge hit' Jill Murphy, *The Bookbag*

'What Harry Potter did for wizardry,
this book does for tales of dragons' *Chicklish*

Also by Lucinda Hare:

'I urge anyone aged nine or over to snap this up . . .
A battle-dragon of a book!' *Fantasy Book Review*

'This is in my top five Young Adult books of the year . . . it will be the hottest thing on the YA circuit' *Falcata Times*

'I think *The Dragon Whisperer* is the best book I have ever read (I have read a lot of books – in our house, we have about twelve thousand!). I think the way the words are written sounds like magic' *Rachel, aged 13*

'I haven't been able to put it down!' *Jessica, aged 13*

'I cannot wait for the next book to come out' *Sarah, aged 10*

Lucinda Hare

Book Two of the Dragonsdome Chronicles

CORGI

FLIGHT TO DRAGON ISLE
A CORGI BOOK 978 0552 56023 8

A Random House Group Company
Corgi edition published 2011

1 3 5 7 9 10 8 6 4 2

The Random House Group Limited supports the Forest Stewardship Council® (FSC®), the leading international forest certification organization. All our titles that are printed on Greenpeace approved FSC® certified paper carry the FSC® logo. Our paper procurement policy can be found at www.rbooks.co.uk/environment.

Set in 11/16pt Sabon

Corgi Books are published by Random House Children's Books,
61–63 Uxbridge Road, London W5 5SA

www.**kidsatrandomhouse**.co.uk

Addresses for companies within The Random House Group Limited can be found at:
www.randomhouse.co.uk/offices.htm

THE RANDOM HOUSE GROUP Limited Reg. No. 954009
A CIP catalogue record for this book is available from the British Library.

Printed and bound in Great Britain by CPI Bookmarque, Croydon, CRO 4TD

Dedicated to the SAS
and the British Armed Forces

Chapter One

Dive, Dive, Dive . . .

'T minus two and counting . . .'

'Ground crew, clear the pads . . . clear the pads . . .'

Red landing lights turned green as the flight of Imperials and Vipers retracted their claws and spread their wings in readiness.

'Stormcracker, Stormcracker, you are cleared for immediate takeoff.'

'Acknowledged, Dragonsdome. Lift off . . . lift off . . .'

'Strapped in?' Quenelda turned to Root who was fiddling with his flying harness. 'It'll be fun!'

Root mumbled unconvincingly as Two Gulps and You're Gone launched into the air, but by then it was too late.

It was a day of yellow haar, the suffocating fog that crept in from the sea. Its smoky coils lay thickly over the loch so that only the jagged snow-capped teeth of the mountains to the north and south of the Sorcerers Glen were visible from the air. In the freezing brilliance of the sapphire sky, a military flight of twenty Imperial Black battledragons of the III First Born, accompanied by three wings of smaller, swifter Vipers, took off from Dragonsdome.

At their apex flew the Earl Rufus DeWinter, Commander of the Stealth Dragon Services, the SDS, on Stormcracker Thundercloud III, his magnificent battle-dragon. At his starboard wing-tip flew a much smaller flame-coloured Sabretooth with stubby wings and a crooked tail, ridden by a young girl and a gnome boy. The Earl's daughter, Quenelda, and her companion, Root, were on their way to Dragon Isle; an unusual achievement since only the SDS and those of royal blood were normally allowed to set foot on that fortress island. But while every other young lady in the Seven Sea Kingdoms dreamed of going to court, ever since she could remember, Quenelda had wanted to follow in her famous father's footsteps and enrol at the SDS Battle Academy on Dragon Isle. It was not only this very peculiar ambition, nor even the fact that Quenelda wore boy's clothes and had flown battledragons with her father since the age of three, that made her a very special young lady. There was another reason – a secret that only her friend, Root, her father, the Earl Rufus, and his dragonmaster, Tangnost Bearhugger, shared. They all believed that Quenelda was a Dragon Whisperer, which meant that she alone could talk to dragons.

It was because of this secret magical heritage that Quenelda, flying her battledragon, Two Gulps and You're Gone, and her esquire, Root, on gentle Chasing the Stars, had recently defeated a rogue dragon belonging to the Grand Master of the Sorcerers Guild. The crazed dragon had tried to kill the Earl Rufus at the winter Royal Joust.

Everyone save Quenelda thought that the injured dragon had simply been driven to madness by its wounds. But she knew differently. Hearing its inner thoughts, she had revealed to her father and the Queen's Constable, Sir Gharad Mowbray, that the dragon had been trained to kill, was a predator at heart despite its harmless appearance. The question, if she was correct, was how and why. The answer was chilling: the Earl and Sir Gharad had agreed that the only explanation was Maelstrom Magic, an ancient and dangerous dark power long forbidden by the Sorcerers Guild. But why the Grand Master would breed such a dangerous and treacherous creature was not so certain.

Quenelda believed that the dragon's hidden purpose was to kill her father, but the Earl would not accept that the Grand Master, Lord Hugo Mandrake – his mentor and friend from childhood – had knowingly dabbled in Dark Magic, let alone wished to kill him. He believed that the Lord Hugo had simply strayed in his pursuit of knowledge, had allowed his passion for breeding dragons to cloud his judgement. Maelstrom Magic was notoriously unstable and difficult to control, and that alone could explain the rogue dragon's dark thoughts and behaviour . . . True or false, it could not be proved until the Grand Master returned from his estates in the north; until the Earl was able to determine his friend's true purpose without revealing his daughter's unique abilities.

In the meantime, Root and Quenelda had been sworn to silence. If it became known that the most powerful man at the heart of the ruling Sorcerers Guild was a Warlock, panic would ensue, and law and order break down. The Third Hobgoblin War was going badly, very badly indeed, and now more than ever the Earl needed to maintain the sense of calm and security among the people.

Recently, the SDS Commander believed, there were

signs that the thirteen hobgoblin tribes had united, posing the greatest threat to the Seven Sea Kingdoms since the Mage Wars two thousand years before. An attack on the Howling Glen fortress led by the first hobgoblin War Lord Galtekerion, had confirmed his belief; and it had only just been thwarted by Bark Oakley, the Earl's chief scout and Root's father, who had lost his life raising the alarm. As a hard year's campaigning drew to a close and winter blizzards set in early, the Earl had decided to launch a daring pre-emptive strike against the hobgoblins at their breeding grounds on the Westering Isles, hoping to catch the creatures just as they were emerging from hibernation in late spring, weak and disoriented. Strike – before they could breed and swarm. Strike – using the ice shelf which had crept so far south that the long-range Imperials and battlegalleons of the SDS could now reach the remote Westering Isles.

Ignoring his physician's protestations that his wounds suffered during the Battle of the Howling Glen and at the Royal Joust needed time to heal before he got back in the saddle, the Earl was travelling to Dragon Isle to inspect preparations for the coming spring campaign. And, by special permission of the Queen as a reward for their great bravery, he was taking his daughter, Quenelda, and her esquire, Root, with him. Root had had to leave his own dragon, Chasing the Stars, stabled at Dragonsdome. The fortress at Dragon Isle was no place for the placid herbivore. An unruly battledragon might fancy such a succulent morsel!

'Wind three knots and rising. Vector heading north-northwest by twenty . . .' The Earl Rufus DeWinter's voice crackled over Quenelda's helmet. 'Five leagues and closing. ETA ten bells.'

'Dragon Isle!' Quenelda whispered, her breath frosting the inside of her visor.

Dragon Isle . . . Two Gulps and You're Gone echoed, the battledragon's rising excitement matching her own. He had not returned to his home roost on Dragon Isle since he had been badly injured in the war.

Normally such severely injured battledragons were put down, but Quenelda, using her extraordinary skill of dragon whispering, had helped the Earl's dragonmaster, the dwarf Tangnost Bearhugger, nurse Two Gulps back to health – an unheard-of achievement. Quenelda had explained to the wounded Sabretooth how Tangnost was going to mend his broken bones and stop infection from making his tail drop off. If she hadn't been able to calm the unpredictable and bad-tempered battledragon as the dwarf set the fractured bones, they and Tangnost's apprentice, Root Oakley, would have all been reduced to three pyramids of ash on the floor. Their success had led the Earl to give Quenelda Two Gulps as her own.

We are close . . . I can hear my brothers and sisters . . .

Quenelda too could faintly hear the whisper of dragons on patrol above and around them as they flew in and out of range. 'We're nearly there,' she said, turning to Root.

The gnome grinned back at her, not even asking how she knew when, in the freezing fog, they could barely see beyond the tail of the dragon in front. He had long since known that Quenelda had a far keener sense of smell, sight and hearing than any other person in the Kingdoms.

Then came the call that Root had been dreading.

'On my mark,' the Earl's deep voice commanded.

'Ready?' Turning in her saddle, Quenelda touched her esquire's arm reassuringly. 'You'll manage. You've done really well. Honestly, there's nothing to worry about. We're only at three thousand strides. You won't have to bail out.'

Root nodded and tried to look braver than he felt, then closed his visor and then his eyes. Ever since Quenelda learned that she was to accompany her father on an inspection of preparations for the coming battle, she had been teaching Root as much as she could about the history of the SDS and Dragon Isle. While endless blizzards raged, they had spent days in Dragonsdome's ancient Circular Library looking through dusty books and chronicles while Quenelda helped her esquire with his reading and writing. And when they weren't studying they had been flying.

In particular, she and Root had been practising diving and deploying dragonwings – 'in case they had to bail out', she explained kindly, while they both knew what she really meant was 'in case Root falls out of his saddle'. They had to be prepared for anything, Quenelda argued, as she demonstrated for the third time how the wings worked. She wanted their first military flight to be perfect.

Root gulped and nervously checked his flying harness again. His first attempt at 'spreading his wings' had ended in disaster, with him hanging helplessly upside down from the branches of a huge pine tree, wrapped in his wings as tightly and cosily as any sleeping bat. The next day he had taken a cold unplanned dip in the loch, having narrowly missed the sails and rigging of a merchant galleon. And then . . .

'Dive, dive, dive . . .' At his signal, Stormcracker, the Earl's massive Imperial Black, rolled ninety degrees to starboard and peeled away, plunging down through the fog below. Root had barely time to draw breath before the world tipped and they were dropping like a stone.

The wind sang in Quenelda's ears as they plummeted down in perfect formation with the SDS. Her spirit soared. It seemed the most natural thing to do – to swoop down and dance with the dragons. This was what she was born to do, where she truly belonged.

Dragon Isle, Dragon Isle, Dragon Isle . . . The name of the fabled fortress thumped through her veins like a heartbeat. She was going home to Dragon Isle!

Standing virtually upright in his stirrups behind her, eyes closed tight, knuckles white, Root hung onto the plunging dragon for dear life. As the force of their descent threatened to pluck him from his saddle, he wondered if Quenelda would even notice that he was gone. Despite his full-face visor and helmet, the wind shrieked shrilly in his ears and his eyes watered in the cold. The speed stole his breath away and left him gasping for air. He gritted his teeth, feeling his lips peel back against his gums. The flying harness that tethered him to the saddle dug painfully into his shoulder blades and waist; his stomach churned and his neck ached. In moments the flight was lost from view as if devoured by a giant dragon's smoking mouth. Root couldn't stand this much longer: his arms were burning with the effort of hanging onto the saddle horn. Then, with a crack, Two Gulps' stubby wings spread and caught the wind, and they levelled out with a thumping jolt scant strides above the cold sea.

'Seven furlongs and closing . . .'

Dragon Isle sprang into three-dimensional view over the Earl's navigator's right-eye lens, runes and marks rapidly scrolling down in a burst of information. He glanced at his forearm vambrace display to check his co-ordinates. Satisfied, he lifted his head. 'Vector approach confirmed and holding.'

'Acknowledged,' the Earl replied.

Within heartbeats, a flicker of blue lit up the fog around Stormcracker, enveloping the Earl and his huge battledragon in a fine latticework of fire. The next second, creeping tendrils wrapped around Two Gulps like tree roots questing for water. Root felt the hairs on the back of his neck stand up – the iridescent light was crawling all over him as if searching for something. In front of him, Quenelda's hair radiated about her helmet like a golden dandelion. Vivid sparks danced in front of the boy's eyes, making him squeal.

Quenelda turned to him with an apologetic grin. 'Sorry, I forgot to warn you. Papa told me. I think we've just passed through a nexus.'

Root looked blank.

'A nexus,' she explained, 'is a defensive shield. They are cast around Dragon Isle like huge invisible nets.'

'Sorcery . . .' Root breathed. 'So they know we're here?'

Quenelda nodded. 'They know. Look behind you.'

Root turned in the saddle. He looked to his right – *starboard*, he hastily reminded himself. Then he looked to port. He shrugged. 'Where?'

Quenelda raised her eyes and pointed a finger. Root looked up. Three battlewings of Vampire dragons in close formation were silently escorting them in. Root hadn't seen or heard a thing.

'What?' His mouth fell open. 'When did they appear?'

Quenelda laughed. 'Oh, about three leagues out, probably before we even passed through the outer nexus.'

Within moments, great jagged spikes of black rock reared up out of the sea all about the flight, bristling with crossbows and catapults set on narrow gantries.

'There!' Quenelda pointed as pinpricks of light glimmered like stars through the fog. As they drew closer, growing pools of yellow light burned through the mist, becoming brighter by the heartbeat.

'Stormcracker, Stormcracker . . .' The flight tower crackled into life. 'This is Seadragon Tower. You are cleared to land in the east lower cavern, vector heading zero six one.'

'Dragon Tower, Dragon Tower,' the Earl Rufus responded. 'ETA minus five and counting. Stormcracker out.'

The Earl's flight, followed by Quenelda, realigned their angle of approach. The fog thinned. Quenelda forgot to breathe. Behind her Root gasped.

Soaring up in front of them, built into the combs and carved out of the coal-black cliffs, was the lair of the SDS, guardians of the Seven Sea Kingdoms. Countless blazing braziers and lanterns picked out its imposingly high towers. Vast cliff battlements, spiralling stairways, cliff dragonpads, buttresses and watch towers climbed the sides of the cliffs up and up towards the great castle hidden in the mists far above.

Dragon Isle!

Chapter Two

Dragon Isle

'Root! Root! Come *on*!' Quenelda was becoming impatient. '*Come on!*' She stamped her foot in frustration. 'We'll be late! You can't possible walk up every stair. There are ten thousand steps to the top of the tower. You won't arrive till next week.'

Root groaned. He knew what she said was true. He had already tried once before, counting one thousand, three hundred and two before his legs had given out on him, and as a result they had both missed a patrol briefing. Still . . . He glared, whether at Quenelda or at the porting disc he wasn't quite sure, and then gave in gracelessly. 'Oh, very well,' he grumbled.

This was the last day of their visit before returning to Dragonsdome in time for the Yule festivities at the Royal Court. In three hectic days they had accompanied the SDS Commander as he toured the barracks, the forges, the armour pits and the roosts, talking to his men and watching them train for the approaching late winter campaign. The two of them had also been fleetingly shown around the cavernous flight hangars and dragonpads, and the harbour caverns crammed with battlegalleons. But these covered only a tiny fraction of this vast island fortress, and to Quenelda's deep disappointment the Earl had no plans on this brief trip to visit the castle where the men of the SDS learned the art and strategy of warfare.

For as long as she could remember, Quenelda had wanted to enrol at the Battle Academy and become a Dragon Lord – those elite few Battle Mages who flew Imperial Blacks. Since the century of its founding, the seven peoples of the Sea Kingdoms had sent the best of their young to learn to fight their common foe, the hobgoblins, at this academy. But young ladies, tradition held, simply couldn't fly dragons, let alone fiery-tempered, unpredictable battledragons. And they weren't capable of Battle Magic. *They should pursue more . . . feminine pursuits*, Quenelda thought with a sneer. *Like . . . like sewing tapestries and dancing*. Well, she *was* a young lady *and* she could fly as if born to it. And one day soon, Quenelda swore, she too would be a Dragon Lord like her father, and this was her first chance to see what that would entail.

Unfortunately for Root, the denizens of the vast

fortress moved about by using porting stones – discs carved with runes and imbued with sorcery that could whisk you from one point to another. Root hated the porting stones: they made him sick, just as flying used to, but Quenelda would never forgive him if they missed a tour of the Command in Control, the CIC – the operational heart of Dragon Isle. Training exercises were already underway: they had seen hundreds of dragons flying over the loch. Back on active duty, Tangnost too was out there somewhere, training rookie Bonecrackers and troll Marines from the Sea Reaver regiment. There had been neither sight nor sound of him since before the jousts, when he and his raw recruits were transferred to Dragon Isle for full-scale exercises with a hundred thousand veterans. Both Quenelda and Root missed him dearly and hoped to see him before they left.

'CIC,' Quenelda said clearly.

There was a sensation of tingling warmth. Root felt his knees buckle, and groaned. The rock about them blurred, then streaked, and the world turned bright white. Root's stomach followed as an afterthought.

'Ugghhhh . . .' His protesting wail died away.

Suddenly they stopped, and Root's knees gave way

again. He felt sick, putting out a hand to steady himself as the world shuddered into focus about them – to reveal a large circular chamber shrouded in semi-darkness. Feeling wobbly, smothering a protesting belch from his stomach, Root followed Quenelda off the porting stone and into the operational centre of the SDS.

A quiet murmur rose up around them in the softly lit tower as they stood there, open-mouthed. Revolving spheres and three-dimensional displays hung and moved and spun about them while sorcerers at their centre stood or sat, touching or dragging or rotating the flowing, merging magical light . . . The massive stone walls of the tower were inset with ancient runes and Quenelda could feel the protective power of Battle Magic close about them. She and Root both jumped as the voices of pilots and navigators out on exercises filled the tower.

'Red Leader, Red Leader, this is red two . . .'

'On approach, vector three niner one . . .'

'Come . . .' The Earl beckoned the pair over to the centre of the room, where a group of armoured Dragon Lords were studying a three-dimensional display of the Sorcerers Glen. Above it, suspended in the air, were layered transparent grids overlaid with neon-blue runes.

'Each battledragon has a unique signature.' The Earl pointed towards the glyphs that moved across the huge tactical display above. The slightest movement of his hand revealed another beneath. 'As does each Battle Mage.' He beckoned a finger and the outline of a flying Imperial appeared between them, Bonecrackers storming up a wing from a battlegalleon. 'Thus we know exactly where each and every dragon is within twenty leagues of the Sorcerers Glen, even when visibility is zero.'

'Is Tempest Talonstrike ready for takeoff?' The Earl turned to his second-in-command, the Strike Commander of Dragon Isle, a man he introduced as Jakart DeBessert. Quenelda looked at the tall blond officer with his warrior's braid, wondering how he had taken the news that his only son, Guy, had lost a hand because of her brother Darcy's bungled attempt to fly a battlegriff.

'Fully prepped, Commander,' DeBessert acknowledged. 'Recruits are boarding now.'

The Earl looked at his daughter gravely. 'Time, Goose, to return to Court and thereafter to your studies.'

Quenelda's face fell. The Court! Her studies! She didn't know which was worse. She sighed theatrically.

'You know that the Queen has specifically requested

that you attend this year's Yule festivities,' the Earl chided her gently. 'You are to sit at the high table – a rare honour.'

Quenelda pouted to show what she thought of the honour. She had conveniently forgotten the Queen's final command on the day of the joust; had put the ghastly idea out of her mind. She would have to wear a dress again. How she hated dresses! And the other young ladies would all mock her and laugh at her rough manners and poor etiquette, as they always had. She hated going to Court! Root saw the light go out of her eyes, the resigned droop of her shoulders. So did the Earl. Unexpectedly, he smiled.

'An Imperial will be taking off for Dragonsdome in half a bell. I expect the pair of you to be on it.'

'What?' Quenelda's protest faltered. 'W-what about Two Gulps? Why?'

'Two Gulps will return later with me. The Imperial will be taking recruits on their first High Sky operation. I thought you might like to go with them . . . ?'

Quenelda frowned, still reluctant to leave her beloved battledragon. 'But why . . . ? What?' Her father's words caught up with her. 'Papa!' She couldn't believe what she was hearing. 'Truly?'

Root couldn't understand her joy. 'You've flown lots of times with your father on Stormcracker, haven't you?'

Quenelda nodded. 'Yes. But only flying at Two Gulps' pace, which is *really* slow. Never in full flight; it's not normally allowed in the Glen because it creates such a huge backwash from their wings – it blows over boats and breaks windows. And never on an operational fully armoured Imperial with battlecrew!' She was grinning from ear to ear, before another flash of realization hit her. 'But . . . you're not coming with us, Papa?

'No. But you won't be returning alone. I leave you in the very best of hands.'

'Tangnost?' Quenelda's eyes lit up. 'He's returning with us?'

Her words were barely out of her mouth when, across the floor, the porting stone rippled. The blossoming light faded to reveal a familiar broad-shouldered outline.

'Tangnost!' Root and Quenelda turned to greet the Earl's dragonmaster.

'Yes,' her father said warmly. 'Tangnost is going to accompany you. I'm afraid I must stay here but' – he raised a finger to forestall her appeal – 'I promise, Goose,

I *promise* I shall be back at Court in time for the Yule festivities in five days.'

Quenelda sighed. As long as he returned before she had to go to the Court.

'But I still don't understand,' Root whispered to Quenelda. 'Not on an operation? What difference does High Sky make?'

The Earl grinned wolfishly at his daughter's esquire. 'Wait and see, lad. Wait and see.' He looked at Tangnost. 'Take care of them, Bearhugger,' he said, before turning back to his officers.

Chapter Three

May You Ride the Stars For Ever

The hangar deck rose slowly up to lock into the landing pad with a metallic boom. The Imperial dragon resting there was already armed and carrying a full complement of armoured Bonecrackers. Head craned upwards, Root thought he had never seen anything quite so huge in his life. How had he *ever* thought Chasing the Stars was scary? She was the size of a midge compared to this giant battledragon. Quenelda stepped forward confidently, heading for the Imperial's head, but Root hesitated on the gantry, trying to still the frantic beating of his heart. He reached out tentatively to touch the tip of a huge tailspike, then suddenly remembered that these mighty dragons had magic of their own and stepped hastily backwards into Tangnost.

'Root . . .' the dwarf said softly. 'No need to worry, lad. I'll take care of you. Follow me.'

The young gnome swallowed, trying to keep his breathing normal and slow as Tangnost led him to the base of the tail and up the half-dozen rungs driven into the dragon's armoured hide.

'Up you go, lad. I'm right behind you.'

It was Root's first ride on one of the great battle-dragons. As he climbed up and up the Imperial's tail, he felt his knees start to wobble, the fear of flying and heights creeping up to ambush him just when he thought he had conquered it. It was like climbing a mountain, a rocky boulder-strewn mountain. The Imperial's pebbled armour plates were utterly different to the smooth hide of Chasing the Stars, or the scales of Two Gulps.

Three hundred nervous recruits were buckling up onto the twin spinal plates as Tangnost led Root the entire length of the dragon's spine.

'Right, lad,' the dragonmaster said, strapping the gnome securely into his seat. 'I'm going to be right there beside you.' He pointed towards the seat behind the navigator's chair, before going to inspect the last of the men climbing up the dragon's wings, roaring, 'This is your first experience of the Drop Dead Manoeuvre. If you survive this final test, you get your SDS wings and are ready for active service! Make sure all your equipment is tightly stowed. This ride is going to rattle every bone in your body.'

'D-D-Drop Dead?' Root squeaked, but Tangnost had moved out of earshot.

Meanwhile Quenelda was greeting the dragon: *May the wind always sail under your wings, Tempest Talonstrike . . .*

May you ride the stars for ever . . .

Tempest Talonstrike's reply was courteous, but then the dragon turned her mind back to her tasks and the commands of the Dragon Lord to whom she was bonded. High overhead, without being aware of this conversation, the pilot and navigator went through their pre-flight preparation.

'Warming up . . .'

'Navigation . . . Wind speed . . . Cloud density at three thousand strides . . .'

'Black One, Black One, this is Seadragon Tower. You are cleared for immediate takeoff. Flight path one six niner . . .'

Talonstrike stretched out her wings, ready to warm up. Quenelda quickly climbed the rising wing to sit down beside her pale-faced esquire, who was fumbling with the helmet he had been given.

'What is the D-Drop Dead Manoeuvre?' he asked

nervously, knowing that whatever the answer was, he was not going to like it.

'Ummm . . . it's like what we did when we flew here. When the dragons lose height rapidly, only instead of gliding down, we drop.'

'Drop?'

'Mmn,' Quenelda nodded. 'Straight as a stone down a well. It's' – Quenelda chose her words carefully to reassure her friend – 'it's not as scary, because on the Imperials it's as if the landscape moves and not you. The dragon's so big you can't see yourself dropping. The Imperial's own magic will keep you safe.'

As Tangnost strode up to take his seat, it took a few heartbeats for Root to realize that Talonstrike had already taken off. Then they fell away from the pads with mind-numbing speed, but it was so smooth that he wasn't feeling at all airsick. *This isn't so bad*, he thought.

Then the pilot gave the Imperial her head. With a sound like a thunderclap, the dragon's great wings rose and fell. The speed was breathtaking. Familiar landmarks streaked past in a blur. Quenelda, so familiar with flying on Stormcracker, had never flown at speeds like this: the mountain peaks sped by and the battledragon ate up the leagues.

'The Corkscrewwww!' Quenelda helpfully informed Root as the world about them tipped and spun three times.

'*Aaaarrrgh!*' Root's petrified shriek was lost among the cries of three hundred recruits, and then they were climbing vertically at a ferocious speed, held in place only by their strong harnesses. Someone's shield was swept away, ricocheting off a spinal plate before disappearing into the blue void.

Up . . .

And up . . .

And up . . .

Talonstrike took Quenelda and Root higher than they had ever flown before, up to where they could see the horizon of the One Earth curving away below. The air was freezing, and the snow-covered highlands, lochs and islands below looked like an exquisitely rendered map in white, russet and heather-purple. As they climbed ever higher, the vivid icy blue about them slowly grew darker. Soon stars appeared, and the heavens spun with them. The battle-dragon glided soundlessly. Frost cracked on her wings.

'Right lads,' Tangnost bellowed into the thin silence. 'Drop Dead!' And then the dragon raised and folded her outstretched wings to her sides and they plummeted down.

Down . . .

And down . . .

And down . . .

And as the dragon's wings levelled out, to her deep embarrassment, Quenelda was heartily sick.

'Dragonsdome to Tempest Talonstrike. You are cleared to land on pad one. Wind light and easterly. Approach vector clear . . .'

'Locked on and closing,' the navigator responded.

As the battledragon swung around the Black Isle and slowed on her final approach to Dragonsdome, Tangnost came for them both where they sat frozen and shaking, blood drumming through their heads, fingers numb, teeth chattering. He helped them with their buckles.

'Come on.' He grinned as they both stood on wobbly legs and followed him slowly up to the withers of the great beast.

'My lady,' the pilot said, unbuckling his harness and

then standing to one side, 'would you care to pilot us in?' He gestured to the elaborately sculpted pilot's chair, the arms inset with a sophisticated array of battle runes and marks.

Quenelda stared. 'Me? Truly?' And then she realized that this was Tangnost's idea, a Yule gift from the heart. She turned and flung her arms about him.

The corners of his mouth kicked up in acknowledgement. 'You earned it for what you did in the Cauldron. Most final year cadets on Dragon Isle couldn't have done as well.'

As Quenelda lowered herself into the chair, the navigator stood up, lifting the fearsome visor of his dragon helmet. 'Root Barkley,' he said solemnly, 'would you like to navigate?'

'Me?' Root's head spun. First he was given a dragon of his own and now *this*. He stepped into the huge navigator's chair with its baffling set of instruments. The world changed as the Dragon Lord placed his helmet on the gnome boy's head. The helmet was heavy, and then the visor's display filled his vision with scrolling graphs and grids and bright runes that flickered swiftly and then were gone.

Heart thumping, the cold forgotten, Quenelda held the reins lightly. She knew that this great battledragon could land without her help, but she was the one in the pilot's seat! She was the one flying a fully operational and crewed Imperial Black towards Dragonsdome's great keep.

'You are cleared for landing . . .' The voice rang in Root's ears. 'Vector approach two zero five . . .'

The Earl's dragonpad was anchored halfway up the keep. Red landing lights flickered on and off. The blast of a horn reverberated across the dragonpads and gantries as the deck crew stood by. Tempest Talonstrike's rear claws were splayed, seeking contact with the decking as the mare raised her wings and dropped the final twenty strides. And then they were home – to a collective sigh of relief!

Chapter Four

The Razorback Brood

The knifing wind blowing in from the sea was sharp with salt and the promise of yet more snow. Wrapped in a heavy cloak and warmed by the Dark Magic that coursed through his veins, the Grand Master, the Lord Hugo Mandrake, stood on the clifftops of Roarkinch and watched the sea break on the rocks below. Here, on this desolate storm-lashed island north of the mainland, lay the true centre of his power. Following his failed attempt to kill the Earl Rufus, the Grand Master was here in the north, supposedly raising two regiments of Bonecrackers for the planned attack on the Westering Isles. Instead, he was making sure that the SDS would never return home from the forthcoming battle with the hobgoblins. Turning abruptly, he crossed his castle's inner bailey and descended the rough-hewn rock steps that led down into the ancient dragoncombs.

It was here that he had first tapped into the Maelstrom; here too that he had conjured an elixir that allowed him to wield the immense corrosive power of dark destruction that would otherwise have long since killed him. Instead, immortality and a new Dark Age beckoned. But first the kingdom's ancient guardians must fall. The supposedly invincible SDS must be destroyed, their reputation and power broken. To whom, then, apart from himself would the Queen turn to guard her northern shores against the hobgoblin swarms? He would first claim her hand in marriage, and then usurp her crown.

To this end, using the Maelstrom, he had been cross-breeding stolen pedigree battledragons and hobgoblins. He gave these evil creatures shape and form and a name: Razorbacks. A dragon conjured to carry its most hated enemy, the hobgoblins. The Grand Master paused to consider a young Razorback brood that slithered and coiled unceasingly below him, the rasp of their sharp spines rattling like shale on the shore. Feeding on a diluted Maelstrom brew, already they were large, each the size of a full-grown bull, growing daily. Soon they would exceed the size of a Sabretooth; but unlike Midnight Madness, the unstable rogue dragon he had unleashed at the Winter Jousts, whose dark side was hidden, these foul creatures were evidently as much hobgoblin as dragon: amphibious, carnivorous, voracious pack hunters who were bound to serve him. And they spewed Dark Magic the like of which the SDS had not seen since the Mage Wars; forbidden Dark Magic. And none would know how to fight it. The Seven Sea Kingdoms would fall and ultimate power would be his!

Passing on, he moved out through the caverns to the shore, where a hobgoblin awaited him. The sea around them boiled with Razorbacks, black against the rocks of the shoreline. Clinging to them like limpets were thousands of pale hobgoblins.

'Have you done as I commanded?' the Lord Hugo demanded of the hobgoblin messenger whom Galtekerion had sent.

'Asss you commanded, lord,' the hobgoblin hissed, keeping its head bowed before the masked warlock. 'One of our championsss was sssacrificed. His body bears the marks of the thirteen tribessss and carriesss the great tooth of the warlord. We placed trophiesss and weaponry from the tribesss about him. His ssssacrifice will be honoured.'

'And you are certain they will find him?'

'Yesss, lord. Hisss body was left in the great cavern at the heart of the mountain in the Howling Glen. The SDSSS sssscouts will find him.'

The Grand Master nodded, finally satisfied that the trap was set. The SDS would take the bait.

'Lord . . .' the hobgoblin said uncertainly, afraid of exciting this warlock's wrath. 'Our warriorssss are sssstarving . . . many are dying . . . those who have gone into winter sleep will never awake in the ssspring.'

'It will not be long. Sacrifice the old and the weak. Tell your master that his warriors will soon feed on rich dragon meat. The Earl is bringing four regiments to the battle, numbering twenty thousand dragons.'

'Even the mighty Imperialsssss . . . ?' The hobgoblin trembled at the name of that most feared of dragons.

'Yes.'

The hobgoblin's pale eyes glowed in the growing dark. 'Lord . . .' it hissed as it looked upon the Razorbacks. 'They will recognize usss? They will obey only usss? Not the Dragon Lordssss . . .'

The Grand Master nodded. 'They will obey only you.'

And you – the Lord Hugo Mandrake smiled as the hobgoblin mounted a Razorback and disappeared below the dark cold waves – *you will obey only me!*

Chapter Five

Becoming Better Acquainted with Dragons

The last note of the bard's harp thrummed to raucous applause. Beneath the holly and berries that adorned the upper table, the Queen beckoned him forward. The bard, an elf from the Eastern Kingdom, bowed gracefully as he accepted a purse of gold, then bowed again to Quenelda, seated beside her father and to the Queen's right. As the palace had been decorated for the twelve-day celebration of the Yule Festival, the Court had buzzed with chatter, finding the Lady Quenelda and her unusual esquire a welcome distraction from the gloomy talk of war.

Quenelda had refused the jewelled and silk dresses and caps offered by the Queen's ladies-in-waiting, choosing instead a simple kirtle of sky blue. Her straw-blonde hair was worn loose, and brushed for once. Quenelda was overwhelmed by all the attention as she stood to acknowledge the applause. Her woollen skirts itched and the pointed shoes that the Queen's ladies assured her were all the rage at Court pinched her toes – they were bound to raise a blister. It was a better curtsy than the one she had managed at the Winter Jousts, but it was awkward and stiff nonetheless. Behind her chair, Root bit back a grin when he saw the hot, jealous glances cast her way by the Queen's younger ladies-in-waiting and her half-brother, Darcy. Only Root and the Earl knew just how much Quenelda longed to be back in breeches and boots and up and away on the back of Two Gulps.

If Quenelda was having a hard time adopting the role of a lady, Root was having an equally difficult time learning the courtly duties of an esquire – one of which was to serve Quenelda at table. He was doing as badly as she was, and had already spilled wine over her twice. He had also nicked his fingers while cutting her a slice of bread that was so thick it had raised loud laughter from her brother.

Darcy was furious at the attention lavished on Quenelda. Once again, his little sister had upstaged him in front of the entire Court, in front of tens of thousands from all over the Seven Sea Kingdoms! And now the whispers centred on him and his failure to take up the challenge to his injured father at the Winter Jousts. Aware of his shortcomings when it came to flying dragons, and angry at his father for ordering him to

Dragon Isle instead of allowing him to remain in the Household Cavalry, he had in that bitter moment of refusal wished his father dead. Then he would be Earl and none would dare laugh at him behind his back.

'Outrageous!'

Further down the hall, sitting at a lower table, the Lady Armelia was also furious. It was too outrageous. When Darcy's young lady had first visited Dragonsdome, his sister had humiliated her and ruined her chances of becoming a lady-in-waiting. And now Quenelda's unladylike display in the Cauldron was being applauded. The girl was a disgrace to the DeWinter name. That was because she had been allowed to run wild like a common peasant boy, instead of being sent to the exclusive Grimalkin's College for Young Ladies. Within its austere and decorous walls, daughters of the nobility were prepared for life at Court and taught the art of enchantment in order to ensnare eligible young noblemen.

And as far as Armelia and the young ladies at Court were concerned, Darcy was still the most eligible and dashing young man around, and her intention was to become his bride. Wealthy beyond measure, and stunningly handsome to boot, it was rumoured that he was shortly to take command of his own troop of unicorns in the Queen's Household Cavalry. Why, if she were to ensnare Darcy, she would be the envy of the entire Court! She might even win the coveted Golden Wand of Achievement from Grimalkin's! Her imagination running away with her, Armelia hurriedly flicked open her fan to cool herself, then realized that the Queen had risen. Everyone was applauding. Quenelda was looking horrified, her mouth hanging open.

'Aquainted with . . . ?'

Within heartbeats Armelia too was in danger of letting her own mouth hang open. Had she heard correctly? To yet another ripple of applause, the Queen was suggesting that all the younger ladies might attend Dragonsdome and receive a tour from the Lady Quenelda to become better *acquainted* with dragons. Armelia had absolutely no desire to become better acquainted with dragons. Certainly she had attended the races and jousts, as one did, but on no account did young ladies actually have anything to do with beasts of burden. That was strictly a manly pursuit. But if she were to aspire to be a lady-in-waiting, with all the privileges that brought, then she must show willing . . .

Meanwhile Quenelda gritted her teeth behind a smile that had frozen in place. All the young ladies attending her? At Dragonsdome?

'Ah, Goose!' The Earl smiled at his daughter's stricken expression. Taking her hand in his, he added softly, 'It is a great honour given in recognition of your bravery.'

'It is?' she said incredulously.

Her father nodded. 'Goose, you've done the impossible. You don't need to come to Court. The Court are going to come to you! If you feel uncomfortable in a dress and dancing, think how they are going to feel meeting these dragons of yours!'

As his words sank in, a slow smile crept over Quenelda's face. She turned triumphant eyes to where Armelia glowered, and inclined her head graciously.

Chapter Six

Oh, Madam!

The foul pool of liquid smoked. It smelled utterly repulsive, even Quenelda had to admit, and what the frog thought about it no one would ever know now. The tip of a hat appeared from behind the burned desk, followed by two outraged eyes and a mouth already opening wide in rebuke. The eyebrows were gone, and the smoking beard had seen better days.

'Madam!'

Quenelda lowered her wand and prepared for yet another telling off. She had no idea what had gone wrong. She sighed. Keeping her promise to her father to study hard for her first wand had seemed easy at the time, when only thoughts of flying Two Gulps had filled her mind. But now she was stuck in the library for endless tedious hours with Professor Stodgepoddle, practising the casting of spells. Elementary spells, as he kept reminding her; spells that should have been learned in the nursery. Well, Quenelda thought sourly, at least she was good at *some* of her studies. Professor Spiraldykes was positively rapturous about her rune casting. He had been rendered almost speechless when she had combined runes to create an Elder rune so complex and powerful and old that none now knew its meaning.

In a state of high excitement that brought colour to his shrivelled old cheeks, he had rushed off to the Circular Library, returning at midnight with a fusty old book. Three days later he found what he was looking for: the same Elder rune carved on the portal of the long gone Ice Citadel, copied in a fading manuscript. His fellow scholars patted him condescendingly on the back. The old fellow's wits were addled, they said, nodding. Everyone knew that the Earl's daughter was hopeless at magic.

Where the rune had come from, Quenelda admitted in quiet moments, was baffling. She hadn't been studying diligently, or been shown the rune by her father on Dragon Isle – as Spiraldykes thought. When the professor had opened the book, it was as if she'd seen them all before, instinctively recognizing the complex glyphs that represented earth, fire, wind, water – and a few more that had long since fallen into disuse: stone, ice, wood, dark and light.

'Madam!' Stodgepoddle pursed his lips. The dratted

child was daydreaming again. 'Casting spells is a complex skill. As with any skill, some are naturally gifted; others' – he looked at her meaningfully – 'have to be *tutored*, have to *apply themselves – practise . . .*'

Quenelda closed her eyes and sighed as the torrent of words washed over her. It wasn't as if she did it on purpose! The difference between grips . . . The complexities of casting . . . It was all so boring . . . After all, magic was everywhere – you just had to dip into it. Wands were a prop for those who weren't very good at magic, like Stodgepoddle. Quenelda stopped abruptly. *What* was she thinking? Where had these strange ideas come from? She frowned.

'Ahem . . .'

It was evident that the tirade had finished, because now the old man was looking at her over the rim of his spectacles, his lips pursed, his eyebrows – or what was left of them – raised in expectation. He'd asked her a question.

'Erm . . .' Quenelda ventured hopefully. That at least should cover most options, and at least it would look as if she was considering an answer.

'Madam, madam.' Stodgepoddle shook his head in

sorrow. 'I fear that we must once again go back to elementary spell-casting. Your grip and technique are all wrong. You are not clubbing someone over the head.' He held out his hand palm upwards. 'Your wand.'

Stodgepoddle balanced the girl's wand in his hand. It was plain elm wood, warped by age and unadorned, not at all like that of Lady Armelia, one of the other young ladies at Court whom he tutored. *Her* dress wand was priceless unicorn ivory inset with gold runes, a powerful wand for one so young. *Now* there *was a proper young lady*, he sniffed. *Elegant, dazzling, enough to set the old heart racing, just as a young lady should. Perhaps it was just as well that this one was plain wood. Heaven knows what damage this wretched child might do with something more powerful. And there she was, eyes unfocused, off daydreaming again. It was too much!* He rapped Quenelda's knuckles, pleased at the way she jumped and glared at him.

'You hold your wand delicately . . . just so, just so' – he demonstrated – 'so that you may cast your spells correctly. Now you try, madam. You rest the end in the palm of your hand, position your thumb to hold it in place, and your first finger — No! No! Have you not been listening? Your first finger here along the shaft of the wand. Now. Attend this.'

And then the old man drew a circle in the air and pirouetted, his robes fanning out ridiculously, before bringing the wand down with delicate grace. 'And then you flick your wrist – just so, as if you were casting a net of gossamer . . .' He handed the wand back to Quenelda. 'The Heron's Dance is quite the thing at Court at the moment, madam,' he said tartly, moustache quivering. '*All* the young ladies are expected to be accomplished. To—'

Quenelda rolled her eyes in horror. Fashions at Court seemed to change every moon. The latest hairstyle, poetry, dancing and romance. And now this ridiculous dance where the wand took the place of the heron's beak and the steps emulated the courting ritual, ending with the joint casting of a romantic spell, showering the dancers in little stars . . . Just the kind of thing that awful Armelia would swoon over. Gripping her wand firmly, Quenelda gave it her best shot.

The Professor ducked as her wand whistled over his head. He closed his eyes and sighed. Earl's daughter or not, he had been tasked with teaching an impossible pupil. She was so bad he barely knew where to start. If she danced like this, they would end up with a decapitated heron! Hardly the stuff of courtly romance.

She holds her wand like a boy, he thought. *I knew no good would come of allowing her to wear breeches and boots. Quite shocking! Wouldn't have happened in my day, oh no! Bad enough when she was a child, but now that she's a young lady*. Supposed *to be a young lady*, he amended, lips pursed in disapproval as he looked at the buckled boots, the patched jacket. Breeding . . . that was what it all came down to; who knew who her mother was?

No – he shook his head – his was a hopeless task. The Lady Quenelda would never amount to anything.

Chapter Seven

Hobgoblin Burial Cairn

'All clear!'

Scouts from the XIII Stormbreakers moved quietly through underground passageways, picking their way over the littered bones and weaponry of hobgoblin warriors killed in the battle at the Howling Glen. For almost a moon scouts had been mapping the maze of tunnels and passageways, first discovered by Bark Oakley, which wound through the heart of the mountains. With them was a team of sappers, better known as the Tunnel Rats – dwarf engineers who specialized in collapsing hobgoblin tunnels – and two squads of Bonecrackers, just in case they found any warriors still alive and lurking. There were more combs here than anyone had imagined, but their task was nearly done.

'Wait!' the lead scout warned the sappers. He could see a slight phosphorescence seeping along the tunnel up ahead. 'Hobgoblins!' he whispered, putting a finger to his lips for silence. Everyone crept towards the spectral green light, with the sound of water growing louder and louder beneath their feet.

Part of the tunnel had collapsed in the fighting, the flash marks caused by sorcery instantly recognizable. The explosions had triggered a major rockfall and brought down part of the ceiling; it had taken weeks to clear. Clambering over the boulders, a scout pointed to where a small arrow was crudely carved into the passage walls. 'Bark went this way.'

'What,' a Bonecracker muttered to groans of agreement as they moved forward, 'is that *dreadful* stink? Even hobgoblins don't normally smell as bad as this!'

As they pushed their way through the rubble, the tunnel suddenly opened out into a vast cavern heavy with glistening stalactites, dully lit by a phosphorescent glow radiating from a boulder in the centre.

The water thundered through the cavern like a thousand drums. The scouts squinted through the haze to where a huge hobgoblin was laid out on the flat-topped boulder in the middle of the torrential river. There was no doubt: this was a hobgoblin burial cairn – a rare find, almost certainly a tribal leader.

The Bonecrackers threw out a grappling hook,

snagging it between two large boulders on either side of the body. Pulling the line taut, three commandos anchored it. Crossing their legs around the rope, they moved swiftly along it, hand-over-hand, to the cairn. Axe raised, one nudged the stinking carcass just to be sure, but the creature did not move.

'Make haste,' said another as his wet gear began to stiffen. 'Else we'll freeze to death!'

The boulders underfoot were slick with ice and treacherous for the slighter gnomes. Striking up several flares, the scouts examined the cairn in the flickering red light. All about it lay battered shields and swords, both SDS and hobgoblin.

'Look – this belonged to the Rokrorin tribe!' A scout pointed to a heavy breastplate and broadsword typically worn and wielded by that tall, heavy-set hobgoblin tribe.

'And Karakin!' another said, lifting the short-hooked swords favoured by that tribe's warriors for hamstringing dragons.

Here and there lay the dragonskull helmets of another tribe, the Charkins. The scouts looked closer, and discovered armour and weaponry from all thirteen tribes set about the body. The standard also bore the totems and symbols of each tribe. They turned to examine the body. Broken dragonbone armour sheathed the huge hobgoblin's chest, arms and legs, and a dragonskull helmet hid his head and face. A great flint sword was clasped to his chest. One of the scouts lifted a dragontooth strung about the hobgoblin's neck.

'This is their leader!' he said excitedly. 'Look at these tattoos!'

'Affirmative. This must be Galtekerion.' Another scout yanked the dragon's tooth from the rotting creature's neck. It came away with a wet slap. 'He must have died from his wounds; never made it back to the sea.'

They called the Bonecrackers forward.

'No!' The battle-hardened troopers drew the line at moving the body. 'It stinks worse than rotting offal. It's falling apart!' One grasped a slimy bone to demonstrate. The ribcage came away from rotting flesh, and globules of innards spilled out, raising a chorus of ripe oaths.

'Then take these tokens and weapons as proof. The Commander will want to hear of this. We'll take as many artefacts and as much weaponry as we can, then the Rats can blow the cavern. Agreed?'

As commandos and scouts removed what evidence

they could, the Tunnel Rats laid their munitions about the cavern with care. Once this and the radiating tunnels had collapsed, then no hobgoblin could take the garrison at the Howling Glen by surprise again. The heavily burdened Bonecrackers pulled out first, followed by the Tunnel Rats, who stopped at every junction to set more explosives. Finally, near the entrance at the waterfall discovered by Root's father, they were ready. Red flags were waved to warn all dragons and patrols in the air away.

'Fire in the hole!'

BOOM!

The cavern in the mountain's heart convulsed as the massive impact of the blast rippled outwards.

Chapter Eight

Dragonsdome

As the new Year of the Sabre-toothed Dormouse began, a luxuriously appointed carriage swept over the snowy spires of Dragonsdome, disturbing a flock of winter ravens. Armelia dabbed at tears that kept welling up and threatening to mar her perfect complexion, irritably waving away the gaggle of minions fussing about her with mirrors and combs. The Earl had carried out his ugly threat, and Darcy had been given strict orders to report to Dragon Isle within the week. Rumours were flying about that the SDS were preparing for a late winter campaign. Armelia hoped they weren't true. Even she knew it was impossible to fly in blizzards and winter storms. What would happen if Darcy were injured, or worse? It was too awful to contemplate. She was quite besotted with him, and his wealth was enough to turn any young girl's head!

To prove the point, young ladies-in-waiting had been chasing Darcy whenever he attended Court, and they all planned to attend Dragonsdome at the first opportunity in the hope of pleasing the Queen and catching his eye. So

Armelia knew she had to prompt a proposal and make him hers before he left. As the Duchess-in-waiting, her status at Court would be assured. The fabled wealth of Dragonsdome beckoned. And so she had immediately agreed to the Queen's absurd proposal – not to see the ghastly Quenelda, of course, but in the hope of catching a private moment or two with Darcy. All she had been waiting for was a break in the endless blizzards.

I hope she doesn't expect me to go anywhere near dragons, Armelia thought desperately as her carriage put down on a lower landing pad, swept clear of snow and ice. *Ghastly scaly creatures . . . Leathery wings . . . Great teeth . . . Bad breath . . .*

The humiliation of her previous encounter with Darcy's young sister made her heart flutter with trepidation, and wonder if she had made a mistake coming here – an entire day at Dragonsdome in the company of the Earl's daughter was not an enticing prospect.

Why, the very thought of Quenelda's exploits in the Cauldron made Armelia shudder. She could feel a heat rash breaking out despite the frigid air. Her own brush with a battledragon on her last visit to Dragonsdome – that same battledragon that Quenelda had flown in the

Cauldron – sent shivers up her spine. An easy mistake to make, after all: one dragon looked pretty much like another – an assortment of scales, talons and teeth. And that ignorant view, unfortunately, was exactly why the Queen had decided that her Court should be better informed about the great creatures that defended the Seven Sea Kingdoms.

Neither young lady, Root observed as the opulent carriage came to a halt and Armelia peered hesitantly out, had made a single concession to the other. Quenelda looked like a stable boy from her head to her toes, while Armelia was dressed like royalty. War had already been declared on their first encounter. This was the opening skirmish in what promised to be a long campaign . . .

She looks like a toy doll, Quenelda thought, as Armelia was assisted down from her carriage by a footman. The girl was followed by a gaggle of twittering ladies. *Doesn't she ever do anything on her own? It must be suffocating.*

Is that her? Armelia squinted at the figure in the shadows. *And that . . . commoner she calls her esquire! How do I talk to someone in boy's clothes?* Armelia thought in near panic as she stepped down, ignoring the bowing footman, who choked back a whimper as she stood on his fingers.

Quenelda regarded Armelia scornfully. *She must have at least six lace petticoats under that dress. She's going to end up cleaning the pad with them, they're so long. How can she get through doors? And you can hardly see her face under all that make-up – and look at all the little girlie ribbons . . . And as for those ridiculous high heels – how can she even walk? I'd break my ankle. And the sickly perfume – it's enough to knock a dragon out . . .*

Sky above! Armelia wrinkled her nose. *She's as filthy as a stable hand, and she smells . . . of rotten eggs? Of dragon?*

Armelia had considered swooning as a means of avoiding the Queen's orders to spend the day at Dragonsdome. Young ladies were taught the delicate art of swooning at Grimalkin's – how to fall to the ground dramatically without causing any real injury. It worked every time, but there were no gallant young gentlemen to hand, and she didn't want to crumple her beautiful dress. And of course, that was exactly what this wretched girl would expect her to do.

Quenelda wilted. *She'll probably want to talk about*

dresses and diets and dancing . . . and gangly young men with a double helping of spots who can't ride a hippogriff to save their lives, like Darcy.

She stepped forward into the sunlight. Her hair was tangled from flying without a helmet. She had chosen the dirtiest, most patched jerkin she could find, and her face was sooty.

Armelia was wearing the costliest gown in her wardrobe, a confection of imported silk and gold-threaded brocade, exquisitely tailored by Foresight and Hindsight's Exclusive Emporium. Buried beneath a mound of rare ice-bear furs, a small fortune in emeralds hung from ear and throat and wrist, chosen to match the colour of Darcy's eyes. The unicorn wand hanging from a ribbon on her wrist had cost her parents virtually all their remaining fortune. The gown was gathered about an impossibly small waist and then billowed out. She surged forward on a wave of lace and superiority.

Quenelda smiled the hypnotic smile of a Spitting Adder about to strike. 'Welcome to Dragonsdome, Lady Armelia.'

'My lady.' Armelia sank into a graceful curtsy, a patronising smile tugging at the corner of her brightly glossed lips. She'd show this little tramp who had never heard of deportment or etiquette how things were done at Court.

Remembering Quenelda's humiliation at the Winter Joust, Root bit his bottom lip. He cast a furtive glance in his friend's direction. Smiling sweetly, Quenelda gave an answering curtsy that was if anything more graceful and even lower. Root's jaw dropped. She had been practising!

Armelia curtsied again, determined not to be outdone. Quenelda's next curtsy was so low she nearly caught her breeches on the buckles of her flying boots. If she had been wearing spurs she would have had a painful accident – which of course was why boys didn't curtsy. Having no option, Armelia sank right down to the ground and looked up to find Quenelda's satisfied smile looking down on her. Realizing she had been tricked into foolishness, Armelia flushed a deeper red behind the rouge. Gritting her teeth, she attempted to rise but found herself overwhelmed by the weight of brocade and beads. Two of her ladies rushed forward to assist.

'Perhaps my esquire . . . ?' Quenelda offered, making no move herself as Armelia floundered helplessly.

Aghast, Root tried to think what an esquire should do

on such an occasion. He had no experience of helpless fluttering girls. Quenelda's requirements were somewhat . . . different. Thinking that his good friend Quester would know what to do, Root stepped forward awkwardly to offer his hand.

'Esquire?' Armelia put a world of polite enquiry into the one word. She deliberately searched the dragonpad. 'I see no esquire.'

Quenelda's words dripped ice. 'Then let me present to you Root Oakley, son of Bark Oakley, heroic scout to my father.'

'But he's a . . .' Armelia let the sentence hang like a gathering thunderstorm.

'A . . . ?' Quenelda smiled even more sweetly.

'Why' – Armelia made a practised dismissive gesture with her wrist – 'he's a commoner.'

'His father died warning the SDS of the attack on the Howling Glen! He saved the fortress! Without his warning many more might have died – including my father, and your uncle!' snapped Quenelda.

'Oh!' Armelia had the good grace to blush. She had not listened very closely to her uncle, a Wing Commander with the XIII Stormbreakers, over the midwinter festivities. War was exciting and romantic – until it came down to details, and his injured big toe was not very glamorous . . . Shamed, she took Root's proffered hand.

Quenelda, Root thought two bells later, was enjoying herself far too much. When she had wickedly suggested to Armelia that she might care to inspect Dragonsdome's art collection, a rival to the royal collection, the young lady had accepted with alacrity, relieved that real-life dragons hadn't been mentioned. Little did she know what Quenelda had in store.

Armelia stifled a furious yawn behind her fan and wriggled uncomfortably. Her corset was digging into her ribs. Behind her, her companions shuffled and murmured restlessly. When she accepted Quenelda's offer, she hadn't expected these endless panelled corridors adorned with vast paintings of warlike DeWinter ancestors mounted on their battledragons. As they paused at each, Quenelda proudly pointed out a host of tedious detail: the different breeds of dragon, the complicated dragonarmour of the period, the weaponry, and the inevitable piles of toasted hobgoblins lying at the dragon's talons. It was perfectly ghastly, and Armelia was just about cross-eyed with boredom. The effort of smiling politely was making her cheeks ache.

Fearsome black SDS armour lined the walls between the paintings. Looking closer, Armelia noticed that the suits all bore dents and ragged tears. The DeWinters obviously died in the saddle and not in bed. She shivered. She didn't want Darcy to be added to the long list of glorious dead.

When Armelia thought things couldn't get any worse, Quenelda led her into a huge vaulted hall. 'This is the dragons' dome! The castle and palace get their name from this room,' she said, with real passion in her voice. 'It was here that the First Alliance was forged.'

Armelia looked vacant, although Root thought it was quite hard to tell the difference from her normal expression.

'Between us and the dragons . . . ?' Quenelda hinted.

Armelia smirked as servants lit branches of candles to chase back the shadows. *An alliance between men and dragons indeed! Dragons are mere beasts, bound to servitude as they should be*, she thought. *Dragon Whisperers and all that nonsense learned in the nursery are mere fables and legends. Everyone knows that! What nonsense this ridiculous girl believes!*

'This' – Quenelda pivoted carelessly on her boot heels, enjoying the way the squeak made Armelia start – 'Stormrider Spitfire, the first Imperial to bear my forefathers into battle.'

Armelia turned gracefully in a swirl of glinting jewellery and coloured petticoats, then gave a small squeak of horror. In the middle of the room, suspended on wires and towering right above her, were the skeletons of dragons large and small, all sheathed in dragonarmour that sprouted a vicious assortment of cutting blades, spikes, tail and talons. Armelia felt rather faint.

'And this is Volcano Taloncrusher the Second,' Quenelda continued. 'A pedigree Firedragon. His lineage goes back unbroken to the Century of the Volcanic Shrimp! You can distinguish between Firedragons and red Saharan dragons by the length of their—'

Armelia's horror-struck expression over what was to follow was frozen in place as a voice shouted out:

'Lady Quenelda!'

Quenelda frowned. That was the voice of Quester, one of Tangnost's most promising esquires, a young man who would one day make a name for himself in the SDS.

'We're in the dragons' dome,' she bellowed, making her guest jump.

'Lady Quenelda!' The handsome esquire's cheeks were red and he was puffing hard as he clutched his sides. 'Roostmistress Greybeard sent to say that Quicksilver Dewdrop has gone into labour as expected . . . but – but something is very wrong. Roostmistress Greybeard believes a babe has turned the wrong way in the womb, but the mare won't let anyone near her . . . She says they will all die if the babes are not delivered soon.'

Guest completely forgotten, Quenelda was already turning away. 'Root, Quester, follow me!'

Armelia looked over her shoulder at the looming skeleton in the middle of the room and quailed. It was so huge! The candles flickered on its hollowed ivory bones, its triple rows of serrated teeth, its massive steel-shod talons. Suddenly it looked as if it was moving! In a fury, Armelia stamped her silver buckled foot and fled to the door after Quenelda, her ladies tripping along behind her eager to escape.

'Lady Quenelda!' Armelia's outraged voice curdled the air.

Leaping down the stairs, Quenelda skidded to a halt

against the balustrade. 'Quester, please escort the Lady Armelia and her retinue to the great hall and see that she is properly cared for until her carriage returns.'

Root breathed a grateful sigh of relief that Quester was to remain with Armelia. His friend had been teaching him court protocol and etiquette, but Root felt intimidated by the aloof young girl.

'No!' Armelia was determined not to fail. If news of this should reach the Queen, then her chances of redeeming herself would be gone. 'I shall accompany you to become better acquainted with dragons!' she declared imperiously, and swept down the stairs, ignoring the dismayed expressions of her companions.

Chapter Nine

The Nursery Roosts

Quenelda arrived at the nursery roosts with Root at her side. The dwarf roostmistress and the stablemaster, along with stable hands and ostlers, were gathered around a stall where a small gooseberry-green dragon thrashed feebly in the straw, her rasping breath sounding like a blacksmith's bellows.

'All was going well, Lady,' Roostmistress Greybeard growled, 'then a babe turned in the womb and now none can be born. She is bleeding inside and getting weaker by the moment. She won't let anyone near her. I fear it may already be too late to save any of them.'

'Where's the surgeon?' Quenelda asked as she discarded her heavy jacket.

'Dragon Isle, Lady,' the roostmistress answered. 'Loaded transports return daily from the north with casualties from the winter exercises. The storms are brutal for man and beast alike.'

Quicksilver Dewdrop . . . Quenelda was instantly at

the distressed dragon's side, laying an ear carefully to her chest. *The birth is difficult?*

Dancing with Dragons . . . It was barely a whisper.

The deep rhythm of the dragon's twin hearts boomed frantically; beneath them, the faltering heartbeats of baby dragons grew weaker by the minute.

You must let the No Wings roostmistress care for you. She wishes to help. Trust me, Quicksilver. We wish to save your babes . . .

Unused to walking any great distance in the ridiculously high heels that were all the fashion at Court, Armelia wobbled to a stop and fanned herself. Her high-heeled boots had repeatedly got stuck between the cobbles, her silk tights had snagged on a buckle, and a ladder ran up out of sight beneath her pantaloons and petticoats. Her ringlets were askew and a ribbon or two had unravelled. She dabbed away the faintest sheen of sweat from her forehead with a lace hanky and hoped that she would not meet Darcy before she had a chance to repair the damage. To her relief, Quester finally pointed out the terracotta-tiled roofs of the nursery roosts ahead.

'With your permission, Lady?' Anxious to be gone, the

esquire ran on ahead, leaving Armelia to be tended by her servants. Gathering her dignity and her skirts, head held high, she walked at a more decorous pace towards the arched doors thrown open to the morning. Ripe odours wafted out, making her eyes water.

'My lady!' a companion protested. 'You cannot step in there! It . . . smells so. There are . . . Why, there are *dragons* in there! It will be dangerous!'

Waving her companions' protests aside and taking a deep breath, Armelia stepped over the threshold and was swallowed in darkness. Her reluctant entourage followed, huddling together for security.

After her exhausting walk through gardens stiff with hoar frost, the steamy heat of the roost took Armelia's breath away. It was unbearably humid and crowded, and stank of . . . dragon? She had no idea. She gave her furs to one of her ladies, who gratefully fled the roost back into fresh air. Once her breathing had slowed, Armelia could hear strange noises overlaying each other in the musty gloom – soft chirps, a shrill fluting, deeper whoops and peeps – and realized that she had never heard the call of a baby dragon. Dragons hadn't featured in her upbringing in any shape or form, and she knew little of giving birth beyond the fact that it was dangerous. She paused as a thought struck her. *It must be dangerous for dragons too . . .*

But even Armelia's untrained ear could hear, above all the strange sounds of the roosts, the frantic heaving of a dragon in distress, and the soft murmur of anxious voices. Allowing her eyes to adjust to the gloom, the girl moved forward cautiously. Following lanterns and voices, she came to the centre of the building. Around her the individual dragon roosts radiated outwards like slices of cake. Peering beyond the shafts of light that streamed in through the windows, she could see Quenelda and a dwarf in one of the stalls, surrounded by a huddle of people.

'. . . an infusion of argon leaf,' the dwarf was saying gruffly to Quenelda, who knelt in the straw at the dragon's side, 'to calm her, and some digitalis to slow her heart. She is very weak. Calm her, Lady, so that I may at least save her, if not the babes.'

Quenelda nodded and turned her attention back to the dragon, which was already quietening beneath her gentle touch.

We must search for your baby . . . We must turn

the head, else all will die . . . You must be still . . .

Only Quenelda heard the dragon's pain-filled response. *As you say, Dancing with Dragons . . . But the pain . . .*

We will give you something for the pain.

Something tugged at Armelia's skirts. She looked down in horror to where a small black and white dragon was trying to eat her dress. 'Get it off! Get it off!' Her voice rose an octave to a high squeak.

'Shoo! Shoo!' Her ladies flapped ineffectually, hitting it with their fans. Armelia kicked it. It scuttled out of reach and trilled angrily at her.

Just then Quicksilver Dewdrop collapsed sideways, chest heaving, knocking Root and one of the stable hands to the floor with her flailing tail. Ignoring the red welt the tail had raised on his cheek, Root helped the ostlers get the almost unconscious dragon into the cradle, amazed at her weight.

Quenelda was rolling up the sleeves of her embroidered shirt when Quester returned, cradling a mortar and pestle so as not to spill its steaming contents. Carefully he strained the contents into a wooden bowl and handed it to Quenelda.

'I need you to give her the infusion a little at a time,' Greybeard instructed Quenelda.

The dwarf turned to the stable hands, who were already moving forward with a pulley and harness. 'Lift her – gently now,' she warned as they raised the dragon.

Meanwhile Armelia was glaring at the small black and white dragon, which had returned for a second helping of lace. One of her more adventurous ladies bent forward to pick the hatchling up, but it scuttled off into a pile of hay, seeking out its parents. The mare stepped forward to protect it. The ruff about her head raised up, and her tail waved warningly. Unfortunately Armelia was blissfully ignorant of animal behaviour, and was not able to understand the body language. The mare was small and did not look threatening, and so, checking that no one was looking her way, Armelia drew back her foot, ready to kick again. Her movement caught Quester's eye.

'Nooo . . .' He lunged forward. 'Don't touch—'

Too late! The mare ducked under Armelia's boot and swung her hindquarters round to face her. Back feet treading the hay up and down with gusto, she raised her quivering tail. Foul-smelling liquid sprayed over Armelia and spattered her companions. They fled, shrieking, abandoning their mistress – all save one, who fainted.

The stench was truly overpowering. Armelia stood there, her mouth opening and closing, coughing and spluttering with outrage. There was a brief intake of breath as everyone at work in the neighbouring stall stared at her, but then the pregnant dragon moaned and they immediately turned back to their allotted tasks.

In the course of her cosseted life, Armelia had never been ignored. It was a new and unpleasant experience – as unpleasant as the liquid that dripped from her hair and nose and chin. Her cheeks burned with humiliation. Turning on her heel, trampling the prone body of her companion in her haste, she collapsed onto a bale of hay.

In the stall, Quenelda was soothing the dragon as the stable hands gently raised the canvas cradle, lifting the mare to her feet.

'Truckleloam balm?'

A gnome apprentice stepped forward with a pail of thick ointment. Scooping up a handful, the Roostmistress rubbed it generously over her forearms. Standing beneath the cradle, she reached up under the dragon's tail.

No! Surely she's not going to . . . ? Feeling nauseous,

Armelia's fragile determination wavered and she staggered out into the yard, seeking fresh air.

Nearly . . . nearly, Quenelda reassured the mare. The dwarf was straining against the dragon, her arm in as far as it could go. Sweat was running down her face. Quenelda was soothing the agitated dragon while trying to watch what the Roostmistress was doing. A sudden gush of blue blood splattered over the pair of them.

'Here . . .' Someone rammed a bucket into Armelia's hands as she stood on the threshold of the stables. Her flustered ladies were feebly attempting to remove the offensive stains from brocade and silk without getting any of it on themselves. The dirty liquid in the bucket spilled over, splattering Armelia's skirts and filling her dainty pointed boots. 'Tip it into the gutter and get some fresh water – from that well out in the courtyard,' the stable hand commanded, pointing outside. Nobody was allowed to stand idly by in the nursery roosts at a birthing. In a daze, Armelia wobbled over to the well and looked at it hopelessly. Water was normally brought to her, chilled in crystal goblets.

'I – I—' she stuttered to no one in particular. A goblin mucking out another stall looked at her and turned back to his task, shaking his head.

'Lady?' Quester approached her carefully, not reacting to the dreadful stench that kept her servants well away from her.

'Allow me,' he said kindly, and he let the bucket plummet down into the hidden depths of the well. A *splosh* echoed up, and the esquire began turning the handle with easy strength. 'Your first birthing?' he asked sympathetically.

Armelia could only nod wordlessly. She was on the verge of hysteria.

'It's always difficult the first time,' he offered kindly, trying not to wince at the awful smell. 'I threw up.'

Armelia looked at him faintly. 'Did you?' Somehow that made her feel much better. 'I thought . . .' She started dredging up what little she knew of dragons. 'I thought all dragons laid eggs.'

'Oh no. Some do lay eggs like snakes and birds, but many give birth to live young, just like most other creatures. It depends on the breed.'

They headed back into the roost. The sawing breaths of the dragon were growing weaker. Armelia followed Quester into the steamy darkness as he strode ahead with the bucket.

'W-w-what is her name?' she called after him.

'Quicksilver Dewdrop.'

'That's a beautiful name,' Armelia said, swaying.

'Here,' Quester offered, coming back towards her. 'Let me get you a seat.' He pulled a big three-legged stool from the shadows and dusted off the cobwebs with his shirt cuffs. Armelia sank gratefully onto it and fanned her face.

The dragon was keening now – a dreadful wailing sound.

'Come on, girl,' Quenelda whispered. 'Just a little more . . .'

Roostmistress Greybeard suddenly withdrew her arm. There was a splatter of mucus, and a gelatinous sac spilled out onto the hay with a wet slap. Within moments, another – and then another – fell into the waiting arms of the apprentices. A rush of rancid air rolled across the stall.

Armelia's eyes fluttered. She felt sick. And for the first time in her life, she genuinely fainted, falling unnoticed over the back of the stool into the straw, feet and frilly bloomers in the air . . .

She swam slowly back to consciousness. She was lying down but her mattress was prickly and she felt sticky.

There were anxious voices, but puzzlingly they were not clustered around her. Nor did she recognize any of them. Someone was washing her brow, but the cloth was rough and scratchy. The water was syrupy and she could feel it gumming up her eyes. She tried to open an eye and found she couldn't, and when she wiped the goo away, a little face was peering enthusiastically at her through sea-green eyes. Its nose was pointed and it had two horns. They were attached to a small yellow dragon, fat as butter. A yellow forked tongue flicked out – a tongue that felt like hot sandpaper. With a squeak, Armelia scrambled to her feet, dumping the baby dragon on the floor. It fled for the safety of a far roost, chirping furiously.

Around her, Quicksilver Dewdrop's roost was a hive of activity, everyone cradling a baby dragon, trying to draw life from the limp scraps in the straw.

'Here . . .' As Armelia staggered to her feet, Quenelda thrust a tiny dragon into her hands. 'Rub her,' she ordered. 'Get her circulation going or she's going to die . . .'

The tiny dragon lay cold and limp in Armelia's arms, curled up like a hibernating hedgehog. She opened her mouth to ask what she was supposed to rub the dragon with, then shut it again. Laying the little bundle of scales gently down in the hay, she bent down and tore the hem from one of her petticoats. She gathered the tiny creature in her skirts, then rubbed it tentatively.

Nothing. The baby dragon remained unmoving in her hands. 'Live,' she whispered. 'Live . . .' Looking up helplessly, she saw how robustly the others were rubbing, and redoubled her efforts.

'Yes! Look!' Quenelda triumphantly handed another baby to one of the grooms; he laid it down in the straw next to the exhausted mare, who gathered it to her beneath a spread wing.

Armelia rubbed with renewed vigour, anxious to show that she too could coax life from the bundle in her hands. 'I . . .'

There was a small hiccup. Then another.

The infant dragon's scales fluttered in and then out. The tiny tail twitched. The baby sneezed to clear its nostrils, spraying blue mucus over Armelia's bowed face.

'It's . . . it's breathing,' she said tremulously, holding up the little dragon, swaddled in petticoats. 'It's alive!' she cried triumphantly. 'It's alive!'

* * *

The dragon mare lay on a bed of fresh hay with eleven babes suckling contentedly. With a warm glow, Armelia gazed down in wonder.

'Is she . . . Are they all going to live?'

'Yes.' Quenelda smiled, teeth white against brimstone dust and grease. It was like the sun coming out from behind a cloud.

Armelia found herself smiling back. Not bothering to locate her perfumed lace hanky, she wiped her filthy hands on her clothes just as Quenelda had done.

There was movement outside.

'Armelia?' Darcy's haughty voice rang out. 'Gods! What is that awful stench? Your servants said you were in here . . .' Stepping into the dark roosts, he looked past Armelia and Quenelda into the stall; then his gaze slowly returned to take in the ripped petticoats, the goo . . . the stench . . .

'Armelia?' Darcy's tone was one of sheer disbelief. '*What* are you doing in here?'

Chapter Ten

Spring Forward

'It's so cold!' Root shivered as he buckled up Chasing the Stars' saddle, stamping his feet on the icy cobbles to get some warmth in them. Comfortably wrapped in her padded winter tack, his dragon nuzzled at him, searching for the honey tablets she knew he would be carrying. Root had been warned by Tangnost that his beloved mount was looking a little plump, and as he eased out the girth strap one notch more, he had to admit the Dragonmaster was right.

As the Month of the Wolf Moon drew to a freezing close, the snow had finally stopped falling. Dragonsdome and the Sorcerers Glen wore a thick mantel of white, the roads and viaducts of the glen were blocked, the loch frozen. Today the overcast sky had cleared, and it seemed as if, after months of confinement, everyone in the kingdom was out and about. But for Root and Quenelda and their dragons, the only place to be was in the air! Snow crunched beneath Root's feet as he took his eager mare to meet Quenelda, who was leading Two

Gulps out of the warmly glowing battledragon roosts.

Soon they were swooping above the crowded ice-locked harbours, and speeding over the loch towards the thick woodland that skirted the northern shore. The air was thick with dragons, griffins and hippogriffs. Seeing a dark opening beneath the snow-covered trees, Root and Chasing the Stars darted in. There was a strange breathless silence beneath the icy canopy, disturbed only when a branch weighted with snow snapped, or a pheasant called. Root and his mount deftly wove between the great pines, startling a herd of deer in a clearing. He could hear the cracking of brittle branches as Two Gulps battered his way through the trees behind them.

'Root?' Quenelda's voice was muffled. 'Root, where are you?'

Taking hold of a laden spruce branch, Root softly urged his dragon behind a huge pine. With a snort of smoke, Two Gulps crossed the little clearing, and then pursuing dragon and rider were almost upon them. Letting go of the branch, Root dodged out of the way as Quenelda and Two Gulps flew smack into a wall of snow. As the dragon collided with the branch, the pine tree shivered in protest, and more snow and frozen needles cascaded down, forcing them to land. Two Gulps shook his head and flamed to show his displeasure, melting more snow and drenching them. Quenelda shook her wet head, cursing as lumps of ice melted and trickled down her back. She could hear Root whooping with delight.

'Right,' she fumed as a large pine cone bounced off her head. Gathering up her reins, she urged her battledragon upwards in pursuit.

Catch him, Two Gulps! Catch him . . .

I am trying . . . came the short-tempered reply as Two Gulps struggled through the pine trees. As they failed to spot their elusive quarry, Quenelda belatedly realized that she might have a fearsome and highly trained battle-dragon of her own, but cave-dwelling Sabretooths did not have the manoeuvrability or the speed of a Widdershanks. She and Two Gulps took to the ground, and he stormed forward over the dense pine needles that coated the forest floor.

'Arghhh!' she screamed as the familiar magenta-blue dragon darted in front of her, and then, in the blink of an eye, vanished between the tree trunks. She looked up, then behind, then to her left, just as Chasing the Stars shot round Two Gulps' starboard flank and disappeared again into the gloom.

Hot on her tail, Quenelda and Two Gulps thundered out of the woodlands into blinding sunlight reflected from banks of snow. Chasing the Stars continued to torment and tease the slower battledragon. She circled and spun in the sunlight, darting about as she had done in the Cauldron, until the clumsier Sabretooth was exhausted. As Chasing the Stars swung beneath him yet again, the bad-tempered battledragon flamed.

'Oi!' Root protested as he felt the warmth brush against his cheek and kiss his mare's flank.

'Oh, Two Gulps!' Quenelda's heart was not in the reprimand. She too felt like swatting the annoying Root out of his saddle. He was as bothersome as a cloud of midges.

'Let's race,' she suggested. Two Gulps could do with letting off some steam after a long confinement in the roosts, and so could she. And of course, she always won, so – that would take Root down a peg or two.

Root's eyes lit up. He was eager to show off his new-found ease with flying. 'Where to?' The young gnome still had to think about the geography of the Sorcerers Glen.

Everything looked so different in the air, and there were so many other things to consider – tops of trees, gusts of wind, bridges, and collisions with other dragons, or bad tempered eagles.

'The Old Broch,' Quenelda suggested.

Root nodded. He could picture the ruins of the ancient circular tower that lay atop a knoll several leagues west of them.

'On the count of three: three . . . two . . .' *Now, Two Gulps!* she whispered, to give her mount a head start. 'One . . . *GO!*'

Chasing the Stars exploded into action. Despite his head start, without the help of a dragonpad, Two Gulps struggled to gain height and speed. The broken tail wasn't helping either. As they piled sideways into another deep snow drift after rounding a stand of rowan trees too swiftly, Quenelda realized with disbelief that she was going to lose. By the time she arrived at the Old Broch, the other pair had landed and Root was leaning nonchalantly against his mount's flank, chewing on a frosted blade of grass.

'We won!' he pointed out – rather unnecessarily, Quenelda thought as she brought Two Gulps down beside him.

'But, Two—'

She opened her mouth to tell Root that it had not been a fair contest; that Two Gulps was handicapped by his broken tail. Then, with an effort, she bit back her protest. Kicking her feet free of the stirrups, Quenelda slid to the ground on her mount's blind side so that Root couldn't see her face. Rummaging in her saddlebags for a flask of bramble juice, she tried to understand why she was feeling as grumpy as Two Gulps.

The answer didn't please her at all. She was *jealous*! It was a new emotion; no one had ever beaten her! No one! Flying dragons was what *she* did. It was an unpleasant experience, and fleetingly brought sympathy for the countless esquires she had humiliated and belittled for not keeping up with her. That feeling passed swiftly, however: Quenelda was not one to dwell on setbacks.

As Root and Chasing the Stars rubbed noses in mutual congratulation, Quenelda realized that the gentle dragon had changed as much as her master. They both had a new confidence since they had come to her rescue at the Winter Jousts. She had fulfilled her pledge to her father and more: she had taught Root only too well, she reflected wryly. Not that she was going to reveal that to her esquire, or anyone else. Quenelda moved round her battledragon and slid her helmet off.

'Congratulations!' She smiled, clasping Root's hand in a military grasp. Not entirely convincing, but it was a good effort, and Root only smirked a little.

Chapter Eleven

Confession

The Grand Master relaxed as he saw the brightly coloured spires of the Sorcerers Guild crowning the city skyline of the Black Isle. Now it was time to rest briefly before the Guild meeting tomorrow to discuss supplies and equipment for the XIII Stormbreakers' fortress in the Howling Glen. He was elated but exhausted. His plans were complete. Right now the hobgoblins and their Razorbacks would be nearing the Westering Isles.

Having summoned the Maelstrom, he had for the first time successfully conjured a stable vortex from its dark depths; a whirling tunnel through the darkness that had allowed him to travel the huge distance from Roarkinch to the Brimstones in a fraction of the time it would normally take. Now he could reach and fight in the coming battle and return before any noticed his absence. His power continued to grow, but it had left the taint of the maelstrom on him; his hands shook and he felt sick and dizzy. His addiction to the elixir was growing; he needed it more than ever.

But as he flew closer, he could see the unmistakable outline of a fully armoured Imperial at rest on the Guild dragonpad. The battlebanners of the SDS and the DeWinters hung limply in the still air, although the Lord Hugo would have recognized that particular dragon anywhere. Then, as he was about to land on an empty pad, he felt it – barely, the faintest prickle on his skin . . . A ward had been cast about the Guild. It was Battle Magic without a doubt; subtle, barely discernible, but very powerful. Without the power of the Maelstrom he would have failed to detect it at all. The Earl Rufus was expecting trouble.

Why?

A shiver of disquiet passed through the Grand Master's body as he handed his mount over to a groom. If Rufus knew of his treason, he would have been intercepted long before he even returned to the glen. He would be languishing in the deep prisons of Dragon Isle in chains, bound by Battle Magic.

How? How could the Earl suspect something? Well, he was forewarned. With a confident stride, and a smile on his face, he descended to his chambers.

'Hugo!'

The Earl embraced his friend, before searching his face. 'You're tired,' he observed, noting with surprise that the dark hair was streaked with silver and the deep indigo eyes so dark they almost looked black.

'I know,' the Grand Master smiled ruefully. 'I'm getting older, and the flying was difficult in this weather! I had two mounts collapse from exhaustion and frost bite. But I've raised ten thousand veterans from the north.' The Grand Master poured some wine to calm himself. 'They are striking out to reinforce all our coastal garrisons as we speak . . .' That much was true, only they would slaughter the SDS and Royal troops they found there.

'My thanks,' the Earl paused, reluctant to raise concerns about a man whom he loved like an older brother. 'Hugo, your dragon at the Jousts . . .'

The Grand Master's heart hammered as sweat trickled beneath his robes. He desperately needed his elixir and tried to still his shaking hands. His thoughts raced. Could his dark magic beat the Earl's battlemagic yet? Could he disguise its use here at the heart of the Black Isle? Chaotic magic always had unforeseen outcomes. He summoned his remaining strength.

'What of it?' he looked puzzled, merely curious.

'All thought the dragon to be rogue, but its behaviour could be seen in a different light. It behaved as a predator might.'

The Grand Master frowned, as if considering this view for the first time. 'That is true,' he conceded. 'But the stallion was spurred to madness by the reckless behaviour of my kinsman, Duke Grenville. It was he who drove the dragon to pursue you, to settle an old score. Thereafter it was the dragon's many wounds that led to so many injuries and deaths. I fear it took fright at the crowds, and that was . . . very unfortunate.'

'Yet it did not die,' the Earl persisted. 'Why did the arrows not kill it? It had the physical strength of a predator even though it had no armoured hide.'

'Ah,' the Grand Master smiled as if delighted to reveal a secret. 'I am discovered! I thought to use my knowledge and experience to breed domestic dragons that were tougher, more aggressive; that could be used by your SDS. I was hoping to have five hundred bred and trained and in the field for next year's Spring campaign; a New Year's gift to you. The Winter Joust seemed such a perfect place to show off the dragon's qualities.'

'Might you have unwittingly drawn upon the

Maelstrom?' The Earl held up a hand to forestall the angry protest forming on his friend's face. 'Hugo, you *know* you have always pushed the boundaries of learning; you ever seek after knowledge and sorcery that would be beyond the power of most to master. You delve more deeply in the ancient chronicles and scrolls . . . Think carefully. Have you unwittingly drawn upon the Maelstrom?'

The Grand Master vehemently shook his head. 'No! Not knowingly!'

'Hugo, will you then subject your findings to Inner Council, your dragons to the Breeders Guild, before we breed any more for the SDS?'

'Of course,' the lie came easily, as did the false smile.

The Earl nodded, satisfied. His daughter must be mistaken, but no wonder. Having to witness the slaughter in the Cauldron, being threatened by a rogue dragon which nearly took her life and his . . . She was still a young inexperienced child, and her imagination had run away with her. Mutually satisfied, they turned to the Inner Council tomorrow and the Earl revealed the astonishingly good news that Galtekerion was dead.

Chapter Twelve
Duchess-in-Waiting

'Ohhhh . . . are those *real* dragon opals?'

'My! What a *large* diamond!'

'Yes, isn't it . . .?' Armelia purred as she tilted her hand just so in the sun, the huge diamond engagement ring sparkling. 'It is but one of the Dragonsdome jewels, and is *quite* priceless. And now that I am Darcy's fiancée' – she spread out her skirts and pirouetted so that the layers of silk stitched with thousands of jade beads could be seen – 'I have been to Foresight and Hindsight's Emporium for a fitting. I am to have whatever I wish for my wardrobe!'

'Ooohhh!'

Armelia contemplated the gaggle of envious young ladies-in-waiting who surrounded her. Duchess-in-waiting! She could barely contain her glee! Tradition now entitled her and her parents to their own rooms in Dragonsdome and at the palace, and a larger retinue of servants and men-at-arms.

And yet it had all promised to be a total disaster when

Darcy had arrived unannounced at the nursery roosts. Armelia had done what all ladies were taught to do in tricky situations: she had fainted. After all, her dress was already ruined, and if she were not careful, her reputation would follow. Good thing she had already laid the little dragon – little *hatchling*, she corrected herself – down beside its mother to suckle. Darcy had had no option but to lift her up and take her outside – to do less would not have been chivalrous. The pleasure of being swept up off her feet, eyelids a-flutter, was somewhat ruined when he unceremoniously dumped her on the nearest haystack. Muttering loudly about his clothes and the stench, Darcy had then headed for the palace and a fresh doublet, leaving Armelia and her ladies to await a carriage. It had not been an auspicious beginning.

But by the time she had soaked in the delicious warmth of a copper bath tub in front of a roaring fire, Armelia was feeling quite restored and had decided upon a new strategy. In the unused wing of Dragonsdome where she had now been given rooms, she had noticed several portraits of Darcy's young mother, Desdemona. Following a scandal that was still the talk of the Court, Desdemona had been banished by the Earl for betraying him – but with whom no one had ever discovered. Darcy didn't talk about his mother much, other than to blame his father bitterly for her early death. He was only six when she had been sent away, leaving him with memories of a beautiful dark-haired woman who granted his every wish in defiance of his father's commands.

Armelia's stinking dress had been removed for burning. Her maids, with Darcy's permission, dressed her in a fresh gown from his mother's extensive bridal trousseau. Having them dress her hair in the same fashion as in the portraits, she swept regally down the stairs as if she already belonged at Dragonsdome.

Darcy was smitten. With sour looks, those young ladies who had arrived for dinner to see how she had survived a day 'becoming better acquainted with dragons' acknowledged that they had been outdone. Darcy only had eyes for Armelia. He knew of her disastrous first encounter with his half-sister, and took little persuading over dinner that Quenelda had quite deliberately humiliated Armelia again in an effort to split them up.

Blinking back tears, bottom lip trembling as she had been so artfully taught at Grimalkin's, Armelia explained that she had been prepared to fulfil the Queen's ridiculous edict and to suffer such indignities because she had wanted to see Darcy before he left for Dragon Isle. Who knows, she trilled helplessly, when she would see him again?

Darcy was furious with Quenelda. 'She is trying to make trouble between us. If you were my wife, all save the Queen would have to bow to you – including my wretched little half-sister!'

Not exactly the romantic and passionate declaration of undying love that Armelia had been angling for; that she had endlessly spun in her vivid imagination. But still . . . Darcy was to be hers, and in time Dragonsdome would follow! Could anyone ask for more?

And yet . . .

And yet . . .

Deep inside, Armelia now harboured a secret she would reveal to no one: she had actually enjoyed herself in the nursery roosts! It was the first time in her entire life that she had got her elegant, manicured hands dirty. A daughter of ancient nobility whose fortunes had fallen on hard times, she had been raised by a succession of nannies and indulgent parents who had lavished every last groat they had on her – including sending her to the exclusive

Grimalkin's College. Alliance to the greatest Earldom would restore her family's fortunes and their rightful place at Court.

But privileged and pampered though she was, Armelia had never done anything for herself. She had never walked in the rain; she had never dressed herself, never washed a dish. Never handled a baby dragon . . .

As for commoners, the servants and soldiers were all but invisible to the ruling Sorcerers Guild. Theirs were the mundane tasks of life, freeing the upper classes to practise their High Magic, to enjoy the fruits of life. Yet Root's quiet dignity and Quester's friendliness had given her pause for thought.

And, Armelia had grudgingly acknowledged, in Quenelda she had met a girl who had thrown off the shackles of society's expectations. A girl who was doing what she wanted to do, despite the nasty gossip that Darcy – and she herself – had spread at court. Given what she had seen of Quenelda, Armelia could very easily picture the Earl's daughter on a dragon flying into battle. *And why shouldn't she?* Armelia thought to herself in surprise.

This revelation had ignited a tiny flame of rebellion

deep within her. Yes, she still wanted Darcy – but perhaps in time she could change him, soften his attitude towards his young sister. And she could certainly try to put an end to the relentless gossip at Court. Did it matter that someone was different?

She had revealed none of this to Darcy, of course, as he slid the wondrous ring onto her finger . . .

Chapter Thirteen

The SDS Have Been Scrambled

'Galtekerion is dead.'

A wave of incredulity swept the Inner Council of the Sorcerers Guild. Had they heard the Earl Rufus correctly? Cheers broke out. Hats were hurled into the air. There had been so much bad news recently. Poor harvests followed by an early winter had drawn thousands to the city. That and the prospect of an early SDS campaign was rapidly eating up the Guild's meagre resources.

The sight of hobgoblin weapons, artefacts and tools had caused muted comment and confusion. The Council had been anxiously awaiting the arrival of the kingdom's most celebrated soldier.

The Earl limped to take his seat. He waited for the celebration to die down.

'He died of wounds taken at the Howling Glen. Our scouts found a burial cairn deep within the mountain. They recovered weaponry about the body from all thirteen tribes – and this necklace.' He held up the dragontooth amulet removed from the dead hobgoblin champion. 'The sign of Galtekerion's overlordship. And see there . . .'

He pointed to a hobgoblin standard next to the door. 'If you look, masters, you will see totems for all thirteen tribes surmounted by a new symbol, the dragon's head, the mark of Galtekerion's overlordship. And these . . .' He held up torques and bracelets of carved bone inset with gold. 'This is Galtekerion's personal rune. Many such were on and about the body.'

We immediately sent out long-range reconnaissance patrols to verify this discovery. The Frost dragons can still fly in this filthy weather. They all report the same thing: the thirteen tribes are riven with infighting, each tribe's champion seeking to take Galtekerion's place. Many are starving, fighting amongst themselves for food. The weakest have slipped into hibernation and died; their bodies litter the ice. There can be little doubt: their Warlord is dead.'

The chamber finally quietened.

'We are going to strike now before they choose another. And we are taking the Tunnel Rats with us. We are going to destroy the spawning pools.'

That left the Guildsmen breathless for a moment,

and then they cheered their Champion's audacity.

'I have spoken to the Queen: the SDS have been scrambled, all our men recalled. We leave for Dragon Isle tonight, and the Howling Glen tomorrow. From there, we fly to our forward base out on the ice. Advance elements, including all our ground attack dragons, are already on exercise there, and Frost dragons have located the islands by flying from iceberg to iceberg.'

'But, my lord,' said a tall balding Guildsman, looking worried, 'we have not been able to move up the supplies and equipment you need. The passes have long since been closed. We were hoping that if there was a break in the weather, we could ship supplies to you for the early spring. And as for more dragons . . .' He fell silent.

'Our battlegalleons and transports have been iron-clad so that they can break ice. My Cairnmore mine in the Brimstones has been shipping ore over the last five summers to the Howling Glen; more than enough brimstone for a short winter campaign. Each dragon will transport their own supplies. As you know, four of our regiments have been practising flying and fighting in blizzards for over two moons. We are using High Magic and Battle Magic as we have never used it before: to keep airborne and operational in winter. The SDS fly tomorrow. We will not fail.'

'I will personally co-ordinate moving what supplies and equipment we can up to the Howling Glen,' Hugo Mandrake, the Grand Master, promised. 'And if possible our galleons will try to support your forward base on the ice with men and supplies from royal coastal castles and keeps, though I fear they are all ice-locked.'

Guild and masters alike stood in tribute to the SDS Dragon Lord. 'May the gods bless you, and fly with you on Wings of Vengeance!'

The Earl stopped on the steps to the dragonpads as his men mounted.

'There is another pressing reason, Hugo, why we fly now. The Narwhal, Orca, White Fox and Ice Bear clans report that the ice shelf is still creeping south. Reconnaissance patrols confirm it. By the time spring comes, unless there is an early thaw in this cursed weather, the ice will bridge the sea from the Westering Isles to the mainland. The hobgoblins must be stopped before they breed and swarm onto the ice, else we will never hold them back. They will come in their millions.'

Ah . . . it was too much to hope that this would go unnoticed . . .

'You wish me to keep this news secret?'

'Yes. It would cause widespread panic. The high passes are still blocked. The roads will soon be a quagmire that would trap everyone. In this weather they would die in their droves trying to reach safety.'

'And your tactics?' The Lord Hugo tried to keep the eagerness from his voice as the Earl prepared to mount.

'We will attack when it is full dark in three weeks' time. Detailed tactics have been hammered out by our Strike Attack Group since the assault on the Howling Glen. The forward briefing with my senior officers takes place tonight on Dragon Isle. Darcy will attend. It is time my son developed an appreciation of the many aspects of warfare.'

'He is flying with you?'

'No.' The Earl's face showed fleeting sadness. 'He would be a danger to himself and those around him. No, Darcy will be attending the Academy with other cadets: he will have to earn the rank that should have been his by right if he had taken his responsibilities to heart. He will temporarily be assigned duties on Dragon Isle, once we have flown. We are taking so many that we leave only a skeleton garrison.'

The Grand Master clasped the Earl in a firm embrace. 'Take care, Rufus,' he said. 'Don't take risks – your injuries are yet to heal fully. May the gods fly with you, old friend.'

As he watched the Earl take to the air, he allowed himself a small smile of satisfaction. *A skeleton garrison? And Darcy being privy to the tactics to be employed?*

Perfect . . .

Chapter Fourteen

The Dragonsdome Ring

'What's happening?' Quenelda stood to one side as her brother stormed past, blind even to her in his fury.

Root cried out as Darcy deliberately pushed him aside, spinning him into the wall. Up ahead, Quenelda ran into her father's study. 'What's happened? Papa?'

The Earl turned from the table as Root entered, rubbing his shoulder. 'Galtekerion has died from wounds in the Battle of the Howling Glen. The tribes are breaking apart, fighting amongst themselves. We are going to strike now, while they are leaderless, half stupid with starvation and ready to hibernate.'

'But . . . but you aren't ready,' Quenelda protested. 'You haven't had time to rest and rearm, to test your winter armour. It's too cold for some of the dragons . . .'

'I know,' he said gently. 'We will lose many men and dragons before we even reach the Isles. Hundreds who are injured will never return home, will freeze to death. I—'

'But why?'

'Because it will secure a victory unlike any we have

known. It will secure peace for generations to come!'

'When do you leave?'

He came to stand beside her, took her chin and tilted it. 'Tonight for Dragon Isle. Tomorrow we fly north to rendezvous with the IV and the XVIII at the Howling Glen. The Ice Fortress is already operational. The engineers and the northern clans have moved huge supplies across the ice. We will airlift apothecaries and surgeons with us, so Tangnost will depend upon your help. Hugo's troops will man and supply the coastal castles, and provide support for our forward base if the weather allows. For the first time ever, Goose' – the Earl's eyes gleamed fiercely in the firelight – 'we take the fight to the hobgoblins!'

At the mention of the Grand Master, sudden foreboding gripped Quenelda. Why, oh why was she not a boy, so she could fight at her father's side? The Earl saw it in her face, the tense shoulders and knotted fists at her side. He gathered his daughter closely to him. 'I know you want to be flying with me. I was going to do this before I left in early spring, to announce before the Queen and Court . . .'

Her heart thumped. 'What?'

The Earl pulled a heavy ring from his finger: two golden dragons entwined. As Root stepped back in amazement, the dragons slithered and separated, forming two rings. The Earl gave one to his daughter and returned the second to his finger.

'Papa!'

'Put it on, Goose. Go on. You have earned it.'

Quenelda tentatively tried the big ring on her thumb. 'It's too big – Oh!'

The Earl smiled as the dragon curled comfortably about his daughter's thumb. She held it out at arm's length, feeling its warm weight. 'I'm heir to Dragonsdome?'

Root was stunned, eyes shifting between the Earl and his daughter.

Her father nodded. 'Yes, you are. Darcy forfeited that right at the Cauldron. All the kingdoms saw for themselves what manner of man he is. He will never be a leader; no one will respect him or follow him in battle.'

'You've told him? That's why he is so angry?'

'Yes. He has been ordered to report to Dragon Isle. He would squander Dragonsdome's inheritance and wealth, not use it to protect the kingdoms. He must never inherit, thus I give the ring to you now so that all may know my wishes should I not return.'

'Papa!'

'Never fear! The hobgoblins do not know we are coming, and we will deliver a blow from which the banners will never recover. The war will be ended, and I will be home far more often to watch my daughter grow up. Ah, Goose, don't cry. Watch for us when the moons wax.' He turned to Root. 'I charge you to care for her until I return, young man.'

'I will, my Lord,' Root said, acknowledging the Earl with a slight bow of his head.

The boy was growing up fast, the Earl mused.

'And Tangnost?' Quenelda asked. 'Does he go with you also?'

'No. Dragonsdome remains in his care. I need him here to keep an eye on everything . . . These are dangerous times.'

Chapter Fifteen

The Battle of the Westering Isles

The SDS Commander sat on the upper slopes of a glacier and watched as his battlegroup deployed about the Killing Caves of the Westering Isles. Below him, the massed ranks of his own FirstBorn Regiment stretched out across the slopes of the dormant volcano at the heart of the island.

Wave after wave of cloaked Imperials took up their positions in support of the heavy cavalry and troll marines now disembarking from transports and battle-galleons anchored close off-shore. Overhead, Imperials flew inland before stopping to hover at five hundred strides.

'Go! Go! Go!'

Ropes snaked down, and barely half a bell later, three hundred strike teams – nearly ninety thousand lightly armed Bonecracker commandos – had abseiled down and swiftly taken up position at the inland entrances to underground caverns and combs that riddled the island.

The Witching Hour approached – the time when magic was at its most potent.

The Earl beckoned his standard bearer forward. 'Give the signal.'

A beam of light streaked into the sky and exploded in twin white starbursts. The whole island was bathed in cold, white, slow-burning light, as bright as twin full moons. The battle had begun.

EEEEEareeeeeeeeeekkkkkkkkkkkkkkeeee!

Like the drumming roll of thunder the heavily armoured Sabretooths, Spitting Adders and Vipers stormed the outer caves, broad chests mowing down hobgoblins like living battering rams, great taloned feet crushing the soft-skinned warriors beneath them as they charged into the gloom, flaming as they went.

Uttering their bloodcurdling clan battle cries, the Bonecrackers entered the fray.

'Fire in the hole!'

BOOM!

The Tunnel Rats, escorted by Bonecrackers, were now deep underground, the steady rumble of their onslaught on the spawning pools reverberating like an earthquake.

Tons of rock fell into the steaming water, rich with minerals that nursed the young hobgoblins in spring.

Galtekerion flinched in the tepid waters of the deep hibernation pools as the thunder of battle pounded overhead, the sounds magnified by water; but he held his warriors back.

'They will use their cave dragons supported by the Bonecrackers to clear the combs,' the Warlock had revealed, 'and drive you into their mounted brigades and Marines deployed on the beaches. And beyond them cloaked Imperials will make sure none make the safety of the sea.

'Hold your experienced warriors back,' he commanded the Hobgoblin Warlord. 'Give them all available food to keep them strong. Sacrifice the old, the young, the weak. Do not let them know – their flight will be all the more convincing. Let them blunt the blades of our enemies, weaken their arms.'

Galtekerion's eyes glowed in the depths. The plan unfurled as the Warlock had foretold.

'Flame! Flame!'

Leaping and screaming, poorly armed hobgoblins

poured out of the caves to be met by a withering wave of dragonfire that vaporized the ice and turned the sand to glass.

As the smoke cleared, bugle notes rang out, and the SDS Commander unleashed his heavy brigades.

'Charge!'

Line upon line of Cuirassiers smashed into the closely packed ranks of hobgoblins trapped between the cliffs and the Imperials.

'Hold the line! Keep in formation!'

With savage joy, the Magma dragons pounded the hated hobgoblins into the sand beneath taloned toes tipped with barbed sheaths, whilst they struck out with their heads to seize limbs and sever heads with a single bite. Their armoured riders used their lances again and again, a swift jab, withdrawal, another, then another, leaving bodies piled in the frozen black sand. But the tide of the hobgoblins kept coming, and soon the SDS cavalry were utterly exhausted.

'Fall back! Fall back to the transports!' the bugles cried.

Streaming forwards in their wake, the desperate hob-goblins slammed into the waiting Marines' shield wall, ten ranks deep.

'Stand your ground!' Sergeants cried as the first battlespells arced overhead. 'Stand your ground, lads!' But as the hour of the Stroppy Capercaille and dawn tinged the horizon, the heavily armoured trolls of the Marines, too, fell back to their waiting transports and battlegalleons, and Imperials supported by Frost Dragons entered the fray. Purple flames blossomed across the shoreline and the hobgoblins faltered. The battle seemed lost.

'Hide in your deep hibernation pools where they cannot reach you. Let them think they have cleared the combs,' the Warlock commanded Galtekerion, 'then rise up about them. Slaughter them and their cave dragons in the combs where the Imperials cannot support them. Then drive those that survive out onto the beaches. Wait until they have landed their dragons to deploy fresh troops and airlift their injured, wait until the dragons are on the beaches and rocks, and then strike! Release the razorbacks!'

'And you, Lord?'

'I will unleash the Abyss upon them . . .'

Galtekerion shuddered as the taint of the Maelstrom swirled darkly about the Warlock like smoke. Who was this sorcerer who sought the dark rule of the maelstrom?

'The trollsss are retreating, Lord, to the transports as you sssaid they would.' the hobgoblin warrior was young and could not understand why the WarLord had not attacked, why so many hobgoblins lay dead. 'The Imperialssss have decloaked and have taken to the field.'

Galtekerion signalled his bodyguard. 'It issss time.' He bared his fearsome teeth. A horn wailed its grating command as Galtekerion and his heavily armed warriors kicked for the surface of the hibernation pools. Webbed feet and powerful thigh muscles propelled them swiftly towards the flame-licked surface above. A hundred thousand hobgoblins shot up and out of the pools, landing in the middle of the attacking Bonecrackers.

'Now, my warriorsssss,' Galtekerion hissed, a huge war mallet in his hands as he crushed a dozen commandos. 'Now we strike back at the Dragon Lordssss. It is they who are trapped.'

Weapons spun and commandos died before they even knew what was happening. Nets dragged the exhausted cave dragons into the deep pools.

In the deeps, the ominous beat of dragonskull drums began.

Boom . . . boom . . .

Crying out their ululating cry, the elite warriors leaped out of the caves and onto the open battlefield, intent on total destruction of the SDS.

The Earl Rufus frowned. More and more hobgoblins were surging out of the combs which should have been completely cleared. There was no sign of his Sabretooths or Adders, and the thunderous detonations of the Tunnel Rats had ominously fallen silent.

Sensing that the tide of the battle was turning, the Commander signalled three wings of his waiting FirstBorn regiment to engage the enemy immediately. Time to see the battlefield for himself.

'Mount up, Time to stretch our wings!'

Brothers . . . sisters . . . Stormcracker sang as he raised his wings and bared his fearsome teeth.

'Dive! Dive! Dive!' The Earl's deep voice carried over the chaos of the battlefield, as purple smoke from Stormcracker's nostrils billowed about him. The cloaked Imperials glided down over the glacier through the churning rainbow smoke, flaming as they went, a lung-searing whirlwind of hot wind, fire and death. Howls of rage and a rain of arrows and darts rose up to greet them.

Death, death to the dragon-eaters, the dragons sang as they battled amongst the hobgoblins surging onto the beaches, crushing and breaking and burning.

Boom . . . boom . . . boom . . .

Galtekerion faltered as wave after wave of hated Imperials materialized on the battlefield, deploying fresh troops and vaporizing his warriors. Doubt niggled at the back of his mind as spells and incantations arced and exploded in prisms of light, brilliant against the darkness, as the Dragon Lords unleashed their battlemagic on the field and his banners fell back against the crumbling cliffs. Bolts of fire rained down, punching holes in his massed ranks. Even with the trap reversed, the battle now hung in the balance.

Boom . . . boom . . . boom . . .

'Stay in formation . . .'

Flanked by his cloaked household guard the SDS Commander banked slowly over the cliffs and beaches, studying the seething battle below. If he didn't know better, he would say that the hobgoblin banners were fighting in wedge formation, heaviest warriors to the fore, the lesser tribes behind with nets and spears.

And they were not creatures roused from semi-hibernation, unarmoured, weak and weaponless, like those who had been driven out of the combs with the first strike attack. These huge tattooed warriors were fully armed veterans from all thirteen tribes fighting together, ragged tribal standards whipping in the wind. Then he saw another topped by a dragon skull in the thick of the press.

'Galtekerion!' he breathed in horror, searching the seething hordes below. The Warlord was clearly alive and held back his best troops, as if he had known all along what tactics the SDS would employ! He was directing the tribes according to their fighting strengths, a tactic hitherto unheard of amongst the undisciplined thirteen tribes. This was a trap!

'Fall back!' he ordered his officers. 'First Born and Nightstalkers, combat retreat. SeaReavers, cover us . . .' The Earl's standard bearer raised his battlestaff. Two balls of red streaked into the air to explode, followed by white.

'Combat retreat! Combat retreat!'

Seeing the SDS waver in uncertainty, Galtekerion roared: 'SSSSSSSSummon them!'

A horn blasted out, the sound carrying far beneath the icy water. Its call was answered by a fearsome cry that promised death.

Chapter Sixteen

Treason!

All about the island, the remnants of the Earl's army were withdrawing under cover of their Dragon Lords onto the already crowded beaches, when carnage erupted about them.

The ice around the transport ships rose up and cracked. It was as if the rocky shoreline were moving beneath the marines' feet, tumbling them into the sea, where hobgoblin suckers pulled them down and down. The large midnight-skinned creatures that surged up were the stuff of nightmares. Sickly green sorcery played and crackled about them as they surged out of the sea, hobgoblins clustered like barnacles between their barbed flanks. The beasts hissed like snakes, dark smoke to engulf the fighting commandos and hobgoblins alike.

'Hostile dragons! Hostile dragons!' the panicked cry sowed disbelief amongst the SDS.

'Alpha Wing – down, down, down!' the Earl ordered, throwing in his last reserves and bringing Stormcracker round. 'Hostile dragons on the shoreline!'

He lifted his staff and bolts rained down on the Razorbacks, driving the creatures back into sea.

'Kill them,' Galtekerion urged his warriors forwards. 'Kill the Dragon Lordsssss firssssst, then the resssst are yourssss to feed on. Ssssweet dragon flessssssh . . . man flessssssh . . .

Boom . . . boom . . .

Arrows and darts rained down on the SDS thudding into shields and piercing armour. Sabretooths and Adders fell first to the black breath, and then the heavier Magma dragons slowed and fell. Only battlemages and Imperials remained standing amidst the ranks of hobgoblins, immune to their dragons' fatal dark sorcery.

'We have them. The Dragon Lordssss will die!' Galtekerion threw in his champions. In the deep waters, canyons and combs, dragon drums beat furiously.

Boom . . . boom . . . boom . . .

'DeWinter! DeWinter!'

The staff in the Earl's hand writhed and took on new form, burning a blazing circle of fiery golden death about him. Bolts sizzled out across the battlefield, striking a full score of Razorbacks, vaporizing a thousand hobgoblin warriors that clung to their barnacled hides. But the creatures they rode roared and barely lost their stride; they seemed to drink in the power of the staff, their mouths gaping wetly in slavering delight as they fell on SDS dragons. The Earl's eyes widened. Nothing should have withstood that battle spell save an Imperial, the last of the dragons with magic of their own. This was no natural born creature; this was spawned in the Abyss, given life by dark sorcery.

KKKKKKKKkkkkkkkkkrraaaaaaaaaaaaaaaaakkkk kkkkkkkk!

Stormcracker charged at three Razorbacks who were blocking the retreat of injured commandos. Sorcery coruscated about the Earl and his dragon, a golden nimbus of energy: a Dragon Lord revealed in his full power. The great Imperial rose onto his hind legs and came down on a Razorback, snapping its spine. A second Razorback's neck was broken by his lashing tail which cleared space for marines and commandoes to gain the safety of his back, and the SDS Commander stunned the third with a powerful bolt, leaving his Bonecrackers to finish it off.

'Sssssssssuround them. Use the netssss. Bring them down!' Galtekerion cried.

All about the battlefield the Dragon Lords were

extracting their troops, but even the mighty Imperials could not fight such overwhelming odds. As the dragons set down to pick up their troopers, hobgoblins swarmed up their wings and legs too, overpowering them.

Rage and dragon flames erupted across the battlefield as first one SDS Imperial was overwhelmed by sheer numbers, then a second and a third, roaring its defiance even as it drowned beneath choking slime. Stormcracker was struggling to keep his wings free of the never ending assault when a huge hobgoblin leaped out of the heaving throng, a juvenile imperial tooth hung about his neck.

'Mine, he isssss mine . . .'

Climbing onto the backs of dead comrades the hobgoblin leaped at the SDS Commander, bringing a huge sword down on him. It ricocheted off the Dragon Lord's defensive nexus, but the force of the blow knocked the Earl to his knees.

'Galtekerion!'

Galtekerion hissed through his gills. The honour of killing this dread Dragon Lord would cement his place as Warlord of all the hobgoblin tribes.

Baring his serrated teeth the hobgoblin struck and struck again. Sparks flew from the Earl's spelled sword as he deflected blow after blow. Shards of brilliant light built at his fingertips. He raised his hand to strike . . .

A wounded Razorback loomed out of the swirling sooty snow and crashed into Stormcracker, enveloping the Earl's battledragon in dark smoke and dislodging Galtekerion who fell away with a cry. Spines penetrated the Earl's nexus, gouging holes in the Dragon Lord's armour and breaking his arm and ribs. His navigator died instantly, skewered to his seat. Others drove deep into Stormcracker's armoured hide.

KKKKKKKkkkkkkkkkrraaaaaaaaaaaaaaaaa kkkkkkkkkkk!

Poison touched their skin and spread through their bodies. The Earl lifted numb hands to his dragon helmet, the seamless join dissolving at his touch. He lifted his helmet with trembling arms and his hands came away dark and sticky with blood. The pain on the right side of his face was growing, corrosive tendrils spreading like a living root and burrowing down like a cancer. The SDS Commander fell back into his damaged pilot's chair, his right arm hanging uselessly. The Earl's nexus sizzled and coruscated with sickly green tendrils that danced about him.

'Combat retreat,' he cried. 'Retreat to Open Sky!'

All about him Imperials struggled to get airborne. The battle was lost.

Far out on the ice, a lone figure raised his arms to the sky. Corrupt magic shimmered about the Grand Master and gathered at his fingertips. The air above the Westering Isles was suddenly freezing, cracking, tearing, as if the Abyss itself was opening. Sickly lightning struck the battlefield, burning through the swirling snow and sooty smoke to reveal only heaped piles of bones and armour where two Bonecracker platoons and four wings of the 4th Frost Brigade had been moments before. Lightning bolts cracked and boomed, searching for the rising battledragons seeking the sanctuary of open sky. An Imperial crashed smoking onto a battlegalleon laden with the wounded.

The Maelstrom is rising!

The triumphant ululations of the hobgoblin hordes filled the air. Dragonskull drums beat frantically, their song echoing throughout the combs, beating like a giant heart, enslaved to a single will.

Boom . . . boom . . . boom . . .

The Maelstrom is rising!

The wind was shrieking, whipping the falling snow, obscuring the battlefield. Frost was forming on the Earl's armour, its ferny white tendrils devouring everything in its bitter embrace. Soldiers and dragons on the beaches froze where they stood.

'Traitor!'

Powerful malicious magic lay thickly on the battlefield as the Earl searched for the traitor. For traitor there was: a Warlock who had turned on his own kind. Now the Earl knew the face of his enemy, the hidden hand behind the hobgoblin alliance, who had enslaved these savage creatures to his will. An Arch Mage who had turned to the dark power of Maelstrom Magic. And that Warlock had a name: his lifelong friend.

'Hugo! Curse you! What have you done?'

Drums beat like a pulse in the Earl's head.

The Maelstrom is rising!

'Stormcracker!' the Earl called in hopeless rage as hobgoblins swarmed towards him over the heaped bodies of their comrades. 'We are betrayed! Retreat to Open Sky.'

'Combat retreat! Combat retreat,' the trumpet rang out, as red flared in the sky and blood flowed into the sand. '*Combat retreat!*'

Chapter Seventeen

Nightmare

It was freezing in the Sorcerers Glen. Ice covered the water in the washbasin in Quenelda's bedchamber. The Earl's daughter turned restlessly in her bed, throwing off the heavy quilt. She was dreaming of dragons, dreaming that she was a dragon . . . dreaming that she was Stormcracker . . .

It was the blackest, darkest night she had ever known. The air was treacle-thick and choked with Battle Magic. Heavy clouds forked with green lightning were gathering in the night sky, obscuring the stars. A concussion of explosions ripped through the air as the Dragon Lords tried to protect their retreating men. Dragons died, their song silenced in her head.

Her twin hearts were thumping, racing. She was wounded, weakened, her side burning. Dark dragons were clustered along the shoreline so that the Earl's exhausted troops and heavy dragons could not reach the safety of the transports. With a burst of raw hatred she flamed, feeling the power of her breath vaporize the ice-bound sea itself, hearing the hobgoblins' high, thin squeals abruptly cut off. Thick dark smoke stung her eyes: Dark Magic from the Abyss – an ancient foe was rising. A Sabretooth was pounding over the ice, trying to reach a departing transport. It died under the combined assault of three dark dragons; then the laden transport was gone too, swallowed by the water.

Rage filled Quenelda as a roostmate staggered and fell beneath the hobgoblin hordes: the Imperial was hidden beneath a mound of heaving hobgoblins, pale as maggots devouring a carcass, the dragon's frantic cries filling her head, then abruptly falling silent.

Time slowed. The wind shrieked. Lazy, fat flakes of snow fell thickly. A dragon flamed. She never saw the Razorback until it smashed into her from behind, killing dozens. Hurtled sideways, the impact punched the air out of Quenelda's lungs. She felt bones crack. Spikes lanced into her side. Hot blue blood spurted into the freezing night. Instinctively she rolled, flaming as she spun, hearing the cries of the injured who weren't strapped in falling away. More deaths . . . Her serrated tail and talons searched for the soft underbelly, spilling the dragon's steaming entrails into the night.

She felt the subtle touch of rein and hand, heard her bonded Dragon Lord's command clear across the battlefield; fearful words that touched Quenelda's dreaming mind and shook her to her core. 'Treason! Treason! Combat retreat!' her father cried. 'Combat retreat!'

Snow weighed down her injured wings – along with hundreds of the wounded, who clung on desperately, trying to reach the safety of her spinal plates. But many fell away into darkness every time her wings beat downwards. The air was brittle, freezing her wings, crackling in her lungs.

'Treachery, treachery,' the Earl cried as he slipped into darkness. 'Fly! Fly for your lives!'

Then the blizzard obliterated everything.

Quenelda woke with a start, a scream on her lips that brought Root stumbling through from the outer chamber, cursing as he stubbed his toe on the great wooden bedstead.

'Treachery! Fly! Fly for your lives!'

'Quenelda?' Root rekindled the fire and lit a taper, his hand shaking so much he could barely hold the candle. He looked down at his friend, smothering a curse as the hot wax poured over his knuckles. Quenelda was thrashing from side to side.

'Quenelda, wake up, wake up, you're dreaming.'

She sat up suddenly. Bending forward, she struggled to draw breath. She coughed and coughed and coughed. Freezing smoke filled the air about her. Root drew back. Such a strange smell . . . He frowned, upturned nose wrinkling as he sniffed: brimstone and the bitter stench of scorched scales. Quenelda pushed back her sweat-soaked hair and opened her eyes. Root dropped the candle in fright. Her eyes blazed so bright that they lit the bedchamber, and at their heart a roiling black that reflected movement and colour from some other place. Dark scales followed the ridge of her right brow and cheek.

Plucking up the guttering candle, Root held it high. 'Quenelda, what's happening? What's happening to you?'

'P-Papa . . .' Quenelda reached out desperately, her voice strangely deep and rasping. Her hand met empty air. 'Papa . . .' she swallowed, trying to find her voice. The dream was so vivid she could smell the brimstone, feel its hot burning sulphur catching in her throat as her dragon soul retreated. Heart pumping, she shivered in the frosty air and pulled the bed furs closer.

'Quenelda?' Root put down the candle, trying not to show his own anxiety. 'You look like you've seen a ghost.'

'They've been betrayed.' Quenelda's teeth were chattering. 'They're dead. They're all dead . . .'

'Hush.' Root held her frozen hand between his. 'It's just a nightmare. Sleep . . .'

Quenelda's eyes closed and her head fell back on the pillows, hair spilling over her face.

'There, sleep now,' the gnome whispered, pulling up the quilt and tucking it about her. 'Don't worry. Another moon and your father will be home.'

Stepping over to the window and throwing back the curtains, he gazed out into the darkness.

Won't he?

Chapter Eighteen

The Maelstrom is Rising

The Lord Hugo Mandrake was exhausted. Each time he drew upon the Maelstrom it was becoming harder to hide the effects of Dark Magic. His eyes were turning blacker; a fine latticework of green veins now stretched over his brittle skin. He had no appetite – at least for ordinary food and drink. His mastery of elemental power was growing; the dark of the Maelstrom was rising at his command. Over-confidence had conjured a blizzard far worse than that at the Cauldron; one that drove even mighty Imperials into the ground and overturned and sank their transports and galleons. But once unleashed, it surged out of control, and now the north beyond the Old Wall – that ancient relic of the First Age, a wall that crossed the highlands – was buried beneath a unnaturally brutal winter.

He had, perhaps, been too ambitious too soon, because the surge of power that had flowed through his veins during the Battle of the Westering Isles had left him feeling sick and scorched inside, unable to stand. Barely able to open a portal in the raging blizzard he had created, he fled the ice shelf before he was discovered, racing through the nexus for the sanctuary of his nearest castle on the Northern Isles, and from there to a keep close to the Howling Glen. The effort had exhausted him. Something was wrong; the toxic elixir that gave him the strength to survive was no longer enough.

The ancient Dragonsdome Chronicles had recorded that chaotic Maelstrom Magic, once unleashed, was ultimately uncontrollable. Housed in the vanished Sky Citadel, the Chronicles had been lost these past two thousand years. Only the Dragon Whisperers, so legend said, had the power to defeat warlocks, and they too had long since passed from the mortal realm, vanished into history.

The candle burned down. The Inner Council were meeting tonight. The city was growing restless, and the watch were fully deployed keeping order. There had already been several incidents of looting as rumours of disaster swept the Black Isle.

The cauldron changed colour. The freezing liquid sizzled as it touched the soft metal. Hand shaking so badly he could barely hold the pewter tankard, the Grand

Master dipped it into the brew. Greedily he drank down the elixir and let the goblet fall with a clang. He sank to his knees within the cloak of concealment he had cast, and wrapped his arms about himself, rocking to and fro, his heart pounding. His skin shifted and moved as if something alive lay beneath it. Hugo Mandrake stifled a groan, doubling up as the elixir consumed him, changing him, mending his broken body.

Chapter Nineteen

The Thaw

A pale dawn tickled the horizon. The endless blizzard had finally exhausted itself, and silence lay in its place. A thaw had set in, and the ice about the island was breaking up. On the ancestral lands of the Narwhal clan, a dwarf fortress almost buried by snow drifts was stirring into life. Sentries in sealskin and furs stamped their feet to warm them and began to wonder if today they would finally learn the fate of the SDS. It was half a moon since the outriders from the SDS fortress at the Howling Glen had come to the island seeking news of the battle that had taken place far to the west.

As the light grew in the east, a sentry squinted and rubbed his eyes. The shoreline was littered with huge shapes, the cry of sea crows loud and raucous in the early dawn. *Whales perhaps*, the dwarf prayed. The clan were near starvation. If a pod of whales had beached, there would be food enough for this cursed long winter and more. Blubber to render into oil for lamps, bones for tools and weapons. Lifting his axe, he roused his fellows.

They left their long houses and made their way through the ramparts and down the cliff path to the shore. Complaining loudly, the sea crows grudgingly gave way to the group.

More colour leached into the sky, giving the grey shapes texture and colour. The dwarf fell to his knees, his axe falling unheeded onto the sand. A cry of horror broke from his lips. The great shapes lying frozen on the sand were not whales.

They were dragons: *battledragons*.

'Launch the swiftest of our longboats, choose our best sailors. We must send word to Dragon Isle.'

Chapter Twenty

The SDS Have Fallen

As every day passed without news, the rumours and counter-rumours grew wilder. Winter's grip grew harsher. Fear and panic spread around the city. Afraid, and on the verge of panicking themselves, the councillors of the Sorcerers Guild were fractious. As the door swung open to admit the now familiar tall figure of the Strike Commander, Jakart DeBessert, the sound died on a wave of hope that this time he would report good news.

'Well?' the Grand Master demanded.

DeBessert was shocked by the changes he saw in the Guild's most powerful sorcerer. The man's eyes were feverish with exhaustion as he rose shakily to his feet. The weight had fallen off him, and his face had a pallid, almost green tinge to it. Dark hair was now turned to silver.

By the Gods, he looks dreadful! He can barely stand. His grief is eating him like a cancer . . . He loves the Earl like a brother . . .

'Well?' The hoarse voice of the Lord Hugo Mandrake broke into his thoughts. 'What has happened? Where are they? Nearly a moon has passed since the SDS departed for the Westering Isles.'

'My lords, we have had word from an Elder of the Narwhal clan that the thaw in the north has brought bodies of dragons and men to their shores. Bodies beyond counting, burned beyond recognition. A few dragons and their riders made it ashore.'

'There are survivors?' The hoarse words were torn from the Grand Master.

'No, my lord – their minds were turned to madness. Clan mages cared for them as best they could, but had not seen the like of their injuries, and before long they all died, as did all those who tended them.'

They bear the taint of the Maelstrom . . .

The Guildsmen were on their feet, a dozen questions on their tongues.

'But they had escaped the battle?'

'Then there could be others . . .'

'Is there no other news?'

'I regret there is more, Masters,' The Strike Commander's words cut through the babble. 'Come the spring, if the ice continues to spread south, the hobgoblins will cross it in their droves.'

The Grand Master cursed inwardly. So far that news had died with the SDS Commander and his men. This Strike Commander was one to watch.

There was a stunned silence, then the frightened Guildsmen surged forward about DeBessert. The Lord Hugo thumped his staff on the floor for silence and turned dark eyes on the Commander.

'Come spring, can Dragon Isle hold the line? Do you have enough dragons? Enough men?'

'My Lord Grand Master—' the SDS Commander began.

The building shook to its foundations. All heads turned to where the Guild pads were anchored. Faint shouts could be heard. Hope kindled in every mind but one. The chamber held its collective breath, hoping beyond hope to see a familiar figure stride through the door. Hearts raced – none more so than the Grand Master's. Grasping his staff so hard it hurt, he gathered dark sorcery about him, ready to open a portal. The harsh clatter of footsteps on stone echoed down the stairwell. All eyes followed their progress as they came closer and closer, everyone eager for good news.

Urgent hammering sounded. The heavy doors crashed

open. A young Dragon Lord burst in, chest heaving, breath as ragged and torn as his armour. He wore the badge of a Group Captain in the Nightstalkers.

'My l-lords' – his horror-struck eyes sought DeBessert's and held them with a desperate intensity – 'I bear word of the battle. My lords, the SDS have fallen. They are all dead, all devoured. The Ice Fortress is also destroyed, and the scent of strange sorcery lies heavy about it. The hobgoblins were ravenous; starving. In the aftermath of the battle, they . . . they *feasted*, my lord. They and their . . . their dragons.'

A gasp echoed about the chamber. Hands flew to mouths and hearts. Hobgoblin dragons? *Dragons?* That could not be. The hobgoblins and dragons were ancient enemies. The guildsmen's cries drowned out the young officer's next words.

'Sir' – he spoke urgently, softly to DeBessert – 'sir, only the magic of our Imperials and Arch Mages could wound or kill them. Sir, what does that mean?'

'Keep that news to yourself,' DeBessert commanded quietly, 'until we return to Dragon Isle. It means that these creatures are spawn of the Maelstrom.'

Shocked to silence, the young man nodded.

'Dragons born of the Maelstrom?' Suddenly the Grand Master was at the young man's shoulder. 'Are you sure?'

'Yes. They are black as the Abyss, covered in poisonous spikes, and their foul breath kills all it touches. But that is not all . . .' The young man swayed. 'There was a huge hobgoblin whose dragon flew the banner of their warlord. I recognized him from the Battle of the Howling Glen. It *was* Galtekerion. He *is* alive! And there is no sign of the Earl Rufus – he must have fallen in battle with his men!'

With a groan, he crashed forward. Only then did they see the barbed quarrels that protruded from his back. As members of the Apothecaries Guild came to help him, the Grand Master staggered and sat heavily on his chair.

'I must attend the Court,' His voice sounded unnaturally loud in the utter silence. 'The Queen must be informed of this latest news. It will cause her great grief, as it does me.' He beckoned a servant forward. 'Have my dragon saddled immediately. I must fly.'

'I will accompany you, my Lord.' DeBessert closed his eyes.

They are all dead? The SDS is utterly destroyed.

Chapter Twenty-One

Holding the Line

The Queen had had a harrowing night. Having learned of the Earl Rufus's fate from the Grand Master, she had been faced with the task of breaking the heartrending news to his daughter. A daughter who loved her father, who dreamed of flying at his side; a daughter who had grown so much in the last year, showing the first hints of who she would become as a woman. By the time the Queen's Constable returned with Quenelda and her esquire from Dragonsdome, the girl must have known. She could not have failed to hear the tolling bells, or see the standards flying at half-mast over the palace. Queen Caitlin had met Quenelda and gently told her of their loss; had explained that many lost those whom they loved in times of war. That her beloved father was dead – to the eternal grief of them all.

Caitlin was prepared for heartbreak. But instead of tears, there had been defiance. A stubborn refusal to believe that her father was dead – and the shocking accusation of betrayal by the Grand Master.

'He's not dead,' Quenelda insisted tearfully. 'He survived. Stormcracker bore him away.'

Sir Gharad looked at her in pity. 'How do you know, child?'

When questioned, Quenelda revealed to the Queen and her Constable a dream she'd had on what she believed to be the night of the battle. A dream of dragon fighting dragon. Dark dragons like Midnight Madness, only worse, far worse. A dream of Stormcracker bearing her injured father away from the battlefield, the cry of treason on his lips. But where he was now, or why he had not returned to the Howling Glen or Dragon Isle, she could not say.

'Maybe he's too badly wounded,' she insisted tearfully. 'Or Storm is too injured to fly, or they are hiding from the Grand Master's men.'

Stunned, shocked, suddenly hopeful, the Queen's heart leaped within her, despite her Constable's gentle restraint.

'Majesty,' Sir Gharad cautioned, knowing what she was thinking. 'Even if the Earl survived the battle he may yet have died from his wounds.'

The young Queen knew he was right. When the weather allowed flying, the SDS Search and Rescue patrols had found nothing; but there were thousands of islands and caves off the rugged west coast where survivors could be concealed. She was foolish, she knew it, but she wanted to believe, like Quenelda, that the Earl was still alive, hidden somewhere, nursing his wounds, waiting until spring came to return home. Nothing could fly in the howling blizzards that now swept the north.

But if they were to believe Quenelda's dream that the Earl had survived the battle, then they must also believe the horrifying, unthinkable news that the SDS had been betrayed by a man at the heart of the kingdom – the Earl's childhood friend and Grand Master of the Guild. But who could they tell and what could they do? Who had the power to defy a warlock? To betray their suspicions would tear Court and Guild apart, and there was not a shred of proof for any of it save Quenelda's word.

The Queen and Sir Gharad decided to reveal Quenelda's dream to the new SDS Commander, Jakart DeBessert. He needed to know – all of it. But no one else, they agreed. Their fears and hopes must be hidden from the Guild – and particularly from the Grand Master himself. An opportunity came as the Dragon Lord was given a private audience with his Queen to confirm his new rank.

On the way he passed Quenelda and her esquire stumbling numbly along the corridor. He looked at their tearful, distraught faces with sympathy. He had lost many friends, but soldiers knew the risks they took. Few considered the price their loved ones paid when they failed to return home from the war.

But that sympathy did not extend to believing Quenelda's story.

'Majesty,' he gently protested as the Queen wept, 'the Earl's daughter is twelve – how can you believe her? It is just a childish dream. A fantasy born of fear and hope.'

When the Constable revealed that the Grand Master was a warlock whose folly had nearly killed the Earl at the jousts, DeBessert was still unconvinced.

'Majesty, the dragon turned rogue through its injuries. The Lord Hugo and the Earl are virtually brothers – you just need to look at the Grand Master to see how distressed he is by this terrible news. And anyway, why would a man who already has everything want more?'

The Queen was determined to be believed: the future of her kingdoms depended upon this. 'Quenelda says that the hobgoblins have dark dragons, birthed by Maelstrom Magic, conjured by the warlock in our midst.'

The new Commander's face froze in place. *Their own dragons? None know that save the Inner Council. Can the rest of the dream be true then too?* Doubt unravelled in his mind. 'But, Madam,' he stuttered, 'how could you know this? I . . .'

Seeing the man's hesitation, Sir Gharad took a gamble. 'Quenelda is no ordinary twelve-year-old girl. She is a Dragon Whisperer, Jakart.'

The constable had once commanded the SDS before injury and old age retired him to Court. His word was enough for a young man brought up on tales of this old knight's legendary valour on the battlefield.

DeBessert's mind raced at this new information. 'The lost Dragonsdome Chronicles are said to foretell the rise of a Dragon Whisperer,' he whispered.

'A Dragon Lord of unparalleled power who would return to protect the kingdoms from the rising darkness in one final cataclysmic conflict . . .' Sir Gharad finished the legend for him. 'Where does it say that it has to be a *man*?'

Chapter Twenty-Two

The Black Cortège

On the Black Isle, the frosted turrets of the royal palace glittered in the harsh late-winter sun. Ravens in their white winter plumage cawed harshly in the hushed silence that hung over the city. No dragons flew beneath the milky sky. The blizzard had blown itself out, and the air was silent and empty of life.

In black mourning robes, Quenelda, the Queen and the royal retinue stepped out onto the terrace beneath a black awning. Her face hidden behind a veil, the Queen stood silent and still, supported by her Constable, Sir Gharad. His right arm lay lightly around Quenelda's stiff shoulders. The Earl's daughter was refusing to accept her father's death, even as she stood on the balcony before the Black Cortège.

To the left of the Queen stood Commander DeBessert and the Grand Master. The Commander's young son, the Lord Guy, stood proudly behind his father. The young man had yet to see battle, having initially been refused active service because of the injury caused by the Lord

Darcy's reckless behaviour some moons earlier. Now everyone who could fight was welcome in the ranks of the SDS, crippled or not, and the boy had been working hard learning to fight left-handed. His animosity towards Darcy was evident in the stiff way he ignored the Earl-in-waiting.

The castle quadrangle to their left billowed hotly with men's breath and dragon smoke. The clash of arms and bridles, the shouts of sergeant-majors as the ranks of the Black Cortège formed up, sounded brittle in the silence.

On a high tower the bugler sucked in a deep breath. Silver notes shivered in the still cold air. With a saw-toothed screech, the black-draped gates of the Royal Household Cavalry swung open. Following a loud cry of command, the Cortège stepped out onto the cobbled square.

Seven regimental standard bearers on juvenile Imperial Blacks rode out first; their battle banners bearing an image of the triple-headed dragon glinted in the wan light. The Imperial Black that followed the juveniles was a magnificent young mare, selected and led by Tangnost.

The high-cantled military saddle on the Imperial Black was empty, the stirruped boots reversed to symbolize a

Dragon Lord who would fly no more. The SDS and DeWinter standards flew above the saddle's high back. A cadet sat astride the great dragon's withers, and with two silver kettle drums beat out the slow funeral march. The battledragon moved slowly forward to the beat of the drum. Smoke poured from her flared nostrils, leaving a vapour trail of purple haze. The crowd that lined the square was silent, overawed by the dragon's size; it was unthinkable that such magnificent creatures could have been destroyed by the hobgoblins. If these great creatures could not defend them, who could?

'Oh, Papa . . .' Quenelda was suddenly crushed by grief. She shivered in her thick black brocade. Hot tears held in check for so long now fell freely down her cheeks at the sight of the Imperial Black, so like Stormcracker Thundercloud III. She tried to swallow and couldn't; her grief welled up in her throat and threatened to choke her. Then a hand found Quenelda's shaking right hand and squeezed it fiercely: Root was standing at her shoulder.

'I'm here,' he said softly. 'Right here behind you.'

He knew that she was still refusing to accept that her father was not coming home. She was also refusing to attend her brother's Knighthood Ceremony and investiture as Earl. Root was afraid. The look of barely suppressed fury and jealousy that he saw in Darcy's eyes when Quenelda had refused had frightened him. He had been the only witness when the Earl had made Quenelda his heir, and no one would believe the word of a young girl and a commoner against that of the Lord Darcy. Once Quenelda's brother was Earl, what would happen to them all?

Then Root's own heart thumped in his chest as seven small Lesser Chameleons followed the Imperial, representing regimental scouts. Had Root's father, Bark Oakley, lived, he would be there representing the First Born.

Stopping at the centre of the courtyard in front of the balustrade, the Imperial turned towards the west and Dragon Isle. The Queen then cast down winter flowers over the Cortège. Quenelda stepped forward and watched them tumble down at the battledragon's feet.

The Grand Master watched over the scene with hidden glee. His predatory eyes settled upon the young Earl-in-waiting, his head bowed in this apparent moment of grief. In the glittering flamboyant uniform of a captain of the

II Royal Unicorn Regiment, Darcy's only concession to protocol was the black-braided jacket and the plume of black unicorn hair that crowned his gold-engraved helmet. The Grand Master knew the boy's grief was false, that he could hardly wait until his father was buried so that he could become Earl.

Darcy's fury at his father's decision to send him to Dragon Isle had been most timely. The young man had needed little persuasion to reveal the Earl's final plans, his detailed tactics, thereby betraying his father just as his mother had before him. *And why not?* The Grand Master smiled inwardly. After all, the boy was truly *his* son, produced during his affair with DeWinter's wife, and would one day fight at his side. Already the dismantling of Dragonsdome had begun. Even now his men were there. The Earl's pedigree battledragons, all save the Imperials, would be his before nightfall, in exchange for a string of golden unicorns and a small fortune in gold. He looked at his son's fiancée, the Lady Armelia, soon to be Duchess of Dragonsdome; a vain, avaricious young lady, eager to spend the fabled wealth of the DeWinters. Well pleased, the Grand Master turned back to the Cortège.

Elegant Frost dragons drew a gasp from the crowds. Wearing white-scaled hauberks that hung to their knees beneath white enamel armour, and full-faced helmets, they looked ghostly. The massed ranks of the elf Midland Lancers behind them marched ten abreast, their long-bannered lances a thicket of steel-tipped colour.

The crowd instinctively drew back from the scaled Spitting Adders of the Deepwoods Light Company as they clattered out of the barracks; their venom led to convulsions and paralysis, then death. The arrival of the Sabretooths, their measured tread vibrating on the cobbled street, broke through Quenelda's misery. As they thumped past, she thought of Two Gulps waiting impatiently for her return. She longed for the solace of Open Sky. At least she still had him – and Root and Tangnost. They were her family until her father returned. She clenched her jaw and balled her fist. *He will return!* she thought fiercely. *He will!*

He's gone! He will never return, Darcy thought jubilantly as he watched the high-stepping unicorns of the II and III Household Cavalry swept by in graceful lines, the dappled white of the Light Brigade and the Heavy Brigade of golden unicorns, soon to be his to command.

And so the Cortège passed by, a bright glitter of scale and helmet and claw wending down the city's great boulevards and avenues towards the harbour.

As the final footsteps faded from the quadrangle, heads turned up: five air wings of Imperials flew low overhead to honour their dead commander. The pebbled armour of their bellies and tails filled the sky, while their wings raised skirls of snow in their wake. The young Imperial at the centre of the square stood on her hind legs and spread her great wings. Tangnost didn't move as powerful gusts of air buffeted the watching crowds. They drew back in fear as the huge battledragon crouched, sprang and slowly rose upwards.

Quenelda gripped the railings of the balcony; she watched the squadrons swing round to come in low over the city. As they approached the Guild Square, the Imperial Black rose to take up formation in their centre. The dragons flew higher and higher, until they were dwindling specks in the sky. Then they were gone, and only a stunned silence remained. Leaning heavily on the arm of her Constable, the Queen turned back to the palace, leaving the drifting snow and the keening lament of the pipes.

* * *

'Let me mull some wine for you, you're frozen!'

Quenelda hadn't moved. After she returned from her father's memorial, she had changed back into her familiar clothes. Since then she had sat silently staring at the fire. Root fussed about the chamber, chatting mindlessly in an attempt to distract her. Both of them jumped when someone banged urgently on the outer door.

'Lady Quenelda! Lady Quenelda!' Quester barged in without waiting to be announced by the footman. 'You've got to get down to the battleroosts. They're taking the dragons away!'

'What?' Quenelda looked at him through dully uncomprehending eyes.

'Men wearing the livery of the Grand Master.' Quester's tone was desperate, his face chalk-white with shock. 'The Lord Mandrake's men. Quenelda, they're taking the battledragons. Dozens have already gone, by force – they are using dragon collars! Tangnost is trying to stop them, but he's heavily outnumbered.'

Root looked from one to the other in confusion as Quenelda rose shakily to her feet. 'Dragon collars?' he echoed. 'What are they?'

'They're vicious!' Quenelda was almost in tears again. 'They're collars forged with powerful spells of *domination* and *obedience*, used to compel dragons, even Imperials, to obey. The collar eats into them, enslaves them. It's brutal. Unskilled trainers use them. But Dragonsdome never has!' She clenched her jaw. 'Come on,' she said, wiping her nose with the back of her sleeve. 'We've got to stop them!'

Chapter Twenty-Three

Whip and Spur

With Root and Quester at her heels, Quenelda burst into the inner courtyard of the battleroosts just as, with a crack of a dragonwhip, a collared Sabretooth rose into the air from the lowered dragonpads. The courtyard and roosts below were crowded with grooms, all in the Grand Master's livery. Orders and shouts overlaid the confusion; smoke poured from unsettled battledragons. Bound by spurred whips and dragon collars, they were being saddled in the dragonpits. Mouth open in protest, Quenelda started forward, but stumbled over something – or some*one*.

Tangnost lay unconscious on the ground at her feet, guarded by two Dragonsdome men-at-arms, who were looking very embarrassed.

'What happened? What are you doing?' Quenelda touched the dwarf's bleeding head. 'Why are you not tending him?' she demanded furiously.

The older of the two shuffled awkwardly, not meeting her gaze. 'Orders, Lady,' he mumbled into his beard. 'Orders from the Earl.'

His companion nodded anxiously. 'The Earl-in-waiting, Lady Quenelda,' he clarified. 'Your brother.'

The soldiers stepped back hastily as Quenelda glared at them. 'And did my brother order you to injure him?'

'He wouldn't let the Grand Master's men in, Lady. Was about to fight them all. Their dragonmaster is a nasty bit of work – he don't fight clean. We had to restrain Bearhugger for his own sake.'

'You've knocked him out.' Quenelda was outraged. 'From behind!'

'Lady, it was the only way.' The older soldier grinned nervously at her. 'Would have got injured ourselves otherwise!'

'You must look after him now,' she ordered them. 'Fetch the apothecary.'

The soldiers jumped to obey, grateful to have a task that was more to their liking. Root looked at Quenelda. She had changed so much of late, more and more of her father revealing himself in her manner. The men respected her; she was still a young girl, but they jumped to obey. He'd heard the scathing remarks about her brother in the eating halls and barracks

'Who's in charge of this?' Quenelda asked.

'He's in the Sabretooth roosts, lady. Tall, thin, in black leather . . .'

'Thank you.' Quenelda gave a smile, though it didn't reach her hollow haunted eyes. Leaving Quester with Tangnost, she and Root weaved through the milling grooms and esquires.

Two Gulps? she called from deep within her mind.

Dancing with Dragons? came the distraught reply. *Strangers – they are taking my brothers and sisters . . . They are compelling them . . . The magic is baleful – it hurts . . .*

Quenelda stormed into the Sabretooth roosts. She stopped on the threshold, unable to believe what she was seeing. Dragons were being harnessed with rings of dull metal. A tall man with his back to them was shouting orders. Aghast, she saw he was wearing dragonskin leathers, along with vicious dragon spurs. He had a long sword strapped across his back, and a whip in his hand.

Eeaaaaakkaaa!

Everyone cringed when Two Gulps called out a greeting to Quenelda as she stormed up to the man, thrusting herself between him and her dragon.

'How dare you lay hands on my father's battle-dragons! *Who are you?*'

The man turned to consider her, casually scratching his lice-infested head. His pale face was cross-hatched with scars, and most of his teeth were missing. Dressed all in black from his boots to the bandolier that was heavy with weapons, he towered above her. On his sleeve he bore the badge of a red adder on black. Bowing mockingly to the young girl, he peeled lips back from gums dark with chewing tobacco and spat at her feet.

'Knuckle Quarnack, Dragonmaster to his lordship the Grand Master, at your service,' he said insolently.

'What are you doing here?' Quenelda's voice was shrill with fear.

The man slowly scrutinized the girl in breeches and scuffed jerkin, a contemptuous smile curling his lips. 'What's it to you, girl?'

'This is my father's battleroost.'

'Well,' Quarnack said lazily. 'Yer Ladyship, I'd say it were the new Earl's battleroosts. Got the pick of your stables for breeding stock, I does. Taking 'em to his Lordship's stud in the North Lands.'

'On whose authority?' Quenelda's eyes glittered dangerously.

'The young Earl's.' The man smiled and scratched at a crop of flea bites on his chin. 'Well, he'll be the Earl in a few days' time. All the same to me.' He reached into his jerkin and held out a crumpled barkscroll.

Quenelda, with Root at her side, examined the carelessly scrawled signature and wax seal with growing anger. They were indeed Darcy's.

Quarnack eyed Two Gulps and You're Gone, who had moved close to Quenelda. 'And this one, lads. *Especially* this one.'

Quenelda rounded on him in fury. 'You can't. He's mine! My father gave him to me.'

'We take him, nonetheless.' Quarnack waved the man to move forward. 'His Lordship's orders.'

Root stepped bravely into his path. 'Lady Quenelda said you were to leave this dragon alone.'

Quarnack pointedly kept his gaze above the boy's head, a smile on his lips.

Root bridled. 'You—'

'Root.' Quenelda softened her caution with a smile as she gently touched his shoulder. She had a better idea. But before she could do anything, another voice rang through the roost.

'Get out of here! Now!' Tangnost's command held a promise of trouble for whoever disobeyed him. 'Leave, or you will regret it. The Lord Darcy is not yet Earl here.'

Quarnack's eyes narrowed, hand hovering over the wand strapped to his right thigh. Tangnost's fearsome reputation gave him pause for thought. The battle-hardened dwarf held his heavy double-headed axe casually in one hand. Behind him, Bonecrackers crowded the door arch, and it looked as if they were in an argumentative mood. It would be a battle between cold steel and magic . . .

Taking advantage of Tangnost's arrival, Quenelda sent out a command: *Fight! Fight!*

There was sudden pandemonium. The dragons assumed battle readiness. Wings outstretched, they reared up on their hind legs, front talons ready to strike, necks extended, mouths open to flame. Without looking, Quenelda could tell from Quarnack's pale face that Two Gulps was treating him to a glimpse of the fire that burned hot in his belly. Smoke lapped about the Dragonmaster's feet.

Quarnack's eyes narrowed as he took a step backwards. How had the old dwarf done that? He had not seen or heard a signal. His eyes flicked to Quenelda. He had heard about the events in the Cauldron – who hadn't? But he had dismissed it all as exaggeration. After all, no one had been able to see much through the snow, just as his master had intended. Lord Hugo's dragonmaster dismissed her and came to a decision. Seeing murder in the man's eyes as his hand fell to the long iron wand strapped to his leg, Quenelda acted.

Flame! A warning only . . .

Flame spewed out of the dragons' nostrils, licking around Quarnack and singeing his eyebrows and nose. He howled with outrage as the Grand Master's handlers ran for their lives. One dived into a water trough to escape the flames.

'We'll be back, little girl,' Quarnack shouted from the arched doorway as he beat out the flames on his burning clothes. 'We'll be back. You just wait and see.'

Quenelda was almost hysterical by the time she reached the Great Hall. Darcy was lounging on the raised dais, boots on the table. The trestles were laden with food and drink, and crowded with drunken young men and extravagantly dressed young ladies. It was more like a festival than a wake for her father.

Quenelda threaded her way through the chaos. 'Why have you ordered our father's battledragons to be sent away?' she asked him desperately.

'I told you that he wouldn't come home one day.' Darcy looked triumphant. 'Now *I'm* Earl. Dragonsdome is mine!'

'No, it's not! Dragonsdome is mine!' Quenelda protested hotly. 'Papa has chosen me. Look!' She held up her right hand with the signet ring on her thumb.

'That rightfully belongs to me!' Darcy shouted and, darting forward, he seized Quenelda's hand. 'Where did you get that? You must have stolen it! It's mine – give it to me!' He tried to wrestle the white-gold ring off her finger.

Quenelda screamed. He twisted her hand brutally, trying to pull the ring off, but he couldn't budge it.

'Papa gave it to me!' she shouted, trying to ignore the ripple of amusement that had swept the hall at her ridiculous assertion.

'And you can't just get rid of all the dragons here! I—'

'Can't I?' Her brother stood up, cutting her off. 'I think,' he said loudly with a satisfied smirk, 'you will find that there isn't much that I can't do, little sister.'

The talk about them gradually stilled. Darcy could not keep the malice from his smile.

'But they've already taken half the battlegriffs and battledragons! The best in Papa's stud. The SDS *need* those dragons.' Quenelda was on the verge of tears..

'So does the Grand Master. He needs all our battle-dragons, including that dangerous mount you ride.'

Quenelda turned white. 'I won't let you take him.'

'And how, little sister,' Darcy sneered, 'do you propose to stop me?'

'I can,' Quenelda said, calmly holding his gaze. 'He trusts no one except Tangnost and me. You won't find anyone else able to get near him.'

High spots of colour marked Darcy's fury. Then, unexpectedly, he seemed to change his mind. 'If you want to stop that dragon of yours being taken to the north' – his eyes were bright now – 'or any of the others, then you will have to attend my Knighthood and Investiture Ceremony in two days' time. Acknowledge me as the true Earl and give me that ring. It's mine. It was never yours.'

That silenced her. Quenelda stared at him bitterly. She would do anything to protect the dragons, and Darcy knew it: *anything*. Two Gulps was a gift from her father, the only thing that was hers in a world suddenly knocked askew. She nodded sullenly and tried to pull off the ring. It coiled more tightly about her thumb and wouldn't shift.

'Let me try again.' Darcy tugged viciously, and then yelped, clutching his finger as the dragon reared and spat flame at him.

'How dare you!' he hissed at Quenelda, who was looking at the ring in amazement. 'How did you do that?' He sucked his bleeding fingers, unsheathing his wand. The air became charged.

'No matter, beloved.' Armelia lightly placed a hand on Darcy's side, glancing warningly at Quenelda. 'You can have another crafted, darling. There are many records of it in the library. None will be able to tell the difference.'

Darcy nodded, and sat down drunkenly. He belched loudly.

'And if you disobey me, there will be no more dragons for you, little sister. You are going straight to Grimalkin's, where they'll knock all that unladylike nonsense about dragons and inheritance right out of you.'

Quenelda felt faint. She turned and ran, the laughter of Darcy and his cohorts chasing her.

Armelia felt a stab of sympathy as she watched Quenelda retreat. 'You will let her keep that dragon, won't you?' she pleaded. She is distraught, and it is all she has left after losing her father.'

'Of course not.' Darcy smirked with satisfaction. 'I told her that dragon would not be taken by the Grand Master, and it won't. I have other plans for her precious dragon.'

He turned to call a servant over, unaware of Armelia's shocked expresion. 'Command my father's Dragonmaster to attend me – now.'

Time to drive an everlasting wedge between Quenelda and Tangnost.

Chapter Twenty-Four

Thunder Rolling Over the Mountains

Thunder rolled over the mountains. Lightning stabbed, its forked branches like blue veins in the sky. Root was soaked to the skin, at his wits' end. He and Quester had searched the roosts and the stables, then the paddocks. No one had seen Quenelda since she had fled the Great Hall.

'She's taken Two Gulps.' Root was shaking with cold and fright. 'She can't fly in this!' He looked at Quester. 'Can she?'

His friend nodded his head, knuckling water from his eyes. 'If anyone can, friend Root, it's Quenelda.'

The storm was ferocious. Quenelda's mood was as wild and unpredictable as the dark roiling clouds, her thoughts spinning like the wind.

Papa, where are you? The same plea kept going round and round in her head. *Where are you?*

The sudden storm had come out of nowhere, forcing Two Gulps to land on the deep snow-bound slopes of the glen. Freezing water ran in rivulets between his gleaming scales, and Quenelda was long since drenched to the bone. She had no idea where they were. She had fled without thought to where she was going, and the big Sabretooth was becoming increasingly concerned. It might be raining, but it was still freezing and could turn to snow in a heartbeat.

We must return to the roost . . . Two Gulps' thoughts were gentle but insistent as the temperature dropped. Quenelda had yet to shed her soft juvenile skin for scales, and Two Gulps was increasingly anxious.

Dancing with Dragons . . . we must return to our roosts or you may also die . . . The thoughts nudged at her. *Dancing with Dragons . . . ?*

The battledragon could feel the Earl's daughter slipping away from him, just as his previous master had done when they were both badly wounded in a skirmish on the Isle of Midges. He did not want to lose her too: they were bonded for life, and he wanted to be at her side when she spread her own wings and flew for the first time.

When he had first met Quenelda, Two Gulps had been confused. She had the soul of a dragon and spoke the language of the Elders, but she was definitely the wrong shape. She was neither dragonkind or mankind, he realized with awe, she was Onekind – what the No Wings called a Dragon Whisperer. And she was powerful: the ancient magic of the Elder Days coursed through her veins. He could see it shining from her like a star at night, and knew that it was up to him to protect her until she came into her power.

Two Gulps gravely considered what to do. He had called out to brothers and sisters, but there were none nearby; no doubt all were settled down in their cosy roosts and caves, where all sensible dragons should be in weather like this. This bitter cold cracked his scales, and his stubby wings had no control in the crazed wind that pushed him this way and that, but he had to protect his mistress. He knelt on the icy boulders and nudged her. *Mount, Dancing with Dragons. We must fly . . .* He blew warm breath over her. She stirred.

T-T-Two Gulps? Quenelda was shaking now with shock and cold. Dimly aware, as if in a dream, she did as he commanded, collapsing over his wings and neck. Two Gulps sprang up into the storm.

The weather and his small wings forced him to fly low, but even so the wind snatched and grabbed at him. Trees loomed, branches slapped at them, and then they were clear and skimming scant strides above the ice-bound loch towards the Black Isle. Hailstones rattled down on the ice. Rising up and up, Two Gulps wove between the spires and chimneys of the city, and was heading over Dragonsdome towards the battleroosts and warmth, when a powerful gust caught him. Dragon and girl were swept up towards the underside of one of the landing pads, where the great chain-link anchors swung. As Quenelda slipped from his water-licked back, Two Gulps turned and swooped after her, arresting the virtually unconscious girl's fall. Then, as he scrabbled frantically, Quenelda began to slip down, leaving him with the empty jerkin. Desperately, Two Gulps lunged and caught her in his open mouth, great serrated teeth holding her tenderly; he scrambled frantically onto the edge of the landing pad careful to keep her safe.

The sky lit up. Root squinted up through the stinging rain, wondering if he had really seen a dragon landing on the Earl's lowered pad . . . Yes, he'd swear just for a moment he'd seen something – some frantic movement.

'Quenelda! Quenelda!' It was useless. The wind snatched the words from his mouth, drowning them out with its banshee shriek. Root turned, peering through the hail. 'Quester, I think she's up there!'

The deep growl of the thunder vibrated through the dragonpads, tingling through Root's hands as he clambered up the outer gantry stairs. A stray tendril of energy coursed through the metal, snapping Root's hand back in a flurry of tiny sparks. With a cry, he stumbled heavily against the steps, his braided hair radiating out like a dandelion. Ignoring his burned hands, Root stumbled on, scrambling up as fast as his legs would go.

'She's up here! She's up here!'

Quenelda lay unmoving on the deck. Two Gulps stood protectively over her, wing outstretched to shield her from the storm, anxiously nuzzling, calling to her.

Dancing with Dragons . . . ?

Root swallowed. How was this protective battle-dragon going to react if they tried to take Quenelda from him?

'Quenelda?' The girl didn't respond to his urgent call. He squinted into her face. Her eyes were open, black and unseeing. He shook her, but still she gazed past him at some inner horizon.

Root realized with horror that she wore no cloak and

her clothes were ragged and ripped. Her skin was chalk-white, blotched with red where hailstones had struck her. She had gone out without a flying suit on! Her face looked thin and pinched. Clumsily Root pulled off his cloak and threw it round her shoulders. It slapped back against his face like a deranged bird.

Quester laid his cloak down on the landing pad. 'You lift under her arms, friend Root, I'll take her legs. We need to get her inside and send for the physician.'

'Here, lads' – a familiar, comforting voice came from behind them – 'give her to me.' Tangnost briefly searched the girl's blank face. He had seen that distant look many times before on troopers who had seen too much for their battered minds to take in.

Root anxiously held out a hand to touch her ice-cold face. 'Quenelda?'

'It's no use, lad. She can't hear you.'

Lifting her effortlessly, the dwarf swaddled her in his cloak. 'Quester, do you think you can take Two Gulps to his roost? Get the flight deckhands to lower the pad down as far as it will go. C'mon, Root,' he said, nodding towards the keep. 'We need to get both of you inside.'

Chapter Twenty-Five

I Go to Dance with the Dragons

Tangnost strode up the wide avenue through the drizzle, the sound of his hobnailed footsteps dulled by the freezing fog. Moisture pearled on his jerkin. *A foul day*, he thought bitterly, *for foul deeds*. Behind him, the dragon surgeon, Professor Willowfellow, coughed loudly into his long grey beard, his sharp-nosed face a mask of outrage.

Dragonsdome's Dragonmaster looked as if he had not slept a wink. His eye was shadowed and bleak. He had failed to deter Darcy from taking his revenge on Quenelda; failed utterly. The Earl-in-waiting had been furious when the Grand Master had demanded to know why his dragonmaster, Knuckle Quarnack, had been driven from Dragonsdome's battleroosts – by Darcy's little sister and his own Dragonmaster.

'How dare you?' Darcy's colour was high. 'How dare you defy my express orders? The Grand Master said you threatened violence . . .'

'My Lord, any violence was of his own making.'

'I am Earl!' Darcy shouted. 'You will obey me.'

Tangnost's temper was rising. 'The SDS are regrouping. Commander DeBessert has ordered that all dragons of fighting age are to be sent immediately to Dragon Isle. They will take to the field come the thaw.'

'Who are you to countermand my orders? It is the Grand Master's lands to the north that will be attacked first, come spring.'

'My lord, none but the SDS may raise an army. It has been the law since the ancient Mage Wars. The Grand Master cannot ignore this.'

'You,' Darcy spat, 'a commoner, to instruct me on the law! You presume above your rank. A time is coming when you and your kind will learn your place in the order of things.' He was in the wrong and he knew it, but to be thwarted in his own hall in front of his friends!

Tangnost regarded Darcy with undisguised contempt and then turned to go. 'Our remaining battledragons must be sent to Dragon Isle. I have work to do.'

But the worst had yet to come. Tangnost had listened to Darcy's next order with disbelief and had immediately refused in horror. But what could succeed in the face of such reckless hatred? Darcy was implacable, bent on revenge.

'You do as I command,' Darcy threatened. 'Otherwise that sister of mine will be sent to Grimalkin's, where they will curb her wayward behaviour. Until she comes of age, it is my right as her brother to see that she is educated as a daughter of nobility should be. She will be sequestered behind the academy's high walls. She'll not see a dragon, let alone fly one!'

Tangnost's weathered face grew pale. Anger sparked in his eye. To see that bright free spirit trapped in a cage . . . Quenelda would languish and die like those wild dragon fledglings that were kept in cages or on the leash as the latest fashion accessory.

'You would barter your sister?' he said contemptuously.

'One way or another,' Darcy threatened, 'I shall clip her wings, or you shall do it for me.'

Gritting his teeth, Tangnost bowed his head bitterly. If he wished to protect Quenelda as the Earl had bade him, then Two Gulps must die – as Darcy had just ordered.

'He dies tomorrow at dawn when she attends my Investiture Ceremony,' Darcy said curtly, and then dismissed Tangnost with an imperious flick of his wrist.

And then my sister will be sent to Grimalkin's anyway, and will for ever curse your name . . .

* * *

Tangnost and the Professor passed beneath the stone-vaulted roof and into the busy surgery, where half a dozen apprentices were already hard at work. Some were immersed in the deep ceramic sinks, cleaning instruments and scrubbing down benches. Two were bandaging a griffin's injured fifth toe in one of the medic alcoves. There were five huge operating cradles slung from pulleys and extendable winches attached to the huge oak ceiling beams. A further four critical-care cradles hung in deeply recessed alcoves; drips and tubes, valves and funnels hung above them.

The bony, bespectacled surgeon crossed to his work-bench, littered with diagrams and drawings, bones, stacks of books and papers. 'Where did I put it?' he muttered as he rummaged about, sending barkscrolls and sheaves of papers tumbling to the floor. 'Tooth and nail!' he swore as a flask smashed on the tiles.

'Professor?' A rosy-cheeked apprentice bowed. 'Are you looking for your keys, sir?' he offered tentatively. 'They're—'

'Ah! I have them,' Professor Willowfellow said, brandishing a large ring heavy with keys. 'How do you want to do this?' he asked Tangnost harshly. His job was to save life, not to take it, and he could hardly believe the dragonmaster had agreed to this. 'Fast and painful, or slow and gentle? He'll just go to sleep but it won't be quick.'

Anger sparked in Tangnost's eye. 'Gentle, damn you!' he snapped. 'I don't want to be doing this any more than you, Willowfellow. It's nothing less than murder, and I know it! But what can we do but obey? We've lost half our dragons to that . . . to the Grand Master already.'

The surgeon's eyes softened. 'Your pardon, Dragonmaster,' he said, bowing his head, the bells on his cap tinkling gently in his agitation. 'I know how you love each and every one of your charges.'

Tangnost shook his head to clear the red mist of anger that clouded his eyes. 'Your pardon also, old friend. This is an ugly business and no mistake.'

The professor nodded and led the dwarf along a corridor to a heavily barred door. A tap of his staff and the application of the correct key, and the heavy door swung silently open. Taking a deep breath, Tangnost stepped into the deep thick-walled vault that housed the raw ingredients for battle munitions, hexes and curses.

Concoctions distilled from dragon venom were sealed with powerful spells.

Selecting one and resealing the vault, the professor led Tangnost towards the battleroosts.

Two Gulps and You're Gone nickered in recognition, smoke curling from his nostrils in welcome.

'Here, boy.' Tangnost laid his hand against the dragon's chest. He could feel the slow beat of the twin hearts.

Boom boom . . . Boom boom . . .

His own heart was racing as he stepped up to the watering trough. He unstoppered the vial with shaking hands and closed his eye. Would Quenelda ever forgive him? he wondered. Would she understand that Dragonsdome would be utterly lost and her life would be changed for ever if he disobeyed Darcy? The vile purple drops swirled on the surface and then were gone.

'Here, boy,' Tangnost croaked, the words sticking in his throat as he encouraged the dragon, his knees suddenly weak. 'T-take a drink, boy . . .'

Supported by Root, Quenelda made her way slowly down the avenue towards the battledragon roosts. She felt lightheaded with fatigue, and although Root had made her dress warmly in a heavy flying suit, she felt cold and shivery. She had no plan other than to flee Dragonsdome and find her father. She was not going to Court to watch her brother made Earl: it would betray her father's wishes utterly. Instead, she and Root were leaving with their dragons; they would be gone before Darcy returned triumphantly. The only thing she had to do was see Tangnost. He was like a second father to her. The idea of leaving him behind, of being without his strength and wisdom, made her heart thump fearfully in her chest. Maybe she could persuade the dragonmaster to come with them? He bore no love for Darcy.

I'm coming, Two Gulps and You're Gone . . .

I am ready . . . The dragon dipped his head to the water trough. Next to him Tangnost bowed his head and openly wept.

Down in Dragonsdome's labyrinth of kitchen pantries and cellars, Quester hastily packed bread, cheese, oats and apples into a saddlebag. Cold slices of smoked beaver and bear followed. There would be water aplenty churning off the mountainside, and Two Gulps would hunt for his own food: there were herds of deer and wild boar, elk and bears. The other bags already held travelling stove and flints, flares, a rope, candles and sleeping rolls. And a dozen feeding bags of honey tablets for Root's cherished mount, Chasing the Stars. Satisfied, Quester set out for the roosts, carrying enough provisions and equipment to last Root and Quenelda for up to a month.

Boom . . . boom . . .boom . . . boom . . . boom . . .

One of the dragon's twin hearts suddenly faltered and missed a beat. He coughed, sending a small flare of flame rolling over the water trough.

Quenelda stumbled and tripped. Scrambling to her feet, she gathered up her helmet.

'Be careful,' Root urged. 'You're very weak . . .'

The dragon's heart faltered a second time.

Quenelda fell to her knees, crying out.

'Quenelda? What's wrong?'

She got to her feet, her face a ghastly white, then staggered backwards as if she had been punched.

In the roosts, the dragon stood stock-still, trembling. His mouth foamed and frothed. With a fearful thud, he dropped to his knees on the metal decking.

As she reached the outer paddocks, Quenelda's knees buckled. With a sharp cry, she fell over again.

'Quenelda!' Root was really frightened now.

The dragon's breathing slowed.

'Can't breathe . . .' Quenelda's breath was coming in laboured gasps, as if she needed to scoop the air up. Black spots danced in front of her eyes. She reached out blindly with her hands. 'It's Two Gulps! Guide me, Root,' she pleaded, fear burning in her eyes.

Abandoning everything, Root went to Quenelda's side and took her weight.

Dancing with Dragons . . . Two Gulps' breath slowed painfully. *Dancing with Dragons* . . .

The dragon was calling out to Quenelda now – fear-drenched thoughts that had never plagued him on the battlefields.

Boom . . . boom . . . boom . . . boom . . .

'I'm coming, Two Gulps! I'm coming!' Quenelda's body jerked in fits and starts as her muscles stopped working. Gauntlets fell unnoticed to the ground as Root tried to keep her on her feet. She felt so tired. She wanted to curl up . . . it was getting dark – and so cold . . .

The night is coming . . .

Hold on . . . hold on . . . Quenelda was weeping, barely able to see where she was going, the world refracted through a prism of tears.

'Two Gulps!' she howled out loud.

Quester nearly jumped out of his skin as the ghostly pair emerged out of the mist, Quenelda's ragged call hanging in the damp air. Dropping the saddlebags, the esquire raced to their side. 'Lady Quenelda, what's wrong? What's happening?'

Root's anguished eyes met his. 'I – I don't know! It's Two Gulps . . . She has to reach him.'

Dancing with Dragons . . .

The dragon raised his heavy head, his dimming eyes searching for the young girl.

Boom . . . boom . . . boom . . . boom . . .

Tangnost looked up, aghast, as the ashen-faced girl stumbled into the lantern light, held upright by Root and Quester. Quenelda's hair was plastered to her sweating forehead. Her golden dragon eyes were dim and unfocused. Spittle frothed at her mouth.

'Save him,' Quenelda screamed, tears coursing down

her cheeks. 'Save him, Tangnost! I know you can! He's dying! *We're dying.*'

'Quenelda . . .' The dragonmaster sprang nimbly to his feet, trying to stop her headlong flight towards Two Gulps. 'You shouldn't be here, lass.' Then her words hit him. '*We're?* What do you mean?'

Pushing past the dwarf with new-found strength, Quenelda knelt beside the battledragon, blindly searching for his head. The stallion raised his head wearily, his hot breath warming her ice-cold hands.

Boom . . . boom . . . boom . . .

Quenelda desperately tried to raise Two Gulps' head, to cradle his great nose in her arms. Forgetting his fear of battledragons, Root flung himself down and used all his strength to wrestle the great head onto her lap.

'What's wrong with him?' she appealed to Tangnost. 'Why aren't you doing anything?' she commanded as the breath rattled in the dragon's great lungs. 'Two Gulps! Don't go! Don't go!'

One great yellow eye opened. A single dragon tear spilled hotly down the girl's arms. Tears tracked down Quenelda's cheeks to mingle with the dragon's as she rocked backwards and forwards in her distress, cradling him as she might a child.

'Two Gulps! Don't leave me!'

Boom . . . boom . . . boom . . .

Dancing with Dragons, it is growing dark . . .

'No!' Quenelda screamed out loud as haunting dragonsong filled her head.

I go to dance with the dragons . . .

Boom . . .

A thousand memories shared in the blink of a closing eye. The last touch of his mind slipped away and was gone. Nothing took its place. With a long sigh, Two Gulps and You're Gone died, the weight of his great head pinning Quenelda to the ground. A yellow scale came loose in her hand.

Quenelda frantically sought the dying spark in the growing darkness. *I'm coming . . .*' Dragonsong took her and lifted her up on its wings. Her eyes rolled back in their sockets, and her head fell backwards against Root's shoulder. She sighed with a slow expulsion of life, raising an arm to Tangnost in silent appeal.

'I'm going to dance with the dragons too . . .' she whispered. Her body sagged as the breath of life left her. Her fiery eyes dimmed and their light went out.

Root screamed.

Tangnost's face was a mask of shock. 'She's dying, man,' he shouted at the surgeon as Root, eyes wide with horror, knelt to cradle Quenelda.

'Quenelda! Don't go!' the young boy cried desperately. 'Don't go! Don't leave me alone!'

'Don't just stand there.' Tangnost shook the professor. 'Do something to help her!'

'I'm a vet, not a physic,' the professor said, aghast, hands shaking with horror. 'What can I do?'

Tangnost looked up on the scene and raised his stricken face. 'Thor's Hammer!' Tears ran down the dwarf's horrified face. 'We've killed the Earl's daughter.'

Chapter Twenty-Six

Dance of Dragons

In this last dance of dragons
Our three hearts beat as one
But I must dance without you
For my time is almost done

In this last dance of dragons
I will fly with you no more,
We will never feel the wind
Beneath us as we soar.

In this last dance of dragons
I grieve to say goodbye,
For I will not be with you
When you spread your wings and fly.

In this last dance of dragons
You know I'll wait for you,
For surely as the sun sets
You must dance with dragons too . . .

The witching hour of midnight was approaching. High in the belfry tower, beneath an inky sky bright with crushed diamonds, the goblins seized their frost-rimed ropes and the cold brass bells began to swing.

The deep sonorous sound shivered out across Dragonsdome twelve times. The last ringing note fell into silence, marking the end of winter and the beginning of spring. Light and dark, day and night hung in the balance, but light would now gain the ascendancy and the days grow longer.

Then the strangest thing happened. As the waning moons rose high over Dragonsdome, first one, then a second wild dragon flew down to perch on the roof, throwing long blue shadows on the snow. The first notes of dragonsong curled around the chimney tops and up into the frigid night air. Soon there were a dozen, then a score, and then a hundred wild dragons alighted on the steep gables and towers of Dragonsdome.

More and more wild dragons gathered on the dragonpads floating above. In their roosts and stables, Dragonsdome's remaining dragons and battledragons all turned towards Quenelda's chambers. Too high for the human ear to hear, the dragons' notes shivered and sang as they searched out the sleeping girl. Snow slid from the roofs in a flurry of mini-avalanches, and panes of costly glass cracked like caramelized sugar as the eerie notes penetrated Dragonsdome's thick walls.

Outside, wrapped in his bear cloak, Tangnost watched them raise their snouts, and wept. Anger burned deep within him like a banked fire in the forge, the white heat hidden deep inside. Guilt racked him: he should have defied Darcy. He should have taken Two Gulps and Quenelda to the safety of Dragon Isle, and damn the consequences.

A song shivered out over the glen, to be answered by a thousand scaled throats. Was this his doing? Tangnost wondered. Was this a lament for a life that was now slipping away?

Rising and falling, rising and falling, the notes wrapped themselves around the Earl's daughter. Sleep had always brought vivid, colourful dreams of times and places she had never seen. Dreams of dragons, explained away as childhood imaginings.

Now, as Quenelda lay unmoving, the yellow scale clenched in her hand, a new dream took hold of her, cradling her in its coils like a hibernating dragon. With a hiccup, her heart changed its rhythm.

Boom boom . . . Boom boom . . .'

It was warm and dark. Quenelda felt soft stirrings all about her. For the first time since the death of her father and Two Gulps, she felt strangely at peace.

Boom boom . . . Boom boom . . .

Come, said a dragon, warm breath a whisper of wind. *You have walked the ways of the Wingless Ones. Come, Dancing with Dragons, let us show you our world. Let us show you your world. Come, dance with the dragons . . .*

She opened her eyes to find herself in a vast dragon-comb warmed by purple flames. She rubbed against other small soft-scaled bodies: her roost litter. Vast coils about them uncurled. Dim light broke into her dark world, revealing an indigo dome pierced by a million stars.

Boom boom . . . Boom boom . . .

In her dream, Quenelda now clung to a sheer cliff edge, looking out over the sea. The air was alive with sounds and smells, dragons tending their new-born fledglings. The crush of dragons on the nursery ledges was tremendous, their warm breath curdling the sharp smell of urine and the pungent fishy odour of dragon dung. The cries of great black-beaked eagles filled the air as they swooped and dived, hoping to grab a fledgling. A female Imperial nursed her brood, a clutch of six babies nestled in the coils of her tail. Gently the mother nuzzled them forward, waddling and clumsy, towards the cliff edge and the frothing sea far below. Small wings, creased and untried, were spread.

Come, the dragons called to her. *Come dance with us . . .*

Then the mare nudged Quenelda on. In that heart-stopping first moment of flight, Quenelda's frantic beating heart was replaced by another two, infinitely older, infinitely slower, with different memories. Her red blood cooled and thickened to blue, moving sluggishly through a web of reptilian veins. Pale soft skin hardened into diamond-hard dark scales that clothed her from tip to tail. Bones thickened and strength flowed through her outstretched arms that became vast curved wings, able to ride the winds. She felt heaven's breath beneath her wings, lifting her, the endless starry night above. Dragonscaled from tip to tail, she swooped down joyfully towards the sea . . .

Chapter Twenty-Seven
Hibernation

Quenelda slept, cocooned from the cold white world outside.

On hearing of the calamity that had occurred at Dragonsdome, the Queen had sent her own physician and commanded the Earnest and Ingenious Guild of Apothecaries to search for a cure. The men in the yellow-tasselled tricorn hats of the Guild, with their weights and measures, pestles and mortars, came and went. Quenelda was forced to swallow potions, but none of them made any difference to the pale girl with sunken, bruised eyes. Warm and dark in her dream, she slept on.

One by one, the apothecaries declared themselves at a loss as to her condition. 'I confess myself baffled,' one said as he looked down at the girl. 'She has virtually no pulse, and its beat is strange and erratic. Her blood barely moves, she barely *breathes*.' He shook his head. 'It's almost as if . . .'

'As if . . . ?' Tangnost pressed.

'It's almost as if she's gone into hibernation.'

Stricken to his core, the dwarf stood watch over the girl he thought of as his daughter, while Dragonsdome and the Seven Sea Kingdoms disintegrated and fell to disaster about him.

Spring came late – too late. The starving hobgoblins spawned and swarmed. Crossing the ice that joined the Westering Isles to the mainland in their millions, they fell upon every living thing in their path. While the dwarf clans of the high-cliffed Northern and Inner Isles fought for their very survival, hobgoblins on their Razorbacks entered the deep sea lochs of the west, carrying their hobgoblin masters deep into the heart of the Seven Sea Kingdoms. Unaware, Quenelda slept on as the under-manned fortresses of the Stormbreakers and Nightstalkers were isolated and besieged, and the hobgoblin banners swept across all the Northern Highlands virtually unopposed.

Abandoning the Howling Glen to the inevitable, their newly promoted Strike Commander, William DeBurgh, Armelia's uncle, rallied his shattered regiment to protect the tens of thousands of refugees mired down in appalling weather on the military road south. Fighting a futile rearguard action, they fell to the last man and dragon. Mustering fresh troops from the Winter Knights, Shadow Wraith and Firestorm regiments, the new SDS Commander Jakart DeBessert, took the field north of the Brimstones to face converging hordes of over a million hobgoblins, and barely halted their advance at the cost of half his command. And there, where a line of crags rose up above the moorlands between the northern Brimstones and the mountains to the east, the SDS engineers began repairing the Old Wall, a relic of the First Age. Within half a moon, cut off by appalling weather that grounded their Imperials, and surrounded by hobgoblins and Razorbacks, the Nightstalkers' fortress fell with no survivors. The panicking Guild called on the Grand Master to raise an army in the name of the Queen.

Hushed voices drifted in and out of Quenelda's hearing. The belfry counted out the hours, then days and weeks, but her hearts beat to a different, slower rhythm. As the Sprouting Grass Moons gave way to the Corn Planting Moons, and the hobgoblins were finally beaten by the Grand Master's newly formed army, Root quietly despaired for his friend's life. The weight was dropping away from Quenelda, from her high cheekbones and slanting brows. There was no longer any doubt: the Earl's daughter was dying. Giddy with relief at their belated victory over the hobgoblins, the rejoicing Guild called upon the Queen to bestow the new title of Lord Protector upon the Lord Hugo Mandrake, with a writ to raise taxes and an army of his own.

The peoples of the Seven Sea Kingdoms had found a new champion.

Chapter Twenty-Eight

The Queen's Apothecary

As spring turned into summer, there was no reason to hope, but Root and Tangnost maintained their vigil beside Quenelda's bed. One morning Root lay sleeping on a pallet as Tangnost sat watchfully by the fire, smoking his pipe, when a guard knocked on the door, interrupting his bleak thoughts.

'The Queen's Apothecary,' he announced, with hope in his voice. Perhaps this one might succeed where all others had failed. He fervently hoped so.

An elderly man shuffled in, leaning heavily on his Arch Mage's staff, back bowed with age, the triple-tasselled hood of the Artful Apothocaries Association leaving his face in shadow. Behind him, three apprentices carried the tools of his trade: a small portable cauldron, brass scales, weights and measures, a pestle and mortar, pouches and jars of ground herbs and leaves and crystals, unguents and pastes. The old man fussed about his apprentices' preparations for a minute or two before turning towards Tangnost. He suddenly straightened and threw back his hood. Keen grey eyes flashed.

'My Lord Constable!' Tangnost made to bow.

'Nay, man, no ceremony here,' Sir Gharad urged him. 'How is the child?' A bony hand was laid against Quenelda's pale cheek.

Tangnost shook his head sorrowfully. 'No change, my lord.'

'We feared it was so.' The old man bit his lip. 'I come bearing urgent news. It is no longer safe for the Earl's daughter to remain here. With his armies successful in the north, the 'Lord Protector' has returned.' His smile was ironic. 'You may have heard the celebrations?'

Tangnost nodded grimly. Eager for victory, the city had gone wild; bonfires and fireworks had cracked and blazed till dawn.

'A triumphal parade is being organized by the Guild, but our Lord Protector is already turning his attention to other matters. Since he heard the tales that Quenelda 'died' with her dragon, the Lord Protector has become most concerned for the child's health. Already he has expressed his wish to care for her. He is to formally seek guardianship from the Queen's Council in three days' time. He claims the Earl wished it. Given their lifelong friendship, it seems a natural enough request. Because the young Earl Darcy supports him, the Council are bound to agree.'

'You can't let that happen!' Root leaped forward to stand in front of Quenelda as if she were about to be dragged away.

'Hush, lad,' Tangnost admonished.

'But the Queen! She—'

'The Queen is powerless.' The Constable balled his fist in frustration. 'She rules in name only. The Council gives Hugo whatever he asks; they are utterly under his spell and cannot see their own danger. Who knows – they may even defy her wishes . . . We cannot take that risk. Many of her servants have been quietly replaced – few can be trusted any more; and the palace is guarded by the Lord Hugo's troops.'

Root was on the verge of tears. 'You can't let him have her – he's a warlock! If he finds out she truly is a Dragon Whisperer . . .!'

'Do not fear, lad,' Sir Gharad said, laying a reassuring hand on the boy's shoulder. 'We are not entirely helpless. The SDS may be diminished, but Dragon Isle still wields great power at the heart of the kingdom, and she will be safer there. Commander DeBessert attends the Queen at this very moment, and stays for the evening banquet in honour of the Lord Protector. While the Lord Hugo is being feted, we make our move. Two cloaked Imperials from the Commander's escort will put down at the Hour of the Howling Wolf. The Queen will say that SDS battle apothecaries wish to see if they can cure the Earl's daughter, and even the Lord Hugo and her Council will be unable to find fault with that. To protest would be to raise suspicion, and anyway, our Lord Protector is a busy man these days, and caring for a child should be the least of his concerns. You must prepare to leave at a moment's notice, perhaps for ever.' He glanced at Tangnost, who nodded grimly in understanding.

'For ever?' Root paused. He shook his head in confusion. 'I don't understand.'

'I fear the Lord Protector will not forgive those who defy him. He cannot touch the SDS, nor are they answerable to any save the Queen. But you – you may never be able to return: your life may be forfeit.'

Suddenly the Queen's Constable looked like nothing more than a very old man; a man who had lost his king, and now his protégé, a man he had loved like a son – the

Earl Rufus. Unless they acted soon, Quenelda too would be gone. In spite of his fear, Root's heart went out to him.

Sir Gharad felt a small hand take his, and looked down to find dark compassionate eyes that also had known the pain of loss. He blinked back tears. You found friendship in the most unexpected of places. He squeezed Root's fingers gratefully.

'Best get ready, lad,' he said, voice cracking hoarsely. 'And be careful; let none know our plans. All our lives would be in danger were we caught.'

Shocked to the core, Root nodded wordlessly.

Chapter Twenty-Nine

Flight to Dragon Isle

Tangnost carried Quenelda, bundled in furs, onto the landing gantry at Dragonsdome's east wing, where two great Imperials waited, black as the night, their hot breath steaming in the cold air. As they and Root reached the upper pad, Tangnost heard wing-beats, saw silhouettes of dragons against the rising moons as they came swiftly from the city.

'Into the shadow, boy – quick!'

The Imperials on the pads shimmered and were gone. Root ducked down, pulling his saddlebags behind him. Over the past few hours he had been gathering his meagre possessions together and saying goodbye to Quester. His friend had chosen to stay at Dragonsdome to try to protect the stable of dragons from further harm, and to let Tangnost know by homing eagle, what was happening in their absence. The parting was a difficult one.

'Someone must care for the few dragons left, friend Root' – Quester had smiled bravely – 'now that Bearhugger is leaving. With their menfolk slain on the

Westering Isle, most of Dragonsdome's esquires have returned home to fight for their families; there are few left to help the roostmasters and roostmistresses here. I'll wait for you, Root. I'll keep watch and wait until you all come home. Until the Earl returns to take back what is his.'

They had clasped each other tightly, reluctant to part.

'Go safely,' Quester said softly as the gnome left the Esquire's Hall. Eyes blurred with tears, he didn't see a figure detach itself from the shadows.

Felix DeLancy could not believe his luck as he headed for the Great Hall of Dragonsdome. A chance! A chance to finally show the young Earl that he was a good man to have in his service, and to take revenge on that jumped-up esquire at the same time. Things were changing at Dragonsdome, and Felix wanted to be a part of it. And now the Earl's Dragonmaster and Root were planning to sneak away in the night with the Earl's daughter! The young Earl would surely reward him for this news; he would be esquire to one of the most powerful men in the Seven Sea Kingdoms, and that was only the start!

Moving swiftly, Tangnost carried Quenelda up the

cloaked Imperial's wing just as a mailed fist hammered on the great doors below.

'Open up, in the name of the Lord Protector.' The voice carried thinly through the silent night.

'Mount up, boy,' Tangnost told Root with great urgency.

'But what about Chasing the Stars?' Root looked distraught. 'I must fetch her first—'

'I'm sorry, lad.' Tangnost's tone brooked no argument. 'We must leave her. Mount up – now!'

The pad creaked as the cloaked Imperial sprang into the air and disappeared into the night.

The state banquet celebrating the Lord Protector's victorious inauguration had only reached the tenth course when a tall thin man entered the Palace, his dark attire in sharp contrast to the jewelled brilliance of the Court. Hugging the shadows, he moved softly between pillars, threading his way amongst servants and footmen, around behind the high table to where the Lord Hugo Mandrake spoke with the Queen. He stood silently until the Lord Protector motioned him forward. Bending, Knuckle Quarnack murmured something in the Lord Protector's ear. His master stiffened. They had been too late. Darcy had failed to post guards and the girl had slipped through their fingers and was no doubt already on Dragon Isle. Someone had forewarned the SDS of his intent, and they needed no one's permission save the Queen's.

'Lord Hugo?' The Queen laid a hand lightly on his arm. 'My lord? Is anything the matter?'

'Nothing, Majesty,' The Lord Protector swallowed down his bile and unknotted his fist. 'Mere military matters that could have waited.' He could hardly reveal he knew of the child's departure without also betraying that his men had gone to Dragonsdome without the permission of the Queen's Council. Well, if Darcy was right, the Earl's daughter was at death's door and it would not matter; but still . . . doubt niggled away at him. When he had cornered her in the castle after the Winter Joust he had been unable to touch her mind; his power had been rebuffed somehow. Or was it that simply there was nothing there? Why would the SDS spirit her away so suddenly? Merely because she was their old Commander's daughter? Perhaps . . . He would have to wait until after the banquet to find out.

He glanced upwards to find Jakart DeBessert's cool

grey eyes studying him. The Dragon Lord raised his goblet and then he turned back to his conversation, leaving the Lord Protector to speculate.

Well, he controlled the army, the Guild and the palace. What possible threat could a dying child and the weakened SDS pose? The Lord Protector turned back to the night's celebrations and reached for his goblet of wine.

Eighteen leagues away on Dragon Isle, Quenelda was settled in her father's old quarters, attended by the SDS's remaining apothecaries and physicians.

'Now what?' Root was shaking from cold and tension, his courage fraying. 'What happens now, Tangnost?'

The Earl was gone. Dragonsdome as a place of refuge was gone. Chasing the Stars had been left behind: he didn't know whether he'd ever see her again. And Quenelda – no one knew if she would ever wake up. Root had heard soldiers' stories of the injured whose bodies clung onto life when their souls had long since departed. He was so very afraid for his friend.

'I don't know, lad,' the dwarf answered truthfully. 'We keep watch and wait. Perhaps now that she is here on

Dragon Isle, she may wake. Perhaps the apothecaries here will work their magic.' *This was where the Earl's daughter belonged.*

'I feel so helpless,' said Root, sniffing.

'I know, lad. So do I.' Tangnost hugged the boy to him. 'But we have each other, and we must believe that Quenelda will come back to us. We mustn't let her drift away, Root. She must know she's not alone. She still has both of us. Come now . . .' He led the boy out. 'Let's get some hot food in you and then a bed. You're almost asleep on your feet.'

Chapter Thirty

The Heartrock

Homesick for Dragonsdome, lonely, and frightened that Quenelda was slipping further and further away from them, Root had begun to explore Dragon Isle; he wanted to take his mind off what was happening in the outside world. Most of the original dragoncombs were now flight decks, hangars and roosts, barracks and mess halls. There were some passageways, tunnels and combs that he was not permitted to explore, where stern-faced cadets in oversized armour blocked his path, but mostly he found he could now wander around unimpeded. The SDS were too busy fighting for their very survival to worry about one lost and lonely gnome.

Trying to fill his empty days, Root took out his charcoal and his birch-bark rolls and began to draw the battledragons, attempting to capture the unique character of each individual, bringing them vividly to life. Soon the quiet youth became a familiar sight in the hangar caverns and roosts. Every evening he would talk to Quenelda about them; tell her their names and those of their flight crews. What he never told her was how many never came home to their roosts, leaving only his drawings to mark their passing.

One day Root went into Quenelda's chamber, and coaxed the fire back to life before adding some more peat. He then lit a branch of candles. Drawing a chair up to the bed, he made himself comfortable, wriggling into the cushions. He had been talking to Quenelda every evening and was losing heart. Sometimes he would tell her what Tangnost had taught him of wind studies, cloud formation or navigation; at other times he would describe where in the great island fortress he had been that day and what he had found, hoping she would hear him and suddenly wake up, curious to know more.

'Quenelda, I've found this old book . . . *Quenelda?*' He stared as if his eyes had deceived him. The book fell unnoticed to the floor, and he leaped to his feet and threw back the quilt and blankets, as if she could be hiding unseen beneath their folds. Then he looked under the bed. Knocking his head in his haste to re-emerge, he ran out of the room in panic.

'Tangnost? Commander?' Root eventually arrived, breathless, at the battleroosts, bent over with a stitch.

'She's gone. I can't find her anywhere!' He anxiously hopped from toe to toe. 'The flight hangars, pads, the roosts, armour pits, the harbour, forges . . .'

'So she's disappeared . . .' Tangnost said thoughtfully. 'And you've looked everywhere for her? Everywhere but one place . . . ?'

'The Heartrock?' Jakart DeBessert suggested, swiftly understanding the Dragonmaster.

Nodding, Tangnost was suddenly certain. 'The Heartrock.' *Where else would she go? She's come home . . .*

'None have set foot within the Heartrock in over two thousand years,' the Commander said gravely. 'If it is so, then we should bear witness. Come,' he ordered his officers.

Root was running to match the dwarf's urgent stride as they stepped away from the porting stone. 'What's the Heartrock?'

'As its name suggests, it lies at the heart of Dragon Isle. You must have seen the great causeways . . .'

Root nodded. They were impossible to miss – slender black viaducts arcing above a deep pit leading into a core of darkness. The guards wore frightening helmets with long snouts and teeth that hid their faces, and intricate black armour that swept back from their shoulders like folded wings. They truly looked half dragon, half man.

'The guards wouldn't let me past . . .'

'With good reason,' DeBessert assured him. 'There are deadly wards woven about the Heartrock, the very rock is imbued with ancient magics.'

'It is where the first Dragon Whisperer was fostered with his six brothers,' Tangnost explained. 'Where Son of the Morning Star was nursed by an Imperial with her brood, so that he grew to become half dragon, half man. None save a Dragon Whisperer has ever unlocked its secrets.'

Root's eyes widened. 'But why should she be there? I don't understand.'

'Only the SDS and the royal line even know of its existence. The lost Dragonsdome Chronicles apparently record its secrets. All that we know of the Heartrock was recorded there. Legend says that only a Dragon Whisperer may unlock the Heartrock's secrets. It is death to any others who try.'

'What?' Root was horrified. *What if we're wrong?* he wanted to ask. *What if she isn't a Dragon Whisperer?*

Tangnost squeezed his shoulder as if he had read the boy's mind. 'Have faith,' he said softly. 'She will come to no harm.'

They turned a corridor and descended widening stairs that opened into a spacious sloping passageway. The glassy black symmetrical tunnel was so flawless that Root knew without being told that this was one of the ancient Imperial combs. Flickering movement caught the edge of his vision. When he looked closer, he realized that the rock face was alive with runes of liquid gold, constantly shaping, merging and re-forming, which travelled beside them, bathing them in a soft glow. The place was alive with the breath of antiquity. Although he knew no magic, the power of it made Root's skin tingle.

'Dragonrunes,' Tangnost said, seeing the boy's wide-eyed glance. 'The lost language of the Elders. None now know their meaning.'

Up ahead of them, the Commander and his officers had come to a halt. Soon Root could see why. Instead of standing to attention guarding the bridge, the black-armoured guards were turned inwards, kneeling, heads bowed, facing towards the Heartrock. The wings on their shoulders and helmets were fully spread, and the eyes of their helmets were burning bright gold. Their swords were unsheathed, the tips resting on the ground as if in homage.

DeBessert shook his head. 'They won't respond. It's as if they are frozen in place.'

They all looked across the stone bridge to where light flickered up ahead. A sheer wall rose in front of them, soaring up into the darkness. Quenelda was standing motionless in front of it, a burning brand raised above her. Finally daring to believe, Root started forward, his joy at seeing his friend alive overwhelming him.

'Quenelda! You—'

Tangnost firmly held him back, a finger to his lips for silence, but the young girl did not appear to have heard their arrival. She continued her quiet scrutiny of the rock face. Puzzled by her silence, Root looked at what she was studying.

The ancient frieze, carved into the rock thousands of years before, was of an Imperial with her brood. The unfolding story written in stone depicted six fledglings and a tiny child within the mother's coils. Then the child became a young man, dwarfed by the six dragons about him.

As Root's eyes followed the narrative illuminated by Quenelda's flickering brand, he became aware of light footfalls and the murmur of many voices as cadets, sentries and officers congregated quietly behind them. Word of what was happening was passing from mouth to mouth like wildfire.

Quenelda moved on to where the young man stood, arms spread, on a high cliff. Then, as he raised his arms and stepped into the void, his arms lengthened and became wings; scales armoured him from snout to spiked tail and he became a mighty Imperial dragon. His six brothers joined him as they flew skyward.

Stepping backwards, replacing the brand, Quenelda spread her arms. The lamps set on the walls died down. A golden nimbus flickered about the Earl's daughter, suggesting the fluid outline of a dragon. Then the lamps flared brightly again. There was a collective gasp. The wall was gone, and a vast darkness was revealed. A wash of biting cold air rolled over them. A whisper of amazement echoed around the combs, and then those watching held their breath as Quenelda stepped forward.

Tangnost stopped breathing. He had waited for this moment since the day Quenelda was born.

Pinpricks of light blossomed. As all eyes were drawn upwards, stars winked into existence until the dome blazed with their light, and the secrets of the Heartrock were revealed. The entire paved floor below radiated out in circles, until its far reaches were lost in shadows; and at its centre stood the legendary dragonbone throne. The aged bones of that first female Imperial were lustrous ivory, polished gold by age. The sorcery trapped within them and in the great ivory fangs, was potent, an almost visible aura. Drawn by its song, the Battle Mages moved quietly forward through the crowd. Even Root felt the underlying hum that raised goose bumps on his arms.

Ringing the throne were six dragons carved of black granite, gazing outwards like sentinels. Each one seemed perfectly rendered, but as Tangnost watched Quenelda approach the dragonbone throne, something subtle changed, and the statues became more than simply stone. Energy radiated from them. There was a sense, he realized, that the statues were merely sleeping, hibernating in the cold depths of timeless winter as Quenelda herself had done; awaiting the arrival of spring with the promise of rebirth.

Awaiting a summons . . .

As Quenelda stood on the lower steps of the throne, there was a grating sound, as if a huge weight of stone were moving.

'They're turning!' Root was standing in front of Tangnost, the dwarf's hands resting reassuringly on his shoulders. Tangnost nodded.

The six dragons now faced inwards. Their eyes burned gold, and purple smoke rose from their nostrils. Spreading their wings till each wing-tip touched the other, they bowed their heads to the young girl. As she came closer, each in turn stepped forward to blow softly on her face, and she rested her head against their muzzles in greeting. As she accepted their fealty, she named them:

'Rashinan whose wings are swifter than wind . . .
Torgrimble whose voice is louder than thunder . . .
Moranth whose breath is hotter than fire . . .
Fafnir whose scales are harder than stone . . .
Abraxis whose talons are sharper than flint . . .
Stoorworm whose power is greater than creation . . .

'My brothers and sisters' – Quenelda's power was such that her whispered words reached every ear – 'the dark of the Abyss is rising. The time will soon come when I will shed my skin and spread my wings. When that time comes, I shall summon you to my side once again . . .'

'So,' Tangnost said, so softly that Root only just heard him, 'the journey has begun. Who knows where it will take us?'

And then, with a clap of thunder, the chamber went dark.

Chapter Thirty-One

Coming Home

Quenelda came back to her own body slowly, rising through the dreams that clung to the edge of consciousness like memories, the whisper of countless dragons a murmur in her mind. She lay there quietly, eyes closed, as her other senses slowly unfurled like a fern touched by sunlight. She was lying on a crisp linen sheet beneath woollen blankets and furs. The smell of pine resin hung in the air, although the wall sconce had long since died and the room was now in darkness. A fire smouldered in the grate.

Physically she felt weak, but there was a strange hot energy that now flowed through her veins, a fire that burned inside. She was somehow changed, but how? She flexed her hands. Instead of talons she definitely felt fingers and toes, which was a relief. No tail or armoured snout. No scales . . . No, that was not quite right, was it? She opened golden eyes and lifted her right arm from beneath the covers. Darkness held no secrets from her reptilian inner self. There, on the palm of her hand, was a gorse-yellow scale. It was soft, but rapidly hardening like a newly laid egg. Even as she looked, it seemed to sink into her skin so that she could see the lines on her palm through it. But when she touched it with a finger, her palm too was as hard as a scale.

'Oh, Two Gulps . . .'

Tears sprang to her eyes as she remembered Two Gulps and You're Gone. He was dead. She knew with utter certainty that he was – although there was a part of him still with her, within her, which would be with her till she died. She squeezed her hand as tears tracked down her face. Two Gulps was gone. Her father was gone.

Then someone close by turned restlessly, and sighed in his sleep. Sitting up, Quenelda could see the figure curled up in front of the hearth. It was Root. Where was she? She looked around the chamber. She was surrounded by warm dark rock hung with tapestries. There were no windows. A precarious stack of barkscrolls lay beside a chair, along with a mug and some pieces of charcoal.

'Dragon Isle,' she said out loud, resisting the urge to spread her wings and hop from the bed. 'I'm home.'

Root jumped awake like a jack-in-the-box, and was at Quenelda's side in two heartbeats. 'You're back!' he said shyly, taking her hand in his. 'I've been so worried. Tangnost told me to be patient, that you'd come back to us.' He grinned at her with sheer joy. Exhausted, and more than a little confused, she found herself smiling back.

'Wait! Let me get some light.' The gnome boy held a taper to the fire embers, and lit candles about the chamber. Coming back, he sat by her side and looked at her. The fire in her eyes had died back to amber. She was pale and thin, but that was hardly surprising.

'I'm starving,' she said, looking about for her clothes. 'Why are we on Dragon Isle? How long have I been in bed?'

Root looked at her. *How do I tell her that the world has changed? Dragonsdome is gone. The SDS is broken. She doesn't remember visiting the Heartrock . . .*

'A while,' he said carefully. 'But everything's all right now. Tangnost is here too. He has stood watch by your bed every day, when he wasn't in the flight hangar and roosts.'

Quenelda's tummy rumbled.

'Why don't I get you some food, and then I'll explain what's happened.'

* * *

'. . . and I've been learning to navigate! I've been sitting in with the cadets. I can read maps and . . .'

Quenelda sat in front of the blazing fire, wrapped in a heavy shawl, with the remains of a meal scattered in front of her. She was stunned. Root had been talking non-stop for over two bells, relating all that had happened to them over the two moons she had been asleep. She had no memory of the Heartrock at all, and the hardest part had been talking about Two Gulps. Quenelda's grief was still as raw as it had been the day she fell unconscious, and Root had held her while she sobbed. Hesitantly he had explained what Darcy intended; that Tangnost was protecting Dragonsdome's heritage; that the Dragonmaster's grief was no less than hers. That Darcy in the end had betrayed them anyway, and the pedigree battledragons and battlegriffs were all gone.

'Tangnost's been tormented since you fell unconscious. He's afraid you'll hate him, but he had no choice. He'll explain.' Root looked at his friend anxiously. 'Will you see him?'

Tangnost paced up and down. This was ridiculous. He

had faced battle a hundred times, and not felt so afraid. He reached the open door, took a deep breath and stepped in. Quenelda swung round. For several heart-beats they stood immobile, staring at each other, each afraid of what they would see in the other's eyes. Then the moment passed, and a twelve-year-old girl's anguished tear-filled eyes met an old dwarf's oak-brown one.

'Oh, Tangnost!'

He opened his arms. In two strides he had her in a bone-crushing bear hug. 'Thor's Hammer, child! We thought we'd lost you!'

Chapter Thirty-Two

Under a Dark Cloud

Tangnost and Quenelda spent the rest of the day talking quietly. As the sun slowly sank westward, Root left to fetch food and drink, feeling content to just listen as Quenelda described her vivid dreams of distant peoples, times and places. His friend was back, and that was all that mattered.

Knowing she must be weak and disorientated, Tangnost gently told Quenelda all that had happened to Dragonsdome and the SDS since she slipped into her deep sleep. Although he wished to protect her from further distress, Tangnost could not conceal the huge changes she would soon see for herself, nor the devastating news that no rumour or evidence had been found to suggest that her father or anyone else had survived the battle. Quenelda also learned of the fall of the Howling Glen and the Nightstalkers, the death of William DeBurgh and the high cost to the SDS of holding the line.

DeBurgh? 'Armelia's uncle?' There was hardly a family in the kingdom that had not lost men in the battle.

Tangnost nodded grimly. The SDS had lost their Commander and three Strike Commanders in little under two moons, but more was to come.

'North of the Old Wall is still lost, but the Howling Glen has been retaken, allowing us a forward air base.'

Quenelda's eyes brightened as he knew they would. 'Then the SDS is fighting back?'

Tangnost hesitated, then blew out a cloud of smoke from his pipe as if to mask his words. 'No. The fortress was retaken by the Lord Protector and the Army of the North,' he reluctantly conceded.

'The Lord Protector?' Quenelda looked baffled and glanced at Root, who was fiddling with his boot laces. He hadn't mentioned any Lord Protector. 'Who's that? What Army of the North?'

'The Guild feared that the SDS could no longer protect them. They petitioned the Crown to let the Grand Master raise an army in his lands. He took personal command and led an army of raw recruits to retake the fortress. Of course, no one save us knows how he truly did it; that the hobgoblins are his to command. Following that great feat of arms,' Tangnost growled, 'the Lord Hugo was made Lord Protector of the realm and is hailed as the new

Champion of the people. He is now the most powerful man in the Seven Sea Kingdoms, and the SDS have been all but forgotten. Most available dragons, troops and gold from the Royal Treasury are diverted north to his lands beyond the Old Wall.'

Quenelda leaped to her feet as Root bit his lip unhappily. 'But he's a traitor!' Her voice rose shrill with denial. 'He betrayed the SDS and the Queen.'

'He has proved himself cunning beyond imagination. Who will believe him a traitor now that he has retaken the Howling Glen and returned it to the SDS? Who would believe us?'

A knock on the door forestalled Quenelda's protest. A young SDS knight entered and bowed respectfully to her. It was Guy DeBessert.

'My father sends his greetings, Lady Quenelda.' Having witnessed the scene at the Heartrock, Guy was still wide-eyed with awe. 'All are glad you are recovered. They tell me that you flew' – he hesitated, knowing mention of her dragon would be painful – 'Two Gulps to rescue Darcy after the battlegriff bolted, and that you executed a perfect Stoner Manoeuvre. I wish I had seen it!' he added wistfully, unconsciously rubbing the stump of his right hand – the legacy of Darcy's foolhardiness. 'I am heartily sorry Darcy had your dragon killed.' Guy shook his head. 'How could he do such a thing to such a magnificent creature?' Seeing tears in Quenelda's eyes, his words tapered away to silence. Tangnost raised his eyebrows enquiringly.

'Dragonmaster.' Finally remembering his errand, Guy stood to attention. 'My lord father asks if you would attend him in his quarters?'

'Perhaps,' Root suggested, 'you'd like to explore the fortress? If you are feeling strong enough?'

Tangnost nodded. 'I will join you both later. Don't tire her,' he warned Root. 'Much has changed,' he cautioned Quenelda gently before he left, 'since you were last here . . .'

Quenelda nodded.

Despite Tangnost's warning, Quenelda was still shocked by the air of despondency that hung over the island like a dark cloud. Always to the fore of the fighting, and stretched to breaking point by recent heavy losses, the elite SDS had paid a terrible price during the Battle of the Westering Isles and its dreadful aftermath. It was now a shadow of its former glory.

As Quenelda and Root took porting discs down into the rock combs, they passed through empty guard rooms, dark foundries, armouries and half-empty barracks. Only the hospital wing was still crowded, overflowing into a barracks room.

The unseen sun was high overhead as Quenelda and Root, now joined by Tangnost, were welcomed to the battleroosts by one of the SDS Dragonmasters – a grizzled and badly scarred veteran called Loki Strongarm, also of the Bear clan and one of Tangnost's second cousins, who limped heavily on crutches. He saw Root's horrified gaze resting on the scar that slashed across his face.

'Took an injury in the Howling Glen,' the barrel-chested dwarf explained, 'when they attacked the fortress last year – a hobgoblin cleaver. That's how I came to be sent here to Dragon Isle. It was quite a battle.' He nodded to Tangnost, one veteran to another. 'Two hobgoblin banners right under our noses! Nearly caught us by surprise, but the Earl's scout gave us warning.'

At the mention of the Howling Glen, Root bit his lip and turned pale. Tangnost reached out a hand to squeeze the boy's shoulder in sympathy.

'That was my father,' Root said quietly, head held high.

'This is Oakley's son, Root,' Tangnost added. 'Now the Lady Quenelda's esquire.'

The dwarf's eyes widened. Grinning, he reached out a hand and clasped Root's wrist in a bone-crunching soldier's grip. 'Your father saved us, son. He was a good man.'

Root smiled weakly, trying not to wince.

As they toured the dragoncombs, Quenelda discovered roost after roost standing empty, the names carved on the archways a mute reminder of how many had died at the Westering Isles and subsequent battles. And there were few to take their place; the maternity roosts could not keep up with demand.

'Just like Dragonsdome.' Quenelda was aghast. *Where had they gone?*

'Just like Dragonsdome,' Tangnost agreed. 'And most juveniles from the Royal studs now go to the Army of the North.'

The Army of the North! Quenelda already hated that name. *Lord Protector, indeed! How could the Queen have done it? No one could replace her father! She knew that those Razorbacks were of Mandrake's creation.*

He was the traitor. Why couldn't anyone else see it?

And the roosts that weren't empty were occupied by exhausted battledragons: Imperials, Vipers, Adders and Magmas, Frosts, Vampires, and the Lesser Chameleons and Thistles used by scouts and couriers; most of them injured in one way or another, their scales and eyes dulled by fatigue. Their anguished whispers filled Quenelda's head. And worse, they were painfully thin, skin stretched over jutting ribs and parchment-thin wings. They looked half starved.

Quenelda turned to Loki. 'But why are they all so thin? So sickly?'

'Brimstone.' The dwarf shook his weary head. 'Shipments aren't getting through, and those that reach us bear low-grade ore – ore that would once have been rejected. The best is requisitioned by the Lord Protector in the name of the Crown. We send couriers, but all the Royal and DeWinter mines are now guarded by the Lord Protector's men, and they insist the shipments are being sent. Guild galleons are raided by pirates.'

Loki sighed with frustration. 'Even our own battle-galleons are being attacked by Razorbacks. We have lost dozens on escort duty. They simply vanish during the night.'

'Indeed,' Tangnost agreed dryly. 'Since the SDS are so sorely pressed, the Lord Protector has taken it upon himself to provide escort duty with Crown troops, to prevent any further hobgoblin incursions . . . but they too disappear . . .

Next they visited the upper flight hangar cavern at the top of the cliffs, built about and beneath the Seadragon Keep. The once glorious pedigree dragons of the Rapid Reaction Force were exhausted; they had flown too many sorties. Racked by coughs and minor injuries, worn out Harriers and Imperials slept fitfully in the flightroosts, ready for immediate takeoff; their sleep disturbed all too often as they were scrambled to repel a hobgoblin incursion. One patrol was sweeping in as another was taking off.

All at once the dragonhorn sounded, its deep sonorous *boom* making the air in the combs vibrate about them.

'Scramble! Scramble! Scramble!'

The flight hangar exploded into action. Already armoured and saddled, ten dragons were roused and led outside onto the cliffside combat pads by ground crew. Girths were tightened, straps adjusted, feedbags removed. Fully armoured pilots and navigators stumbled out of their hammocks and raced towards their dragons, swiftly climbing the rungs set into the dragon saddles and girths. Settling into their high-backed combat seats, they buckled on helmets, clipped dragoncloaks to flying harness, slung black swords about their hips, their battle staffs already holstered at their knees

Dwarfs pounded out of the northern barracks, collecting shields and axes and war mallets from the racks as they ran, without missing a step.

'Go! Go! Go!'

Behind the two SDS Dragon Lords, two-score commandos mounted two at a time, storming up the dragons' great tail plates. One tripped and fell, sending another half-dozen sprawling down the wing in a tangle of weaponry.

Quenelda could feel Tangnost's concern, though the dragonmaster said nothing. There was nothing to be done about it: after all, there were too many half-trained recruits, too many veterans, too few overall to fully man each dragon.

Ground crew cleared the pads. The dragons powered up, great wings sweeping up and down, warming aching muscles, stretching tendons. Landing lights winked from amber to green.

'Wingwraith, Wingwraith, you are cleared for immediate takeoff. Wind westerly, twelve knots and rising. ETA on the Isle of Storms, sixteen bells and counting.'

'We are good to go.'

'Good hunting, Wingwraith. Seadragon Keep, over and out.'

Within moments, Imperials and swifter Harriers of the SDS were swooping down, gathering speed before arcing up into the air and heading for the Westering Ocean.

Chapter Thirty-Three

Broken and Burned

The hospital wing was worse – a nightmare of suppurating burns, torn limbs and broken bodies. The dragonsmiths, surgeons and their esquires were on the point of collapse. Young cadets from the Battle Academy above had been summoned away from their studies and textbooks to assist; but the hollow-eyed youths were stumbling with weariness.

As they moved amongst the roosts, the stink of burned flesh made Root gag, but Quenelda cried out in horror. Hands held against her ears, she reeled under the waves of pain and anguish from the injured dragons that washed through her.

She turned to the nearest dragon. Swiftly she then moved from roost to roost, till her head ached.

'I would like to help nurse the injured,' she said to Loki. There is still a deep infection beneath these wounds.' She gestured to Storm from the North's chest. 'The poison is gone, but it will need your care and knowledge to heal her. Warrior Windsong has a hairline fracture to her third torlock bone. Crunch Beneath my Talon has an arrowhead lodged beneath his quipsom, which is why he's so agitated . . . and the stitches around Pounce in the Night's amputated hind leg need to be redone. They're too tight, perhaps an apprentice stitched them – and they give him a lot of pain. And . . .'

'Well, I'll be blowed, Cousin Tangnost,' the watching Dragonmaster said, dealing his cousin a thumping blow between the shoulders that made Root's knees feel like buckling in sympathy. 'I wouldn't believe it if I hadn't seen it.'

The grizzled dwarf held out a hand to clasp one of Quenelda's in a rock-hard grip. 'You're welcome here, Lady Quenelda, most welcome. We are short-handed as you can see; lost four score surgeons and hundreds of dragonsmiths on the Westering Isles. We need all the help we can get!

'But how?' He turned to Tangnost as Quenelda moved off. 'How can a child know these things?'

'No!'

They both turned at the sudden loud command.

Shouts and the sound of thrashing wings and talons scraping on rock had drawn Quenelda to a roost deeper in the cavern, where a surgeon and two esquires were trying to treat a badly injured young battledragon.

'No, no further,' the surgeon repeated as Tangnost arrived, Loki trying to keep up on his crutches. 'This is no place for you to be – it is too dangerous'

Held by restraining ropes, the highly agitated Frost colt, Winter Wingwraith, was struggling so violently the cradle he rested in was on the verge of cracking. He had livid black burns across one wing and neck, deep, angry bubbling wounds that seeped and stank, foul against the pure white of his scales.

'Can you save him?' Tangnost held Quenelda back in an iron grip.

The grizzled battle surgeon wearily shook his head. 'No. We have lost three from this patrol alone, he is the last.' He coughed harshly. 'I've never seen such virulent sorcery. We don't even how they have become infected. They are scouts; they've not fought in any engagements. I've tried everything I know, Bearhugger.'

'Whoa there, boy!'

The colt reared up, knocking an apothecary to the ground. Eyes rolling in their sockets, the colt was frothing at the mouth, hearts racing so fast Quenelda could hear them from where she stood. Soon, like the others, she knew his twin hearts would burst.

Hush . . . Quenelda focused solely on the struggling colt, trying to shut out the background cries and whispers. She felt something new stir deep within her in warning; knowledge that wasn't quite memory, a thought that was not quite hers. Darkness snapped in her mind as she jerked her hand back. Maelstrom, the corrupt taint of the Maelstrom!

How do I know? Where have these memories come from? They are not just dreams are they? But I do . . . somehow I recognise it now . . . ancient darkness . . . it has come again . . . the Abyss opens . . . the Dark is rising . . . She shivered with foreboding. *What is happening to me? What am I? These are not my memories . . .*

She moved forwards, pulling against the anchor of the dwarf's arm 'Let me go to him.'

'No. This is beyond you.'

'What's wrong?' Root was puzzled. 'Why don't you let her go? She can help.'

'They're dying,' Tangnost answered grimly, his eye on the surgeon.

'I know,' Quenelda argued. 'That's why—'

'*Not* just the dragons, Quenelda; everyone who comes into contact with them dies.'

'Dying?' Root was horrified. 'I don't understand . . .'

'None do, lad,' the surgeon said wearily, running a hand through thinning hair. A hank came off in his hand. He barely noticed.

Aghast, Root and Quenelda studied him and his young esquires in the dim light. They all looked like living ghosts with dark sunken eyes and green tinged skin hanging in waxy folds. They were racked with coughs, their movements jerky as puppets with broken strings.

'Once they go blind we give them a soldiers' death,' Loki said softly. 'A swift death.'

Root gulped, feeling sick.

Tangnost nodded. 'Believe me, it's a kindness.'

'But I can help him. He's only slightly infected. I can—'

The dwarf shook his head. 'Quenelda, no,' he began. 'You have little knowledge of healing, no experience of chaotic Battle Magic. You do not know the danger that—'

'I *do* know,' she repeatedly stubbornly. 'And I can help!'

The surgeon shook his head in despair. 'You are too young, Lady, to know what is impossible. This is beyond us. All knowledge of the Maelstrom has long since been forbidden. We do not know how to treat such deadly wounds.'

'Let me at least try,' she urged Tangnost, her dragon eyes flaring, drawing a gasp of amazement from the surgeon.

Remembering the Heartrock, and hearing the ancient certainty in her voice, Tangnost reluctantly released her and prayed to his gods that the blood and power of the Elders truly ran in her veins.

'Bearhugger!' The surgeon was aghast, tried to prevent the young girl without touching her.

'Shardlake, this is the Earl Rufus's daughter. Let her stay. She may be able help.'

The surgeon searched the dwarf's face. 'Very well,' he conceded, reluctantly allowing Quenelda into the roost. He had heard the tale of the Heartrock, but like many did not know what it truly meant. 'If it were any man but you asking, Bearhugger . . .'

Quenelda gently moved forwards. Head bowed, she blew gently on the colt's nose, calming him.

I am burning, Dancing with Dragons! Burning . . . burning . . . The dragon's flanks were heaving.

'Where did he fall sick?' *Why did I ask that?*

'Off the Isle of Midges.' The battle surgeon frowned. 'Why?'

The ice! Drifting icebergs . . . The ice is poisoned. The residue from the battle of the Westering Isles, from the Ice Fortress . . . it still kills . . . how long after the battle?

'It's the icebergs. They're tainted.'

Tangnost's eye narrowed in thought. He nodded. 'That's it, lass! You've put your finger on it.'

Root looked lost.

'Frost dragons are scouts, lad, in the frozen north. They fly huge distances across the Westering Ocean by landing on icebergs,' Odin explained.

Tangnost agreed. 'With such a dreadful winter, sightings have been logged as far south as the Isle of Midges.'

'We'll tell pilots at the next briefing not to set down on the icebergs. It means we'll lose our long range reconnaissance capability in the north west, but—'

Hush . . . Shutting out their voices, Quenelda reached out a splayed hand to touch the damaged scales; they were achingly cold. She snapped her hand away and raised her left hand. The scale from Two Gulps pulsed warmly, its golden glow spreading.

Hear me . . .

Memories flooded her as she spoke the ancient language of the Elders with power, so that her words reached every injured and exhausted dragon throughout the great fortress. *Be calm . . . be rested and at peace . . .*

The struggling battledragon suddenly quietened beneath her touch. Throughout the fortress and on the high cliffs above, in the tilting yards of the Academy, the dragons fell still. Eighteen leagues away the Lord Protector shivered as the pulse of magic swept the glen. Somewhere there was a shift in the magical field, he could feel it. What could it mean?

Hush . . . she whispered to Winter Wingwraith, *now I'll take away the pain . . .* Quenelda's fingertips tingled, then a pulse of magic blossomed about her hands, swathing the dragon in a healing cocoon of spun sorcery, a radiant swirl of fierce white energy, bringing with it a release from pain. The Frost dragon shuddered, and his frantic panting slowed as Quenelda drew out the corrosive smoking poison. The darkness fought against her, but as it crackled about her hands she clenched her fists and it was gone with a clap, banished back to the Abyss. The dragon's sweat-drenched muzzle drooped, and he sagged in the cradle as Quenelda sagged into the strong arms of Tangnost.

'Steady, lass, steady,' he rebuked her gently. 'Don't try too much too soon . . .' *Legend says Whisperers are healers . . .*

'He's asleep,' the surgeon said, stunned, 'and the wound, it's clean!'

Trembling with exhaustion, Quenelda let Tangnost and Root help her to her feet. There was a thud as one of the esquires keeled over, the battle surgeon immediately at his side. He looked up.

'Lady?' There was a wealth of hope invested in that single word.

Quenelda knelt beside the shuddering body. The boy was barely older than she was. He was all skin and bone, his pale skin was blotched with sickly green sores that wept black ooze. His eyes had begun to cloud over. She focused on him with a desperation borne of weariness; knowing immediately he was beyond her help, but determined to try.

Laying a hand on his chest, she frantically searched for

the dying spark of life, but she had no strength left and the enveloping dark surged forwards, searching for another victim. Her strength was drained, her knowledge exhausted, it was too much for the young girl. She broke the bond and fell back with a cry.

'I – I can't!' she cried, distraught. 'He's too ill . . . It's too late! I don't have the power,' she wept in Tangnost's arms.

'Peace, Lady,' the Surgeon comforted her. 'We all knew the price, and thought it worth the risk.'

'Come,' Tangnost commanded Root as he guided Quenelda away.

'Sergeant?' The Surgeon beckoned a soldier over, tears spilling down his cheeks.

Root hung back, unwilling to leave. 'But – but you can't just kill him,' he was crying too.

Loki pulled the boy away as the sword arced down. 'Carrock was his only remaining son!'

Chapter Thirty-Four
Nightmare

Twenty-three bells sounded, the Hour of the Creeping Lynx. Deep within Dragon Isle it was hard to tell day from night any more, and Quenelda was worn out. She was learning to ignore the countless whispers in her head, to focus on those dragons that mattered most at each moment of time, but the effort left her with blinding headaches. And when she finally fell into bed exhausted, sleep did not come easily, and brought with it the same relentless nightmare that she could not shut out.

Darkness closed around Quenelda. The familiar walls of her chamber faded. Now it was cold and dark, but she slowly made out glowing orbs of light inset into the rough-hewn walls. The air was thick with brimstone dust, clogging her eyes and nostrils, thick on her cracked tongue. She was shackled and chained and starving, the weight of cold iron heavy about her neck. Her limbs burned; her wounds wept into the dust. She felt the grating misery of starvation and captivity and a longing for Open Sky had driven her to the edge of madness.

Dancing with Dragons . . .

The shared whisper was so faint that she could barely hear its anguished plea. She reached out.

Who are you? Where are you?

But the mind faded beyond her reach, and each time it grew weaker, and Quenelda felt a sense of unbearable desolation and loss.

So cold . . .

So alone . . .

Chapter Thirty-Five

Two Gulps Too Many

Tangnost sighed. The world as they knew it had changed. The impossible had happened. The SDS had been annihilated, betrayed by a sorcerer who now ruled the kingdoms in all but name, and none but a handful knew the truth. North of the Old Wall, all but one of the SDS fortresses had fallen to the hobgoblins. Amidst all the ruin and despair, there was one spark of brightness to offer the fatherless young girl Tangnost now took under his protective wing. As they arrived at the maternity roosts, he prayed to his gods that he was doing the right thing.

Only cave-dwelling dragons were raised on Dragon Isle itself – ancient home to Imperials, and now also to Sabretooths and Spitting Adders. The roosts deep inside Dragon Isle were dark and warm, the tang of raw meat overlaid by brimstone and phosphor. Tangnost led Root and Quenelda to where a Sabretooth mare was lying on a bed of broken rock and shale; her litter of nine a faint gleam of talon and scale in the darkness, that slithered and flamed as they played and pounced on each other in mock battle.

'When were they born?' Quenelda's question was a whisper, as if everything depended upon the answer, which it did.

'Five weeks ago.' The elderly roost master Tam Brandywine glanced curiously at the Earl's daughter.

Root could see her hands shaking. He moved up next to her to shield her from curious eyes.

'Are they . . . ?' Quenelda barely dared to breathe. These small fiery Sabretooths could only belong to her beloved dead Two Gulps. Why else had Tangnost brought her here?

'Yes,' Tangnost said huskily, tears welling.

Quenelda put out her hand to clasp his strong hand in silent thanks. Root realized that she, too, was crying, and decided to put his arm about her as well.

The roost master studied them surreptitiously in the gloom, dwarf and gnome and girl: the legendary Bonecracker and Dragonmaster who had defied the Lord Protector to spirit away a girl who was now his daughter in all but name; the dark-haired gnome who had somehow been raised from commoner to esquire; and the dead

Earl's daughter who had wanted to fly in the SDS since she was a babe. An unlikely trio, yet their deep affection and love for each other were obvious to any who saw them together.

But – he sighed – *it just wasn't normal.* The ruling sorcerers never mingled with commoners, the different peoples of the One Earth never mixed, save here on Dragon Isle, and girls never flew with the SDS. Everyone had their place and their allotted tasks: it had always been thus. To challenge such social strictures, to attempt otherwise, would only end in grief.

Quenelda stepped over the wall and raised her gaze to the Sabretooth mare. So this was Two Gulps' mate. She bit her lip.

Firestorm Bright Eyes – may the wind sing under your wings . . .

Dancing with Dragons, the young mare acknowledged. *May you dance with the stars . . .*

Your litter-pack are strong and many . . .

My mate was strong . . .

Quenelda closed her eyes, unable to stop the tears from falling. The mare moved forward, surprisingly delicate, picking her way through her squalling fledglings to where Quenelda stood, her brow gently coming to rest against the girl's. Quenelda placed her hands on either side of the scaled head and blew softly. The Sabretooth blew gently back, ruffling her hair.

'Odin's beard!' Tam was stunned. 'Ain't never seen nothing like it, Dragonmaster.'

My mate was proud to bear you into battle to save Thunder Rolling over the Mountains. . . Now your scales are hard – you will take revenge on those who took his life . . . ?

I swear it . . . Quenelda's eyes flared gold in the darkness.

Root found that he was no longer afraid, but the roost master stumbled backwards with a cry, tripping over a cauldron of coal and falling heavily to the floor.

Ignoring him, Tangnost in turn reached up to hold the mare's bridle, blowing softly on her muzzle.

One-Eye . . . He could not hear the mare's welcome, but she blew softly back.

Head resting against her, Tangnost spoke, his voice muffled. 'We decided to breed from Two Gulps early; since he became your mount, your Lord father wanted his pedigree bloodline for the battlefield as soon as possible, so he was put to stud with the best mare we have.'

He lifted his head, lantern-light catching his craggy face as he looked down at Quenelda. 'Your Lord father was going to give you the pick of the litter to train; the rest were destined for the Academy and esquires to raise. The Commander says the pick of the litter is still yours as your father wished, and I'll teach you how to train him for battle as your father intended. Only now he will be your mount, so choose wisely.'

Quenelda nodded, knowing what a tremendous privilege was being granted to her. With so many dragons injured and dead, the SDS were nonetheless still allowing her to choose the best fledgling. She considered the little dragons that were mock-fighting, tumbling and cuffing each other at her feet. Small bursts of flame lit up the dark warmth as she knelt down.

'In you go, lad.' The roost master beckoned a roost-hand forward. 'Fetch him out.' He pursed his lips with satisfaction, and nodded knowledgably at Tangnost. 'Pick of the litter for 'er ladyship.'

The stable hand put on some heavy leather gauntlets and moved into the roost beside Quenelda, talking soothingly to the mother all the time. 'There, Bright Eyes . . .

Just having a look at your young 'uns . . . there . . .' He waded through the mass of small scales and talons, armour clicking as they came into contact with his ceramic plates. There were grunts and excited squeaks, and a few hastily smothered oaths, before the boy emerged with a small dragon struggling furiously in his arms. It was trying to turn its head so it could flame him. Another was enthusiastically hanging onto the bottom of his armoured leather kilt. A third was being dragged along upside down, its teeth firmly clamped around the boy's ankle. He had lost a gauntlet, which was being eaten by a plump pear-shaped fledgling in the far corner of the roost.

'Aye, they're a feisty bunch,' the roost master said proudly. 'Going to do us proud, they are. Fighters one and all. Well,' he amended, muttering darkly in the direction of the plump baby dragon, 'most of 'em, anyhow . . . Time that one was culled.'

The stable hand brought the struggling fledgling over to Quenelda, cheerfully wiping the blood from his nose where it had managed to catch a sharp little talon.

'This here's the one for – for you, miss — Ouch! Gerroffmyear . . . Strong lower back, powerful hindquarters, long toes – he'll crunch a hobgoblin or two. Well – ouch! – developed jaw! And look at these teeth, Lady. OUCH! Letgoofmyfingersssssss . . .' The stable hand smiled gamely through gritted teeth. 'Ow!'

As soon as he released it, the fledgling barrelled away to attack one of its litter-mates, and the pair rolled and spat fire at each other under their mother's proud gaze.

But Quenelda's eyes were fixed elsewhere – on the dragon slowly waddling over to her. Fat as a butter barrel, it had finished the gauntlet and was coming over to inspect what she was offering on her outstretched palm.

'Oh no, Lady.' Tam was horrified at her choice. 'I thought she was a good judge of dragonflesh,' he muttered to Tangnost behind a hand. 'No, Lady,' he said more loudly. 'That one's no good. Doesn't fight, just eats. Too lazy. Too heavy.'

Food . . . ?

Quenelda looked into the quietly intelligent eyes that held her gaze as it gently took the proffered honey tablets one by one and ate them with obvious delight.

More . . . ? it asked hopefully.

Quenelda emptied her pockets, and the little dragon

emptied her hand. Its distended stomach rumbled and it burped happily. Behind Quenelda, Root, Tangnost and the roost master all ducked behind the roost wall as a toxic flame rolled over them.

'Phew!' Root nearly gagged. 'What's it been eating?'

'So far today: scale oil . . . the lamp . . . a leather apron . . .' The roost hand thought about it . . . 'a pair of claw clippers . . .'

They risked a look. Quenelda hadn't moved. Although her jacket was smouldering in several places, not a single hair on her head was singed, causing the roost master to rub his eyes in disbelief, and Tangnost's one eye to narrow in thoughtful speculation. Root beat out a spark on her jacket that was threatening to take hold. Quenelda appeared not even to have noticed. She had eyes only for the fledgling.

This baby Sabretooth was the one. Quenelda knew it; had known it from the moment she saw him. He was so similar to his sire. He bore the same red blaze behind the left eye as Two Gulps had, the same oversized canines. Her eyes travelled over scale and claw. The same large golden scales in a mosaic pattern tapering to the tail . . . And no – it wasn't possible. Quenelda drew a sharp breath.

'What?' Root frowned. 'What's wrong?'

'The tail . . .'

All eyes looked at the stubby little tail currently being used by the baby Sabretooth to try and lever himself out of the pen to get at the brimstone scuttles stacked nearby. He jumped and bounced off the wall, big feet in the air, crooked tail thrashing helplessly.

There was a short silence, broken by Tam.

'Aye, born with a crooked tail to boot, lady. Another reason why you don't want this 'un. Runt o' the litter, 'e is.'

Both Tangnost and Root ignored him. He looked at them in bafflement. All three of his guests were staring fixedly at the fledgling's crooked tail.

The little dragon gave up the impossible task of escaping and waddled over to the empty brass scuttle, sniffed it and began to eat it with apparent relish. There was the sound of crumpling metal. Root winced.

'Is there anything he doesn't eat?' Quenelda asked.

The roost hand shook his head. 'Don't think so, miss,' he said cheerfully.

'Will he ever get airborne?' Root asked dubiously.

'Don't think so, sir.'

'Wing-to-weight ratio . . .' Root nodded knowledgeably, earning him a surprised glance from the roost master.

'I want him.'

'Lady?' Tam was taken aback. 'But, Lady—' he began, till Tangnost squeezed his arm warningly and nodded.

'I want him,' Quenelda repeated defiantly.

A quiet smile played over Tangnost's lips. He had been right. This fledgling was most like his sire, Two Gulps and You're Gone. 'What are you going to call him?'

Quenelda grinned, making his heart ache.

She looked back down at the plump fledgling.

'Two Gulps Too Many . . .'

Chapter Thirty-Six

The Call of the North

And so the hours merged into days, and the days into weeks, as Quenelda and Root worked in the roosts, helping surgeons and dragonsmiths, healing the injured and tending the dying; and for the first time since the Battle of the Westering Isles, the number of battledragons available for operations exceeded the number in the hospital wing. But there was that other voice, that other desperate appeal for aid that didn't come from Dragon Isle; the voice she constantly heard in dreams, that now haunted her every waking moment.

Lonely . . . so lonely . . . The faint whisper filled her head, with its desperate song that yearned for wind and rain and Open Sky.

So dark . . . so dark and cold down here . . . Darkness all around . . .

Where are you? Quenelda cried. *Who are you?*

But no one answered.

'What's happening? What's wrong?'

Echoes from the harbour bell were fading as Tangnost, followed by Quenelda and Root, walked along the north jetty in the great harbour cavern. Two merchant galleons flying the DeWinter banner had limped in with deep gouges in their caulked timbers. On one, the mizzen mast was smashed, rigging tangled, rails splintered. The bolt-throwers mounted on the stern and aft castle decks of both galleons lay empty, evidence of a desperate battle. The wood of the port hulls was scorched and still smoking. The injured were being carried down the gang-plank as cranes swung in to lift the precious cargo of ore from the holds.

'All that remains of another brimstone convoy from the DeWinter mine at Cairnmore,' the harbourmaster reported. 'A patrol found the survivors at daybreak and escorted them home.'

'Razorbacks?' Root asked, wide-eyed.

'Razorbacks,' Tangnost agreed. 'The shipping lanes are becoming unsafe.'

Loki arrived, metal-shod crutches sparking on the stone wharf as the ship's Captain walked wearily down the gangplank.

'We were attacked by hobgoblins, with those cursed

demon dragons of theirs.' The Captain ran his hand through salt-stiffened hair, and spat. 'Abyss knows where they found those foul creatures. We lost ten ships in the night. Two just went straight down. There one heartbeat and gone the next.' He nodded gruffly at Tangnost. 'Your idea to carry a Sabretooth on board saved us. Those slimy maggots weren't expecting that when they swarmed over the side. But we need to metal the hulls, for they nearly fired the brimstone in the hold!'

Their words were drowned out as nets opened to pour brimstone into the huge waiting cauldrons. Loki picked up a lump of dusty ore and hefted it in one hand, expertly examining its colour and weight before handing it to Tangnost. 'High-grade amber, but still a fraction of what we need.'

Tangnost nodded. 'Times are desperate.'

Loki nodded. 'Worse than you think, cousin. A courier arrived at dawn. There have been two more explosions at royal mines.'

'Two! Thor's Hammer!' Tangnost exploded. 'It's sabotage, no matter what the Lord Protector says!'

'What does he say?' Quenelda asked coldly, hostility evident in every syllable.

'With so many mines to the north of the Old Wall overrun by the hobgoblins, we have to delve far deeper than before,' Tangnost explained. 'The Lord Protector says that the lower seams are more dangerous to mine. That the dust builds up in the deep galleries.'

'Since when did a Sorcerer Lord know anything about mining?' Odin spat. 'I doubt he's been anywhere near a mine, and it is our folk who are dying!'

Tangnost nodded. 'We need to discuss this. Even with so few dragons operational, things are becoming desperate.'

Maps were spread out in the Dragonmaster's quarters. A few had brimstone mines marked on them in Tangnost's careful hand.

'These here are DeWinter mines' – he pointed – 'marked in red. So far there have been no accidents, though output has dropped. Royal mines are clustered here, here and here, and to the north, and these are on Clan lands belonging to my people. The two nearest us, south of the Wall, are now damaged by explosions.'

'And these ones?' Root asked, pointing to the far north.

'Those belong to the Lord Protector and are beyond the range of the Howling Glen. They are all infested with hobgoblins, he claims,' Loki said.

'Or not . . .' Tangnost said darkly. 'He claims that only three of his mines remain operational, and thus he requisitions ore from the Royal mines. But I wonder . . . I think he is stockpiling ore.'

'Why?' Root asked.

'There is only one reason,' Tangnost said grimly, drawing on his pipe. 'To put an army in the field. War!'

'Do Razorbacks need brimstone to survive, like normal dragons do?' said Root.

Tangnost shook his head. 'We don't think so, lad.'

Root shivered. His encounter with a rogue dragon at the Winter Joust had been terrifying, recalling his childhood fear of dragons. To have such great creatures as your friends was scary enough. To encounter dragons whose only desire was to eat you – whose dark smoke dissolved you like acid . . .

Quenelda was peering intently at the map. 'This is Cairnmore?'

Tangnost nodded. 'The quality of its ore is first class. It's one of the few mines in the area that hasn't been attacked by hobgoblins, or suffered an "accident".'

'But output has dropped drastically,' Loki told her.

'Can you not bring it overland?' Root asked.

'We could, lad,' Loki said. 'The problem is that ore is heavy – heavier than gold. This dreadful weather makes many roads impassable; even the military roads have collapsed under the weight of ice and flood-melt, and the refugees' wagons get bogged down to their axles. And it takes time, lad, a lot of time, to bring in a brimstone convoy, which makes them easy targets for the hobgoblins.

'But' – Quenelda frowned – 'the military roads are still protected by forts, aren't they?'

'They are mostly garrisoned by the Lord Darcy's or the Lord Protector's men,' Tangnost explained. 'Convoys are still attacked by hobgoblins or mercenaries, or so they say. So few convoys to Dragon Isle get through.'

'My nephew is foreman at Cairnmore,' Tangnost said. 'We have sent a dozen couriers warning him to be on his guard against sabotage. I suspect none of our dispatches are reaching him.'

So lonely . . .

so cold . . .

A fading whisper of thought, light as a cobweb, touched Quenelda's mind and was gone. Soon it would be too late. Soon the voice would be silenced for ever. She had to act now!

'Let me go,' Quenelda said suddenly.

Root stared at her. 'Let *us* go!'

Tangnost looked at her, careful not to show any pity. The Earl's daughter was still too pale, too thin. Her bruised eyes had a haunted look more often seen in battlefield veterans – which was no surprise after what she had been through. She needed something to do, something to believe in once again.

'Let us go, Tangnost,' she repeated, on the verge of tears. 'No one would notice the two of us. I – I don't know why, but I need to go north . . .'

'This dream of yours?'

She nodded. 'Someone is calling and calling to me. The answer lies out there, I know it does. Please, please let me go. I *have* to go, Tangnost.'

He knew it would have happened anyway one way or the other. She was stretching her wings.

'Do you think you could manage on your own? It is further away than you think. And yes, the highways and the Northern Way at the heart of the kingdoms are again secure, but you would have to leave them to reach the mine. You have never stayed out overnight in the wilds, never had to forage—'

'I have,' Root chimed in, his voice quietly determined. 'We – my warren – moved camp with the seasons, taking what we needed from the land as we went. I can find food and water wherever we are,' he added confidently, as Quenelda shot him a grateful smile.

'We can manage, Tangnost, I know we can,' Quenelda pleaded.

'You can go, *but*' – he held up his hand – 'you must take a battlegriff, and both of you must be disguised, so that none recognize you, or link you to the SDS or Dragon Isle. Should the Lord Protector's men find you, none would dispute his right to take you into his household. Wear old clothes and old tack; carry nothing that points to Dragon Isle. That way you should be safe. Many visit the mines at the behest of their Lords. With a helmet on, no one outside of the Sorcerers Glen would know you. Quenelda. Cut your hair short and you will pass for a boy.

'We must prepare. Root, go to the map room and put

your recent learning to good use. Memorize your route, the forts and way-stations for food for you and fodder for your mount. Quenelda, come, we have much to plan.'

So lost . . . so alone . . .

But this time she could answer.

I'm coming . . . I'm coming for you . . .

Chapter Thirty-Seven

Beyond the Sorcerers Glen

Root swallowed down his apprehension as he studied the maps and his brass compass. His family had been slaughtered by a hobgoblin war band when he was six, and until he came to Dragon Isle he had never left the safety of the Sorcerers Glen. Eighteen leagues long from east to west, where it met the Inner Sea, it had been his whole world. The Brimstones looked very far away; it might take weeks if the weather was bad. He swallowed nervously.

Since his father had died, Root had had to overcome his fear of dragons and had befriended the gentle Chasing the Stars. Together they had fought a rogue dragon intent on murder, and then he had fled Dragonsdome for sanctuary on Dragon Isle, forced to leave her behind. But he had not had to confront his fears and nightmares out in the wide world beyond the Sorcerers Glen. He gritted his teeth. He wasn't the same helpless boy he had once been, and Quenelda needed him, now more than ever. Ignoring his worries, the young gnome studied the map, re-checked his calculations and plotted their journey.

Although she had left the Sorcerers Glen many times, Quenelda had always flown with her father on Stormcracker. Twice, when she was ten summers old, she had accompanied him as far as the Isle of Midges, where the dwarfs had been building an eighth fortress, abandoned since the ambush that had killed her grandfather. But no further than that. How many times had she dreamed of such an adventure; dreamed of coming to the rescue of the SDS? This furtive departure was not what she had imagined.

Quenelda longed for the solace of Open Sky. It was where she belonged, and yet she still held back, dreading taking to the air without her beloved Two Gulps. He would have loved to fly north to battle. Root, increasingly anxious about the fate of Chasing the Stars, silently let her know that he understood her inner conflict only too well.

Quenelda raised her palm and flexed her hand, amazed at the gorse-yellow scale that armoured it. Although her battledragon was dead, she knew he was still part of her. His strength was now her strength; his dreams invaded hers. She looked at herself in the mirror. She had grown taller over the last six moons since the SDS fell in battle, but she was still painfully thin, the bones of her cheeks and slanting brow more visible. And the eyes that gazed back at her seemed those of a stranger.

But there were still some who would remember the Earl's daughter in boy's clothes. Lifting a knife, she took a hank of hair and sawed at it until it stuck out, short and ragged, about her head. Few people, even her brother, would recognize her now.

The battlegriff, I've Already Eaten, was being prepped for takeoff. He no longer looked as if he came from the SDS stable. Tangnost had chosen a dappled grey with subdued blue colouring, and gave orders that he should not be groomed for a week. Due to a poor diet, his wings and flanks had already lost their normal sheen; now he looked rather grubby and was unlikely to attract any unwanted attention. The tack, found in a dusty storeroom, was battered and much repaired. Old saddlebags and gear were tied down sloppily in a tangle of ropes.

Both Root and Quenelda wore patched breeches and

jerkins beneath faded old hooded cloaks. Root reflected that this was just what he had worn all the time before he was made up to esquire. He had chosen a helm with cheek pieces and nose guard; Quenelda a half-visored bronze helmet padded with leather.

Root checked through their hammocks and bedrolls, all wrapped in a layer of waxed leather hide. Water flasks . . . Travelling stove . . . He glanced up to where the fodder bags and honey tablets were stowed out of reach of the battlegriff's questing beak. The dragonwings strapped to the rear of each saddle were patched and faded. Military rations for a month, to which he had added gnome scones, crab apples and oatcakes. Finally they were ready.

'Here, hide it well.' Tangnost handed Quenelda a barkscroll for his nephew. As she hid it in the folds of her jacket, he gave them their last instructions. 'This warns my nephew, Malachite, to be on his guard against the Lord Protector's men. I have asked that he raise the clans to escort the next load overland. It will take far longer, but it will be harder for the Lord Protector to divert or seize it on a busy military road: too many witnesses, and he will not risk open war with the clans. Keep it hidden, and hand it to no one save Malachite himself.' Tangnost pulled a ring of red gold from his finger; it was fashioned in the shape of a bear's paw. 'He will recognize this token of your true intent.'

Quenelda nodded. The ring was too big for any of her fingers so they strung it on a leather thong about her neck, and she tucked it in beneath her jerkin. At last they were ready to leave.

'Take care,' Tangnost warned them as he adjusted the battlegriff's girth strap. 'Don't draw attention to yourself.' He clasped them both a final time and gruffly bade them farewell.

As dawn tickled the far horizon, the travellers took to the air. They would be clear of the Sorcerers Glen by the time the sun rose.

The battlegriff was very like Chasing the Stars to fly. As they rose into the crisp air, Root longed to see his companion again. One of Tangnost's homing eagles had arrived at Dragon Isle just before they left, bearing a message from Quester informing them that Root's beloved dragon was well, but pining for him. Other news was not so good: Darcy's behaviour grew ever more reckless. He was squandering a small fortune on balls and banquets, dragon fights and hippogriff-racing; and he was neglecting duties owed to the Crown as the Earl of Dragonsdome.

As they approached the expanse of the Inner Sea, Root looked back. Dragon Isle, with its hangar decks, its battlements and towers, was fast disappearing into a blue haze. Only the great spires and copper domes of the castle stood out, gleaming in the early morning sun.

With the raised cobbled military road to their left, they followed its straight lines for three days as it crossed open farmland. Despite the good weather, the military road was already clogged with refugees heading for the safety of the Sorcerers Glen before the passes were closed and true winter set in.

As the crescent moons grew fat in the night sky and the weather held fair, Quenelda decided to keep flying later and later into the night – anything to shut out the nightmares. The battlegriff wasn't used to night flying, and they had collided with an owl and a flock of bats before Quenelda agreed to Root's hesitant suggestion to put down for the night. Root noticed she hardly ate anything now, and he heard her restless tossing and turning each night, crying out to the voice in her head. No wonder she had a headache all the time.

She was exhausted, driven on by her inner voice.

Cold, so cold . . . How I long to see the stars again . . .

On the fifth day, the military road branched and they turned north, away from the coastline, following the Great Northern Way for a further three days. As they reached the lower slopes of the Brimstones, the great forest began to thin out. Soon the terrain was punctuated by steep ravines and gullies, and the heavy smell of sulphur permeated everything. The air grew steadily colder.

The next morning, they couldn't see a thing. Tired, irritable from lack of sleep, Quenelda was not in the mood to allow any further delay just because there was no longer a road to follow.

'You can still navigate can't you?' she snapped unfairly as Root tentatively asked if they were going to wait till the fog thinned. 'You've got a map and compass, haven't you?'

Reluctant to let her down, Root simply nodded miserably. He had been studying hard, but theory and practice were two different things. They took to the air; it was thick as pea soup. Root desperately wished he had one of the SDS navigator's helmets, that he had the three years training it took to fly Imperials. Without it they were virtually flying blind!

Then a wind rose in the gullies and ravines, buffeting them from side to side, pushing them up and sucking them down. Root began to feel airsick again, but manfully gritted his teeth. He could take it! Quenelda needed him to be tough!

The haar thickened.

'Aahh!' Root couldn't help crying out loud as a branch nearly knocked him from the saddle. Without realizing it, they had lost height and had almost collided with a ragged pine tree split by lightning. Quenelda herself was more than a little scared – not that she was going to admit that to Root.

Alone . . . so alone . . .

The battlegriff too was becoming increasingly grumpy. He hadn't been cared for well for many moons, and was out of sorts before they even set off from Dragon Isle. Drenched from beak to hoof, he badly needed a groom and to hunt a tasty beaver or two to pick his spirits up.

'I'm not sure if we're still on course,' Quenelda tried half a bell later in an offhand tone of voice, hoping that

Root would suggest they put down before she had to admit her stupidity.

'No, no,' Root chimed up cheerily, waving the compass at her and nodding manically. 'We're still headed in the right direction!'

Quenelda cursed inwardly, and encouraged the reluctant battlegriff on.

The wind rose further.

'Rather rough going,' she finally ventured over the banshee shriek.

The battlegriff agreed wholeheartedly. He was flapping for he it was worth now; only an ignorant fledgling would be out flying on a day like this. He was exhausted, although he certainly would not be admitting that to Dancing with Dragons.

They might, Quenelda thought half a bell later, still be flying in the right direction, but before long she was no longer certain that they were making any headway. She had the sneaking suspicion they might even be being pushed backwards. The head wind was wicked.

Root had the sneaking suspicion that they were going backwards. He wasn't certain, but Quenelda hadn't said anything, so it must be his imagination.

Then the haar briefly thinned, revealing a lightning struck pine tree that looked all too familiar.

'Err . . .' Root began, pointing to starboard.

'We've been here before,' Quenelda finished for him as a unexpected gust gathered them up.

'I'm putting down,' she shouted over her shoulder. 'This is getting too dangerous.'

She fought to control the battlegriff as they dropped height into a deep ravine, not even sure where the ground now lay. Root cried out and gripped his saddle pommel as a vicious cross wind caught them and spun them about like a sycamore seed.

'Gently, boy, gently does it,' Quenelda's heart was in her mouth as she coaxed the stallion down, petrified he might break a limb or a wing. Why on the One Earth had she made such an unwise decision? Her stupidity might yet kill them all.

Boulders loomed darkly out of the mist and the wind howled like ghosts. Talons extended, the indignant battle-griff landed in a shallow depression beneath a stand of bent pines in a flurry of soggy feathers. Kicking his stirrups, Root slid down his flanks onto his knees where he retched miserably into the scrubby grass.

They slung their hammocks on the lower branches of a great pine tree with the battlegriff roosting below. During the night, the wind rose even more so that their hammocks swung and dipped. Root was petrified, flinching at every creak and groan of the trees, the uncanny yelp of foxes and the plaintive call of the curlew bringing back memories of the night he had spent alone in the forest after most of his family and the entire warren had been slaughtered. He fell into an uneasy sleep.

'Hide . . .' he was burbling. 'I must hide . . .' Sweat poured from him as he twisted and thrashed in his sleeping roll. The sound of the creaking branches turned into the cry of his mother as she had tried to protect his brothers and sisters. The shriek of the wind became the savage cries of the hobgoblin warriors as they sent their young into the burrows and hunted down everyone throughout the warren, flushing them out into the open where they were set upon. The bramble thickets caught on his clothes as he tried to burrow beneath their protective thorns. He was caught, he couldn't move. Something was emerging out of the shadows, reaching out for him . . .

'Root?' Deep in shadow, Quenelda was perched on the

branch above the gnome looking down on him. 'Root?'

Root jerked awake to see a pale hand reached forward. He screamed, batting it away.

'Root! Root! You're safe! It's just a nightmare! You've had a nightmare.'

The youth shivered.

'Here.' Quenelda reached for one of her blankets. 'Listen, I'll light the lamp.'

And as she watched her friend nurse a drink of mulled cider, Quenelda realized how selfish she had been, bringing him on this journey. She had never given a moment's thought to his fears, he had seemed so confident.

'I'll keep watch,' she promised, as Root's head finally nodded. How would she feel out here if most of her family had been massacred by marauding hobgoblins? She wasn't the only one with nightmares.

The dense cloud was, if anything, worse the following morning, but the wind had dropped. Cautiously they took off, Quenelda flying as low as she dared so that she could at least see the ground, even though that increased the risk of collision. The drenching moisture weighed down their flying cloaks and their spirits. But within two bells there were more problems.

'Quenelda, I don't know where we are any more.' Root looked at his compass but the needle span as the first drop of rain fell.

'It must be the brimstone . . .' He pursed his lips. 'Tangnost warned me the ore would make the needle go crazy, but I'd hoped by then we'd have landmarks to sight by.'

Huddled miserably together beneath the battlegriff's outstretched wing, the rain drummed down and the moisture laden air soaked through their heavy cloaks and sleeping rolls. Root tried to start a fire with his flint and tinder, but couldn't coax a spark. They shared cold food and mugs of rainwater. Huddled together against the flanks of the battlegriff they pulled their capes about them and tried to rest, but the desperate whispers Quenelda kept hearing were louder now and she could not sleep.

Who was it calling out to her? What did it mean?

Lonely . . . lonely . . .

So cold . . .

So dark . . .

Chapter Thirty-Eight

Bubble, Bubble, Toil and Trouble

They woke to a bright cold morning and the sounds of birds in the trees. The yellow fangs of the Brimstones rose up into the brilliant blue sky. Overhead, huge mountain buzzards were slowly rising on the thermals. Root climbed a rocky outcrop to get his bearings.

'There it is!'

As Quenelda joined him, he pointed to the expanse of water that should lead to the mine. 'We're close,' he guessed, checking the lie of the loch against his crumpled map. 'Very close now. Perhaps a half-day's journey?'

Flying low, they skirted the mountain. Soon there were no trees – no vegetation of any kind; just the stark chalk-coloured stone of the lower slopes sweeping down to the sea loch, threaded through with saffron-yellow seams of ore.

Shortly after the Hour of the Irritated Bumblebee, Root lowered his telescope and tapped Quenelda on the shoulder. 'Ships . . .' He indicated a cluster of distant sails gleaming in the low sun beneath a yellow haze. 'They must be taking on cargo. Maybe all is well.'

As I've Already Eaten drew closer, the northeast wind carried faint shouts and roars, and, beneath it all, a sound like rain falling on a tiled roof: the steady hammering of mallet and pick on the rock face. As they drew closer, the noise grew louder and louder.

Whips cracked. Voices shouted. Metal screeched. Commands were bellowed. Pulleys swung and chains rattled. The noise was so loud it rattled Root's teeth.

The Cairnmore mine was shaped like a crescent moon cut deep into the mountainside, and it was covered in scaffolding. A group of miners' huts lay in the dunes to the left, down by the long wooden jetty. Behind, amongst the marram grass, half buried by sand, was a large graveyard. Root shivered. Mining brimstone was obviously hazardous, even for mountain dwarfs.

Seven ships were anchored inside the curving stone harbour wall, five of them Guild merchant galleons, with two armoured SDS battlegalleons providing an escort. Two clippers, a half-league out in deeper water, were standing watch as the six galleons lying deep in the water weighed anchor. They flew the Lord Protector's new coat of arms: the coiling red adder on a black background, slashed with a golden unicorn on russet.

'He has no right to the royal coat of arms!' Quenelda began furiously. 'He's not married the Queen yet! He—'

Lonely . . . so lonely . . .

So dark . . .

No stars . . .

The voice drew her back to where a dozen mine shafts, framed by scaffolding and ladders, burrowed into the cliff face. Crude metal rail tracks snaked from the vast entrance down to the jetties, where teams of old and injured dragons were hauling great wagons loaded with heavy ore down to the ships. Others were dragging the empty wagons back. It took Quenelda a moment to work out what was wrong. It was the breeds. In utter disbelief, she turned I've Already Eaten towards the jetty for another pass.

'They're using old battledragons in the mines!' Quenelda was outraged.

'What?' Root shouted. He had turned in his stirrups and was watching the mine as they swung upward in an arc. Figures were running out of the cavernous entrance. He could faintly hear shouting. Then the ground convulsed. Panic rippled outwards as more and more miners turned to flee, jumping from the scaffolding in their haste.

'Look! Look!' Root pulled on Quenelda's arm. 'Something's going on.' He unbuckled his helmet to hear better. 'Look. I think—'

There was a huge muffled *boom* followed by an ear-splitting *crack!* The hillside rippled, then part of the quarry face blew out in billowing clouds of splintered wood, boulders and ash. Vast chunks of burning rock arced into the sky.

'*Aaarghh!*' Quenelda screamed. Everything around her turned bright white, then yellow, leaving her stunned and blinded, with a pink after-image imprinted on the backs of her eyes. Next second, the rippling aftershocks of the explosion tossed the big battlegriff and his riders sideways. Then they were swept away like driftwood on a storm-lashed beach out to sea.

Root's helmet was blown out of his hands. A hot wind hit him like a bunched fist, and then everything went black.

Quenelda felt her tether rope snap, then the breath was punched out of her as she hit the water. Battlegriff and girl thrashed around in the churning tide as debris rained down on them. Stinging salty sea water poured into her mouth. Fingers frantic with haste, she tore at the strap of her helmet, while trying to free her feet from the stirrups.

'Root!' Quenelda spluttered when she surfaced among the freezing waves and called to her friend. Her ears were ringing, and she the sour taste of sea water was in her mouth. Her flying harness was getting tangled in her mount's claws. Quickly slicing through the leather with her flying knife, Quenelda flung herself over the saddle and groped for the gnome's safety line. It was no good; she couldn't get a grip . . . then it came away in her hands.

Yellow dust hung in the air like a choking haar. She couldn't see anything beyond a half-dozen arm spans. Flaming chunks of ore and rock were raining down about her as she searched for her friend. Taking a mouthful of dust-choked air, Quenelda plunged down into a sea of turmoil. Noises hammered against her head, amplified by the water. Bubbles rose noisily, disorienting her. The water churned and sucked, then boomed as the merchant galleys in the harbour broke up and sank with a tearing of timbers. It was as if time itself had slowed and she was swimming through treacle.

Root . . . Root. Where was he? Fronds of dark kelp

wrapped about her. She pushed it away from her face. There! Root's distinctive red jerkin stood out against the shingle like a bright red fish. Blood was clouding the water about him. Kicking with all her strength, Quenelda tried to make for the unconscious gnome. She wanted to reach down to him, but somehow, despite her flying gear, her body wanted to float to the surface. It was like swimming against a strong current. With a final effort, Quenelda tugged at Root's harness and managed to grab his hair braids. Desperate now for air, she kicked upwards. Stones and boulders were still raining down as she surfaced, churning the water; she realized that one had gashed her forehead, spilling hot blood down her face. Salt stung her eyes.

The galleons anchored at the stone wharf were all on fire. One was already sinking, its caulked timbers ripped open by the tons of exploding brimstone in its hold. Shredded sails and blazing rigging fell to the deck, spilling bodies into the sea.

Trying to keep Root's head clear of the waves, Quenelda struck clumsily shoreward towards I've Already Eaten, gagging on the water that slapped into her mouth and up her nose. There was a second explosion from another burning ship as the fire reached its cargo of brimstone.

Boom!

Sea and sound raced outwards. The concussion deafened Quenelda; waves smacked her face, more sea water went up her nose and into her mouth. Her head rang. Shrapnel fizzed and popped over her head like a swarm of hornets, peppering the beach with a lethal storm. The sea was so cold. The weight of her flying cloak and boots was dragging her numb limbs down. There was a dull second *boom*, and a huge boulder crashed down, sending a massive wave over Quenelda's head, driving her under again. She panicked as her legs became tangled in the kelp beds. She had to let go of Root for a moment.

Kicking frantically, Quenelda released her brooch, and the weight of the cloak fell away into the clouded water. Grabbing Root again, she struck out for the shore, but she was exhausted. Then a foot touched rock! Quenelda sighed with relief. She could stand now. Roughly hauling Root by his flying harness up onto the dunes, Quenelda turned back to the panicking battlegriff, who was in danger of drowning as his feathered wings became waterlogged.

'Softly, I've Already Eaten.' She calmed him with her hand, trying to keep those lethal claws from injuring her. *Hush . . . hush . . .* Hanging onto a stirrup, she urged the creature onto the shore. Hooves struck rock, and the animal surged out of the water. *Gently – you're safe now. Trust me . . .*

Sailors were coughing and retching about them as Quenelda dragged herself, Root and her mount up onto the sand. Tethering I've Already Eaten to a bleached tree trunk washed up on the beach, she collapsed and lay there, shaking.

Waves tugged at her boots as the tide slowly withdrew, taking the badly injured and dead with it. Ash floated down like yellow snow. Her ears were bleeding and she couldn't hear properly. Chest heaving, Quenelda blinked, trying to clear the after-image from the back of her eyes. She retched, hot liquid spurting up to burn the back of her throat. Her limbs were trembling with exhaustion, but she had to get moving.

Root . . . Root . . . how was he? Was he badly injured?

Scant feet away, a seagoblin collapsed noisily on the sand, but not before Quenelda had spotted Root lying motionless beneath him. He was still breathing as she pulled him out from beneath the cursing goblin, but blood was coursing from a head wound. Examining it, Quenelda found a nasty bump and a long shallow gash just above his hairline. Searching through the pouches of her flying belt, she picked out a small jar. Her leaden fingers fumbled with the lid, but eventually she managed to paste some of the thick ointment over the wound. That should stop the bleeding and prevent infection.

Behind her, I've Already Eaten was shaking out his wings, preening with beak and claw, tearing out smoking feathers. Back on firm ground, he ignored the shouts and explosions – he was accustomed to them and wouldn't panic now. Quenelda swiftly checked him over too, treating a deep gash on his left flank with the same ointment.

Untying a sodden saddle blanket, Quenelda dragged Root until he was sitting upright against the battlegriff's flanks, sheltered by a hind leg and an outstretched feathered wing.

Protect him, she commanded the battlegriff, wrapping the boy in the wet blanket and then staggering up the steep dunes. The sand clung to her boots and breeches, slowing her down. Before her she saw a scene from the Netherworld: crying children were stumbling aimlessly around the small cottages that clustered near the outer rim of the mine. Somewhere, a bell was tolling urgently.

Terrified mountain goblins, trolls and dwarfs emerged from the mushrooming cloud of choking dust that hung over the devastated mine. Only their red-rimmed eyes and the dark gashes of their mouths were visible beneath the thick layer of yellow ash. The stench of burning flesh reminded Quenelda of the hospital roosts. Were there no healers? No Mages amongst the miners' families?

Tying her flying scarf around her mouth and nose, eyes streaming, she staggered towards the screams. She was immediately plunged into a world of madness.

An injured cave dragon was stampeding, crushing everything and everyone lying in its path. It pounded down the sand dunes and disappeared from sight. Quenelda headed to where shouts and cries filtered dully through the smog.

The mine entrance was gone. In its place was a gaping hole in the mountainside filled with chalky ash that coated hair, eyelashes and tongue. Smoke, thick and oily as sheep's wool, brought Quenelda to her knees. Miners stumbled out, tripping, falling, crying, abandoning equipment as they fled. Grabbing what looked like a cone-shaped mask, Quenelda experimentally put it over her nose and mouth, and immediately began to breathe more easily. Wiping away the blood that still streamed from the cut over her eye, Quenelda managed to tie on the mask as fleeing miners bumped and jostled her.

The passageway she clambered through was chaotic. Timbers that had shored up the ceiling and sides were reduced to splinters. Spars lay on the ground, their ragged edges snagging at Quenelda's boots. To one side, the metal rails running into a tunnel were buckled and bent. Water gushed down from broken flumes and aqueducts, quenching fires as it pooled. A dead dragon lay crushed beneath the debris. Checking for a pulse between the great splayed toes, Quenelda moved on, the voice whispering desperately in her head.

Climb . . . climb. . . climb . . .

Where are you? Where are you? she called desperately, searching through the smoke. The chill of the day outside was a memory; deep in the mine the air was searing hot. Lungs burning, Quenelda paused for a rest at a junction where several mine shafts met. Sweat prickled inside her sea-soaked clothing. Flames and tarry black smoke poured out of a dozen fissures in the fractured rock face.

Two of the tunnels were blocked; others had partially collapsed. Water was gushing from a cracked trough, raising clouds of steam as it quenched the hot stone. From one wide tunnel Quenelda heard the lash of a whip and a bellow, and followed the sound. The ground sloped gently down into a huge central cavern with seams radiating outwards like the spokes of a wheel. A group had gathered about a blocked shaft.

Traces were slung round a huge boulder. Grunting, sweating miners, mostly trolls and dwarfs, hauled on ropes, their hands and shoulders raw. Meanwhile an overseer lashed a bellowing cave dragon – Quenelda noticed that one of its hind legs was broken. Three other dragons lay dead or dying in the rubble, their traces cut away. The boulder was barely moving.

'Show pity!' she shouted, her voice raw, as she saw the severity of the cave dragon's injuries. 'Show pity!'

In answer, a troll swung his heavy pit mallet and the bellowing ended abruptly.

A broad-shouldered dwarf in a singed leather hauberk was shouting orders. He wore a battered miner's helmet and carried a great mallet slung over his shoulder. His hair was singed, and half his face glistened where the cheek-guard of his helmet had been torn away by the explosion.

'Odin give me strength,' he cursed as he took a gulp from his water bottle. 'I can't be in three places at once! Gimlet, get down to level ten and see what damage has been done. Get a team down there. Targe' – he turned to a dark-haired dwarf beside him – 'go and check the water troughs. I want to know if the aqueduct is intact there. We have a lot of fires to put out.'

'Aye, Malachite.'

'Well?' the dwarf foreman snapped suspiciously to the masked stranger who appeared out of the dust. 'Who in Odin's name are you?' Without waiting for a reply, he turned away. 'Follow me. Be quick about it. That's six shafts down and two hundred miners trapped or dead, and those good-for-nothing animals won't move the rubble. The whole world's wanting brimstone, and there'll be hell to pay if we don't get another shipment out.'

Quenelda opened her mouth, then closed it again. Maybe she could learn more if they didn't know who she was. Picking up a fallen globe lamp, she followed Malachite down a gallery blasted to smithereens by the explosion, and on into the burning heart of the mine.

CHAPTER THIRTY-NINE

Lonely, So Lonely . . .

Climbing . . . climbing . . .

At first she didn't see it beneath the choking clouds of dust and the mounds of shale. The creature's thoughts were rambling and confused. The explosions and sulphurous smoke had triggered old memories of battle.

Climbing . . .

Quenelda peered through the roiling dark, her hearts suddenly racing. Sucked up by the main airshaft, black smoke poured out of a cracked seam, making it impossible to see clearly more than a dozen strides in any direction. Flames licked out of dozens of fissures, feeding on precious air. Even with her mask on, Quenelda was struggling to breathe. The floor was covered with semi-conscious miners, thrashing around and gasping like fish out of water. Ten heartbeats passed while she stood frozen to the spot.

Lonely . . .

So lonely . . .

Quenelda's head jerked up. 'Stormcracker Thundercloud?' Her whispered words were barely audible beneath the crack of hammer on stone, the lash of whip and the bellowing cave dragons.

'Stormcracker!' The cry of love leaped across six lonely moons and an ocean of loss. 'Stormcracker!'

The dragon managed to lift his weary head a half-dozen feet from the ground before the cruel bit cut into the soft scales around his mouth. His scales were dull and caked with dust – dozens were cracked or missing, leaving raw ulcers oozing beneath the dirt. His folded wings looked parchment-thin. Quenelda could see the blue blood in the dragon's veins moving sluggishly. And he stank dreadfully: of fear, and loss, and a longing for Open Sky.

'Stay clear of that one,' the foreman warned, seeing Quenelda step forward. 'That's a battledragon. Dangerous he is – won't let any near him. Waiting for the nearest Mage to slaughter him.'

'Slaughter him?' That stopped the girl in her tracks . . . *What? Why?*'

'We don't have the power to kill an Imperial. Few do, save the Mages, and only a handful of them. He's dying anyway. His mind and body are broken.' Malachite sighed and shook his head. ''Twill be a kindness in truth – Oi, come back!' he shouted. 'Come back, you crazy fool.'

Clambering awkwardly over the jagged spoil, ignoring the knocks to her shins and knees, Quenelda stooped down to touch the rasping skin. It was hot and flaking.

'Oh.' She stood stock-still, hot angry tears pouring down her cheeks unnoticed. So this is where her father's dragon was – condemned to a lifetime of servitude in an ore mine. For Quenelda had no doubt: this was indeed Stormcracker Thundercloud III, her father's beloved battledragon. The dull gold eyes opened, but it was clear that he saw nothing save his inner thoughts.

'Come back.' The dwarf had climbed after Quenelda while she stood motionless. Laying a heavy-gauntleted hand on her shoulder, he pulled. The leather knot unravelled and Quenelda's mask fell off. Malachite blinked, then rubbed his eyes with sooty knuckles as if he were seeing things. He tentatively reached out his hand. 'But you're just a boy! What are you doing here, lad? You shouldn't be here. Come away . . .'

Gripping her elbow he tried to pull Quenelda away, but she twisted free, and he fell, his spurs striking stone.

At the familiar hated sound, the dragon hissed a blast of foul odorous breath that nearly knocked Quenelda off her feet. Several of his teeth were broken and rotting; others were missing altogether, leaving decaying bone and gum. The dwarf fell again in his haste to get away, his helmet bouncing away across the rocky spoil.

The dragon's mind quested out blindly through the smoke-filled air and the bedlam around him. *Lonely . . . so lonely . . .*

Quenelda placed her hands against the dragon's hot dry muzzle.

Stormcracker, she cried, grief-stricken. *It's me. Oh, Storm!* She knelt in front of the great dragon and leaned her head against the filthy weeping muzzle and hugged him.

'Stormcracker,' she wept out loud. 'What – what have they done?'

Malachite watched with amazement. Who on the One Earth was this young boy?

What have they done to you? she whispered, the power in her voice finally reaching through the dragon's starved indifference.

Dancing with Dragons? The tendril of thought was so

faint, Quenelda could barely sense it. *Is it truly you? Why has it taken so long for you to come for me? I called and called and called. All these lonely seasons in the dark . . .*

His face and back were seamed and scarred with the lash, but Quenelda laughed for sheer joy as the stinking black viperous tongue flicked out and licked her. The massive tail unravelled, armour plate rattled against chains. Boulders bounced into the pit of the floor. Scooping her up gently, the dragon slowly lifted Quenelda in his coiled tail, higher and higher, till she hung above his massive withers.

'Thor's Hammer!' Malachite breathed in growing disbelief as a single tear rolled down from the yellow eye, dropping into the rubble.

Behind him, dwarfs and trolls were running for weapons mounted on the wall, and a deep horn sounded the alarm. Its blast echoed and re-echoed over the background boom of explosions. Gravel and dust vibrated. Some miners were arming themselves with dragonspikes and whips, as if such puny weapons could harm an Imperial Black.

Straddling the dragon, Quenelda could now see the powerful marks of *captivity* and *servitude* moving through the cold iron collar that had dulled Stormcracker's senses and blunted his magic. And in recognizing them, she knew with certainty that an Arch Mage had sold this SDS dragon into servitude; someone with great power had committed this crime. Only in her lifetime had the practice been banned, but many had yet to change their ways. But this was a DeWinter mine. There should be no battledragons enslaved here!

She flinched as another section of tunnel collapsed on miners trying to clear it. Cries and shouts rang out as everyone turned from the dragon to rescue their comrades. Stormcracker's head swung round, searching for fresh air.

Hush . . . An idea had just struck Quenelda as she *soothed* and *calmed* him. *I am going to buy your freedom.*

Freedom? Open Sky?

Open Sky, Quenelda promised. *And home, Stormcracker. Home to the roosts of Dragon Isle* . . .

Home . . .

She pulled off her mask. 'This dragon can help,' she shouted, trying to be heard above the chaos. She coughed as a wave of dust choked her throat. 'I – I know he can. But in return' – she stared fiercely at Malachite, willing him to agree to her bargain – 'I want his freedom. You must pass ownership to me.'

'Help? How can he help?' The dwarf ran a hand through sweat-soaked hair. 'He's no use to anyone.'

'I can ask him to help.'

'Ask?' scoffed a huge troll holding a dragonspike, his voice muffled by his mask. 'How are you going to do that, boy?'

'Like this. Flame!' Quenelda commanded. *Flame* . . .

The dragon roared a primordial scream of rage and fear; a throaty liquid rattle. Feeble flames licked out through his muzzle – but enough to set tar-soaked timbers alight. They all ran then, tumbling breakneck down the shale, crowding into the mine shafts. All except the dwarf foreman, who stood his ground. A veteran, Quenelda suddenly realized. Was he a Bonecracker? Surely she could appeal to him? Bonecrackers formed lifelong bonds with their dragons; they protected one another in battle to the death. Surely . . .

Stormcracker coughed, a wrenching, jarring cough that rattled his ribs and shuddered through his bony frame. She had to get him out of here. She had to get him home to Dragon Isle. He was dying.

'Strike his chains,' Quenelda screamed. 'Strike his chains.' A rage was burning through her like a fever. 'Then I promise he'll work for you!'

Strike! Strike! the dragon echoed feebly.

'He's a brute,' Malachite shouted back. 'He's wild. Unchain him and he'll kill us all! A rogue, we were told by the Lord Protector's men. That's why he was delivered here.'

'You're the brute, not him. Strike his chains.' Quenelda was weeping now. The dragon hissed at her distress. 'He can help. He can help clear the rubble, those boulders. Save your miners.'

The dwarf paused, considering the offer. He shrugged and nodded. Things couldn't get any worse than they already were. Overriding a chorus of protests, he gave the order.

Grunting and sweating, cursing and trembling, dwarfs and trolls swung their mallets down upon the pegs that locked each link. The sound of steel on steel rang out, but it was too slow. Too slow!

Sorcery thrummed through Quenelda. Her fingers

tingled and white sparks crackling with energy played about their tips. With a surge of power and an angry gesture, Quenelda brought her fist down. There was a blinding flash. The chains broke with a loud *crack*, fragments of metal ricocheting off the walls. Miners screamed as they were caught in the hailstorm. The baleful magic in the links earthed, and the *binding* spell was gone, leaving cold iron.

The dragon shifted and shuddered as the chains of captivity fell away. Deep inside, suppressed magic flickered weakly back to life and seeped through his blood into his body. Slowly, tentatively, the broken battle-dragon unfurled his great wings, the pain making him hiss in distress. As his wings spread, Quenelda could see why. The membranes that webbed his wings between each finger-bone were torn and ragged. The armoured plates were crazed with fractures. A broken yellowed radius bone stuck out, and several wing talons were missing. Huge lesions were clearly battle injuries; others the result of mistreatment and brutality. Bones cracked, and tendons stiff with disuse creaked as the dragon found his balance. Clouds of dust rose into the choking air as he moved forward.

Miners scattered. A few kinder souls, mostly the dwarf veterans of the war, stood their ground and cheered. Malachite stood stunned by what he had just witnessed; the boy had broken a spelled collar! Only a powerful sorcerer could do that, and the binding of this one had been particularly potent. Balancing astride the dragon's spinal plates, unaware of what she'd just achieved, Quenelda now fought to undo the huge buckles that strapped the cruel dragon-muzzle in place so that Storncracker could not feed from the ore he hauled. It was crusted with filth and stuck fast, fuelling her rage. Once again sparks began to arc from her fingers. A brimstone mine! How could they? They were starving the dragons in a brimstone mine! How else could they control Imperials? The Seven Sea Kingdoms needed brimstone above all else, but at what cost? How dare Darcy! Her father would never have allowed this. Her eyes flared liquid gold, and smoke threaded from her nose, mingling unseen in the dust saturated air.

Her rage communicated itself to Stormcracker. The injured dragon hissed. Malachite swallowed, gagging as the rank breath rolled over him. He opened his mouth to shout – to tell the boy to stop; to point out that the muzzle contained twelve-inch incisors and a bite in excess of forty thousand pounds of force. But then shame made him hesitate. He had never been easy with battledragons being sold into servitude and shackled after a lifetime of service, had never agreed with the young Earl's command. Shaking his head at his own madness, the dwarf stepped up to help.

Feeling ridiculous, he unsheathed the great knife strapped to his back, slicing through the dirty brittle leather that the boy couldn't reach. The enormous jaws beside him opened achingly wide, revealing rotten stumps and an ulcerated tongue. Then, to his shame, Malachite fled, tripping and stumbling down the shale, certain that jaws that could bring a mammoth down would have no problems devouring a morsel like him. If his chains were struck, might not the Imperial unleash its magic upon the mine? But the dragon was only interested in the brimstone, gulping down every lump within reach of his sinuous neck.

Slowly . . . Don't eat too much . . . Quenelda had to use all her powers of persuasion to stop the dragon gorging on the ore. *You'll be ill if you eat too much . . . You will be fed again soon . . . You'll never go hungry again. I swear it, Stormcracker! I swear it!* She clenched her fist. A tendril of magic shot sideways to earth on a miner's axe. The dwarf was blown off his feet. Malachite swallowed. What had he just unleashed?

Reluctantly the dragon raised his head.

Slowly, Stormcracker . . . Quenelda cautioned as he slid down the shale. *You are ill and weak . . . gently . . .* The dragon's legs gave way and he slid down amongst a cloud of rubble and dust.

The foreman stepped out of the way of bouncing rubble to move up beside her.

'Water,' she coughed. 'We need water.'

'Over there.' Malachite pointed to where an underground river was channelled through a series of runnels and troughs carved into the bedrock.

Quenelda led the stumbling battledragon to drink, scooping up cupped handfuls to splash over her face, washing away layers of choking yellow dust. Then, lifting a ladle, she too drank her fill, clearing her raw throat.

How do you feel, Storm? she whispered as the dragon lifted his dripping maw. *Do you have enough strength to do as I ask?*

We fly to our home roost?

Soon, she promised. Soon . . .

'A harness!' Quenelda shouted. 'We need to hitch a harness . . .' She slid to the ground, burning the skin from her palms on Stormcracker's dry, abrasive hide. 'Down, Stormcracker, down.' The dragon sagged to the ground.

'Hitch the traces,' she said to the foreman. 'He won't harm you.'

Several of the more powerfully built trolls hitched the heavy chains to the great metal mine harness. Dwarfs swung irons around a huge boulder and clipped the two together.

'Up, Stormcracker, up. Pull.' Remounting, Quenelda urged the battledragon on. *Stormcracker, pull.*

Step by hesitant step, the dragon threw his weight forward, away from the blocked tunnel. Nothing moved. The harness creaked. Then dust sifted down from cracks in the ceiling.

Then – 'It's moving! Boss, it's moving,' yelled one of the dwarfs. Almost imperceptibly, the huge boulder shifted; then, as Stormcracker got into his stride, it broke free. A pile of collapsing rubble followed.

'Hold it, hold it,' the foreman yelled, holding his mask to his face.

Grappling irons were engaged as the boulder swung down. Miners unhitched the chains while others started shovelling ore into wagons. Quenelda stayed by the dragon's head, calming him. They filled a dozen huge wagons.

Malachite sent men ahead to clear debris from the rails and shore up collapsed ceilings. 'Hitch them up, lads. Ready? Take them away.'

The dragon slowly pulled the wagons, one by one, out through the tunnels to the great cave, where they could be harnessed to those cave dragons that had survived the explosion. Every so often Quenelda had to stumble up out of the suffocating dark mine, out into the bright dust-choked air of the quarry, where clan healers and families were hard at work tending the injured and dying. How had Storm survived this? Quenelda wondered. No surprise the great dragon had been driven to madness. But she barely rested herself before returning time and time again.

The roiling smoke thinned as the fires in lower levels were quenched, but the aqueduct was broken in dozens of places and the heat radiated through the rock tunnels and up through the soles of Quenelda's boots. Time became meaningless in the smoking subterranean world. After what seemed to Quenelda like an eternity spent clearing shafts, she heard a rhythmic noise.

'I can hear tapping!' she shouted to Malachite. 'There . . .' She cocked her head to one side. 'Can't you hear it?'

The dwarf frowned, shaking his head. 'Hush up, lads!'

'Hush! Hush! Listen!'

Silence slowly spread through the mine.

'We can hear them!' a voice cried! They're still alive! Some of them are still alive!'

A ragged cheer went up, and was passed through the choked shaft by word of mouth. Everyone who could wield an axe or lift a boulder set to with renewed frenzy.

'How can you hear anything, lad?' the foreman asked as he accompanied Quenelda outside. 'You must have hearing like a bat.'

'No. Like a dragon,' Quenelda realized as she turned to lead Stormcracker outside for the last time. 'I have a friend to tend to on the beach.' She looked upwards towards a sun smothered by smog. She had no idea what time it was. 'We all need a rest.'

Malachite stood and watched as the massive dragon

followed her down to the sea, his powerful tail cutting a swathe through the layers of debris. He turned thoughtfully back to his men. They had a rescue mission to complete.

CHAPTER FORTY

Rising from the Ashes

Two bells later, the impenetrable dust-choked sky was rapidly darkening. Braziers and still smouldering fires lit the wreckage like the aftermath of a major battle. Stormcracker was outside, drinking from a pool of water that had leaked from the broken rock face. Suddenly a cry went up.

'They're alive! They're safe!'

Word rapidly passed from mouth to mouth as family and friends flocked forward to greet the survivors emerging from the ruins of the mine. Flaming brands flickered across the strange scene that met them outside – a huge dragon, with Quenelda astride him.

'Owe it to the lad, there,' Malachite said gruffly as the ragged cheers died down. 'And the dragon. Without his strength we would never have reached you.'

The foreman offered Quenelda his hard, callused hand. When she gave him hers, he frowned, puzzled, and turned it over, his thumb rubbing the hard scale on her palm; but then he remembered his manners.

'Malachite Thornaxe of the Wildcat Clan.' He bowed. 'I and my family are for ever at your service.'

Quenelda nodded, and tried to take her hand back. The dwarf let go reluctantly, eyes travelling from her palm to the huge dragon. 'You can have your battledragon and welcome, lad, though there is no saddle or bridle so I do not know how you will control him. But we can give you dry cloaks, such food and water as we have for you and him.'

Malachite accompanied Quenelda as she and Stormcracker made their way slowly through the rubble to where Root was curled up beside I've Already Eaten. Still dazed and groggy, the gnome looked up as the huge, skeletal battledragon collapsed in the sand before him. He tried to get to his feet, but fell over too.

'Is that . . . ?' Root rubbed his eyes as if the knock on the head was making him see things. 'An Imperial? Here?' Mouth open in disbelief, he took in the dreadful state the battledragon was in. Then he looked at Quenelda, noticing how distressed she was. He stared at the dragon. 'Quenelda. It's not . . . ?' he began uncertainly.

'It's Storm,' she said simply.

Horrified, Root struggled upright. 'Storm? But how?

Why is he here?' He could not believe that this pitiful, broken creature was the Earl's battledragon. He moved round to where the dragon's head rested on the sand.

Puzzled, Malachite watched Root tentatively reach out to touch the battledragon, then turned his gaze back to the exhausted boy. *Had he heard right?* he wondered. *Quenelda? Wasn't that a girl's* name . . . ? Malachite glanced about him. Quenelda bent forward to hear his soft words against the raucous cries of carrion crows and seagulls.

The dwarf hesitated. 'May I know your name, lady?' For despite Quenelda's gear and appearance, he recognized the manner and quiet confidence that came with rank and privilege.

'And ask how you come to be here today?'

Quenelda was so exhausted that she did not notice that her disguise had been unveiled. In all the chaos she had almost forgotten her mission!

'Quenelda . . . My name is Lady Quenelda DeWinter. I—'

The dwarf's brown eyes had widened. Quenelda! He had heard the story of the Earl's daughter and the Cauldron. Who had not? Rumour said that her brother had poisoned her battledragon and that the girl had died with him. Disappeared, folk said, like her father. Sleeping, said others. But who else could she be? Her voice alone should have forewarned him; this, and the fact that she looked like a boy.

He stepped back to search her face, his voice husky with emotion. 'We were all your Lord father's men here, Lady Quenelda. No matter what the new young Earl says, or commands.'

Quenelda nodded and gestured to the dragon. 'S-stormcracker . . . Stormcracker.' Her voice cracked, and hot tears finally flooded her eyes, tracking down her dirty cheeks. 'H-he's . . . He was my father's.' She stopped to swallow. 'My father's own battledragon.'

The hard-bitten dwarf was stunned. This was the Earl's own mount? 'Abyss below!' He raised horrified red-rimmed eyes to hers, which suddenly blazed in the growing dark. Malachite's heart was racing. He knelt in the sand.

'Forgive us, Lady. We were attacked by hobgoblins two moons ago. Caught them tunnelling into the lower levels, riding the water that fed into our aqueducts. All our cave dragons taken or killed. With marauding war bands, more and more dragons are being taken each day – there are none to be had. The Grand Master's galleons transported three Imperials and a dozen others in the dead of night in a wild storm. The dragons just appeared as if out of nowhere. The men wore the badge of the striking adder, but they bore the seal of Dragonsdome. They had written orders from the young Earl, sealed orders. Said the dragons were rogue, but rather than killing them, they had bound them into servitude. The other two Imperials died of their wounds long since.'

'But the law forbids it!' Quenelda protested hotly. 'Battledragons are turned loose in their wild roosts and eyries when they are too old to fight. And Imperials – they are banned to all save the SDS!'

'Lady' – Malachite urgently raised his hand to stay her anger as sparks played about her fingertips – 'they said that after what happened to the SDS, the Guild no longer forbade it; that we had to find dragons where we could. Said the Grand Master's brimstone mines in the north were flooded or damaged, and his army and the Nightstalkers needed our brimstone urgently. By whatever means.'

Quenelda nodded dully. She could barely take in his

words. The day had been one horror after another, and now it seemed as if her brother and the Lord Protector were behind each and every atrocity. It wouldn't have happened if her father were alive. The world had gone mad. She had a horrendous headache from the heat and stench in the mine. Her throat was parched, her stiff clothes heavy with the weight of ash and dust. She swayed.

Malachite put out a steadying hand, compassion in his eyes. 'Are you unwell? I'll call a healer . . .'

Quenelda shook her head. 'No, they are all needed by your people. I'm just tired . . .' She had come for a purpose. She tried to gather her thoughts. The bell tolled the Hour of the Wild Boar, but dark was already falling, the sun a faint red haze through the thick smoke.

'Here . . .' The dwarf unslung his bottle and uncorked it. 'Go on.' He urged her as the young girl hesitated.'Go on. Drink!'

Taking the flask with shaking hands, Quenelda raised it to her lips. A fruity fizzy drink washed down her throat. It was followed by a warm glow that spread out from her stomach.

'Dwarf cider.' Malachite grinned at her surprised reaction. 'Go on, lass – drink some more.'

Quenelda gratefully gulped the golden liquid down, feeling some strength return to her limbs. Then she tried to focus.

'Tangnost Bearhugger, Dragonmaster of Dragon Isle, sent me. I bear a message from him too dangerous to entrust to a courier.' She pulled out the leather thong about her neck to reveal Tangnost's ring, then searched for the letter. It came out rather soggy and crumpled and barely legible.

'Messengers from Dragon Isle disappear, the SDS no longer knows whom to trust. Tangnost wanted me to warn you, but I was too late. The explosions across Dragonsdome and royal mines this year . . . Dragon Isle . . . They believe the Lord Protector is behind them – not hobgoblins.'

'Neptune's Beard! His soldiers have been all over the mine in the last week. They came with orders from the young Earl. Said that they had heard of trouble; that they were here to protect us; that their presence would deter any hobgoblins.' The dwarf looked around, frowning. 'Haven't seen none of 'em since the explosion.

Thought they were all dead. But maybe we won't find them amongst the bodies either.' Quenelda swayed on her feet. 'Sit, lass, before you fall,' Malachite ordered. 'Grackle! Reaver!' he shouted to a group of dwarfs who were tending the injured. 'Round up those who are still on their feet. Set a guard about the mine. There's mischief afoot. This was no accident!'

He turned back to Quenelda. 'My thanks, Lady. No one will get past my lads now. They'll be spoiling for a fight after so many deaths. Tell Tangnost not to worry. Two weeks ago some of the lads opened a new gallery: a rich seam and not too deep. And we'll put the word out to the Wildcat, Weasel, Capercaillie and Red Squirrel clans. Our kindred will come, and when the ore's mined we'll escort it overland ourselves. This will be one shipment you can depend on.'

Quenelda nodded wearily and turned to Stormcracker. She looked as if she were sleepwalking.

'I'll send a healer, Lady.' Malachite touched her shoulder, concern in his eyes. She was so young; too young for this nightmare. First her father, next her dragon, and now the most famous battledragon in the Kingdoms found languishing in his mine.

'I'll fetch you some food, you must eat too.'

But Quenelda wasn't listening any more. She had already turned her attention to Stormcracker, who had collapsed on the sand, his damaged lungs sounding like foundry bellows. She stood, trying to reach out to heal him, but he was so big and she was so tired. The light in her eyes faded, and with it her remaining strength.

'I have to get Stormcracker away. He needs to breathe clean air – this dust will kill him. He's on his last wings.' Quenelda shook her head in frustration. 'I don't know if he can even fly, but we must get him to Dragon Isle and their battle surgeons.' She divided the last honey tablets from their saddlebags between the battlegriff and Stormcracker, who gulped the morsels down. 'He's half starved,' she explained to Root, 'but if he eats too much it will kill him.' She turned back to Malachite. 'We have to try to get him away from here – now, when there are none of the Lord Protector's men to see it.'

Malachite nodded. 'That you do, lass. Who knows when his ships will return?' He looked at her doubtfully, unwilling to voice his thoughts. Could this broken creature actually fly? Could a mere child fly in the dark?

Quenelda tried to ignore the doubt and compassion in

the dwarf's eyes. The dragon had barely been able to stretch his wings during his captivity. And the hollow, light dragon wing-bones, the caratack bones, were notorious for breaking in elderly and ill dragons. But, no – she gritted her teeth. This was her father's battledragon. Even if they could never return home to Dragonsdome, he could at least be cared for in the roosts of Dragon Isle for the rest of his life. And if he died . . . better to die under the Open Sky than the in shackled depths of a mine.

'We have to try.' She bit her lips.

However, if the Grand Master was behind the massacre of the SDS, it would not do to be caught with her father's battledragon, to betray that he had been found. Many might not be able to tell one Imperial from another, but the Lord Protector most certainly could. She had no idea if Stormcracker had the strength to cloak himself with invisibility, but she doubted it. The marks of binding and captivity might have gone, but his power had been drained by them.

She looked at Root, who had slipped into an uneasy sleep. His face was white with fatigue and pain, his dark hair bleached by ash. Could he help her? She roused him.

'We'll have to fly by night and rest up by day,' she said,

watching him anxiously for his reaction. 'Do you think you could manage to fly solo on I've Already Eaten at night? We have to leave here, now!'

Root bit his lower lip. The battlegriff was not his own gentle Chasing the Stars, and had a wickedly sharp beak and piercing eyes, but I've Already Eaten looked as bedraggled as he was, and would protect his rider to the death. He nodded.

Come, Stormcracker . . . Quenelda urged the dragon to unfurl his wings fully. Carefully climbing up between his damaged tail plates, she first checked his upper wing-bones for injuries, paying particular attention to the great shoulder blade, wing-carpus, and the fragile hollow bones of the six metacarpels and phalanges. It was hard to see in the flickering light of the pine-resin torch, but she realized that the dragon's skin was stretched parchment-thin over his ribcage; his once powerful muscles were cruelly wasted, his tendons standing out in taunt relief, ready to snap.

Fly for me, Stormcracker, warm your wings . . .

His first attempt at flight ended in miserable failure. Wings stiff with neglect and crusted with ore-dust would not respond, and the half-starved dragon was barely strong enough to even lift them. When he could, the air flowed straight through countless rips and tears. A shudder ran down his armoured spine and along the wings, and his injured hind leg collapsed a second time.

Quenelda almost cried with frustration as the once proud dragon's head drooped. She was still standing there hopelessly when miners and their families flocked down onto the dunes beside her, lanterns flitting like marsh flies through the haze. She watched in amazement as, with buckets of water and brushes, they washed away the accumulated weight of dust and debris, tenderly cleaning Stormcracker's wounds and sores, then patching them up with heavy canvas and pitch. Children ran up to the huge dragon, tentatively reaching out to offer titbits of food with tiny hands – smoked fish and haunches of goat, dried strips of reindeer and elk, a brace of hares, a pheasant – before running away again, overwhelmed by his size. Stormcracker gulped it all down gratefully with the tip of his tongue.

Then an off-shore breeze blew, rapidly strengthening, thinning the heavy dust.

Storm, the wind grows . . . can you try again?

Wumph . . . whumph . . .

Eyes narrowed, she watched critically as Stormcracker tested his wings, almost rising from the beach as the breeze took him. She turned back to Root, who was adjusting the battlegriff's stirrup straps to suit him better.

'He's no different from Chasing the Stars,' she said, trying to reassure him. 'I'll guide him. He's highly trained. He won't let you fall. You just rest if you can – get some sleep.'

Root nodded and instantly winced. The egg-sized bump on his head was throbbing, and he'd lost his flying helmet in the explosion. The dwarfs had given him the smallest mining helmet they could find, but it was still too big and too heavy for him. It just made his headache worse. He wasn't happy at the notion of flying a battle-griff on his own, but he knew Quenelda had to ride Stormcracker.

'I'll guide both of them . . .' Quenelda was so tired she could hardly think straight. 'You can fly beside me, off my starboard wing. Let's mount up.'

What little light was left was fading fast, draining the smoky landscape of colour. Quenelda turned the dragon into the rising wind, waiting till it caught beneath his wings. Daring to hope, she cried out:

'Fly, Storm, fly!'

Miners raised their masks, and they and their families bade them farewell.

Whumph . . . whumph . . . whumph . . .

Sand and dust rose in swirls, the backdraught shifting the heavy brimstone dust. A sudden gust filled the dragon's wings and, like a kite, lifted him skyward into the darkness.

With a sense of peace, Quenelda knew that for the first time since her father had disappeared, she had found a missing part of her heart. Together at last, the girl and the crippled dragon rose into the night sky, followed by a fearful young gnome on a wounded battlegriff.

Chapter Forty-One

Dragoncombs

The temperature was dropping rapidly. Down below, the loch dwindled to a ribbon of mercury, then vanished into the pooling shadows. As they rose through the heavy layers of dust, constellations like diamond scatter pins winked into existence overhead.

Root huddled miserably in his heavy dwarf cloak, clinging to the saddle's pommel for security, trying not to think about the huge expanse of darkness below him. It was his first solo flight at night – a heart-thumping mix of exhilaration and fear that pounded through his veins, leaving him shaking from head to toe. His head throbbed horribly and he was seeing double, though he hadn't mentioned that to Quenelda. His neck ached, and the wet dragonwings dragged at his shoulders.

Storm, fly . . .

Quenelda was intent on Stormcracker, coaxing the sick dragon forward. Desperate to get back as swiftly as possible, and to avoid any possibility that the lone uncloaked Imperial would be sighted, she chose to strike out as the crow flies over unknown country away from the military roads to avoid detection. But within a bell, as the trees thinned, giving way to open moorland, the great dragon had begun to tire and falter. They were lost, and Root could barely stay in his saddle let alone navigate. Weakened by battle, starvation and brutal confinement, the battledragon's flight faltered.

I must rest, Dancing with Dragons . . .

I will find a place . . .

'Root? Quenelda called. Root do you know where we are?'

'Wha-what?' The young boy started awake. He had fallen into an uneasy sleep, trusting the battlegriff to follow Quenelda. He squinted at the stars but was still seeing double and nearly fell from his saddle.

'Root, we are going to have to put down soon. Storm's exhausted.' Quenelda searched the moor below, trying to find a suitable place to put down. She had been too hasty taking off as dark fell, and she knew it. Why hadn't she waited for dawn?

Then her heart thumped as a ripping sound rent the air. The canvas and pitch patches were giving way one by one! Dark league after dark league of moorland and stands of pine trees passed below them as Quenelda fought to keep as much height as possible above the treacherous bogs and marshes. If Storm put down there, he would sink into the mire and they would never get him out again. This must be what it was like trying to land after a battle, Quenelda realized, with an injured and exhausted mount. She bit her lip. Once again she had assumed that because she could fly, that would be enough. When was she going to learn?

Then a memory came to her from her other self; from her dragonworld memories. Long, long ago in the Elder Days, there had been Imperial dragoncombs in the glen ahead – combs rich with yellow seams of brimstone and cold pure water from the glacier. This was why she had chosen this way!

'Root, head for the larger of the two glens. There are dragoncombs there.'

The boy was too injured and exhausted to ask how she knew. He nodded his head and then wished he hadn't, as a wave of sickness took him. He clung on miserably as the mountains rose up on either side of them.

Quenelda knew the combs were there, but her memory came from long, long ago when winter lay permanently over most of the land. As a girl she had never been to this place before. How could they find the right waterfall in the dark, steep-sided valleys below? Quenelda wondered. She looked up at the rising moons sailing behind a lattice-work of clouds, and tried to take her bearing from the handful of stars still visible. But the stars too had travelled across the heavens since she last stretched her wings. Then one of the moons rose higher, and the river below leaped out like a pale scar on the black landscape, all milk and dark moonshadow. And suddenly she knew where she was. There it was: a glittering shower of foam that burst out of the mountainside, to crash down a deep gorge in a spill of liquid froth.

With a gentle thought, she turned Stormcracker towards it as yet another wing patch began to tear.

'We're going down, Root,' she shouted. 'Hang on and follow us! I'm making for the waterfall!' With her dragon eyes, she could see I've Already Eaten's silhouette above her against the sky, but the boy had been slouched forward in his saddle and might not have heard, so she sent the thought to his battlegriff, bidding him follow her.

Then Stormcracker's wings gave way completely and battledragon and girl were whirling round and round, spiralling out of control. It ripped a scream out of her lungs. She knew in her heart of hearts that if they crashed Stormcracker would not survive the impact, let alone fly again. Her fingers tingled, sparking as bright magic gathered in her hands. Hot fire rose in her throat, but panic drove coherent thought from her. Fiery red bolts spun about her as she flamed her anguish. Parts of the mountain exploded in shards of rocks. Gorse bushes went up in flames.

Root clung on for dear life as I've Already Eaten followed the flaming, plummeting forms of Quenelda and Stormcracker towards the waterfall.

Storm! Storm! Fly! She commanded him, but it was no good. Stormcracker had no magic or strength left to give. The ground reached up to greet them.

Chapter Forty-Two

Dragon Down

Then a golden nimbus of light blossomed about Quenelda. Fire flowed through her veins. Arcing from her fingers, it struck out like a huge spider's web, strong as steel, light as a feather. It cushioned the great dragon in flames that did not burn, slowing their dizzying descent, and cast them gently through the waterfall.

The freezing water instantly doused her fire. Combs and darkness closed in around them, and Stormcracker collapsed, throwing an exhausted Quenelda over his withers onto the floor, driving the breath from her lungs.

Root ducked as a final fireball scorched past him . . . and then . . . and then icy spray embraced him, water battered him, drowning his scream, and they were through, and it was pitch black, and he was deafened and soaked and shivering with cold and fear. Weakened and tired, I've Already Eaten barely managed to avoid Stormcracker but caught a hoof on the spines of his tail. Claws flailing, hooves skidding on the wet rock, the battlegriff came to a halt scant strides from where Quenelda struggled to her feet.

Root spat out water and knuckled his streaming eyes.

'Are you all right?' he shouted in the darkness as he dismounted. 'You're not hurt?' The battlegriff was already fluffing up his feathers and stamping his hooves to keep warm.

Storm? Storm? Quenelda quested as she got to her feet, but there was only silence. The effort of landing had used the last of Stormcracker's energy. He had collapsed into unconsciousness. She stumbled around the battlegriff to where the dragon lay unmoving. He was shuddering, his mind wandering again down a nightmare of endless dark tunnels. Laying her hands against his cheek, Quenelda bowed her brow and, to Root's consternation, began to weep.

'Quenelda?' The gnome moved hesitantly to her side. 'What is it?' he asked gently. 'What's wrong? Are you hurt? Is it Storm?'

'He – he c-can't fly!'

'But he just did.'

'But it took every last ounce of his strength. He's

unconscious. I asked too much of him. He's dying, and it's all m-my fault!'

'Let me light a fire,' Root suggested. He felt dreadful, but he still took charge. 'To get us warmed up. Then we can have a look and see how he is.'

He found sodden kindling and heather in the battle-griff's saddlebags. Getting out his flint, he struck a tiny spark, which danced in the damp dark, then died.

'The wood's too wet!' he muttered. This rescue was all going so terribly wrong. 'Everything's soaked. It's not going to light.' He struck the flint again.

Fire. Without thinking Quenelda formed the simple elemental rune in her mind. The wet wood smoked, burst into reluctant flame, and then suddenly blazed up.

'Whoa!' Root rocked back on his heels as the rising heat almost singed his nostrils. 'I must be getting good at this!' He was impressed with his efforts – he'd never managed to start a fire like this before! With him around, Quenelda need never worry about these mundane tasks.

Lighting their last pitch-soaked brand, Root went over to inspect the dragon. Stormcracker's breath rattled in his lungs, plumes of breath condensing in the freezing air. He looked like a bag of bones, shiver after shiver running through his wasted body. Lifting the brand, Root carefully moved round behind him, appalled by the damage that had been done to the mighty creature. The tranquil black water of the cavern lake behind them flared to gold, then faded back into greater darkness. High above, the ceiling reached down with sparkling needles that dripped with the slow seconds of centuries. Dark tunnels yawned around the cavern's edge in every direction.

Root filled the kettle, then brewed some dandelion tea, throwing in some nettle for strength, and motherwort for protection, from his pouch. The hot tea brought some colour back into Quenelda's cheeks, but she still miserably acknowledged the truth.

'He can't fly any further. I've asked too much of him, Root. He's never going make it back to Dragon Isle. He's never going to fly again!' She wiped away tears. I should have recognized his voice calling! I should have rescued him sooner. We're too late!

'But—' Root opened his mouth to protest, to comfort her, then saw the terrible certainty in her eyes. She had lost Two Gulps. Now, when she had finally found him, her father's battledragon was dying, his injuries beyond her fledgling powers.

Quenelda was crying quietly. 'He'll have to be put d-down. He can't be left to suffer like this.'

'I'll fly back to Dragon Isle,' Root offered, keeping his clasped hands behind his back so that Quenelda wouldn't see them shaking, hoping she would put the wobble in his voice down to the cold. 'I'll fetch Tangnost. He'll know what to do!'

Chapter Forty-Three

When the Wind Blows the Cradle Will Rock

As the grey of early dawn revealed the mountain ridges and glens, it also showed the state of I've Already Eaten. The battlegriff was clearly tiring and in distress. His feathers were scorched, and spattered with congealed blood; his right wing had been badly burned by falling brimstone and, to Root's alarm, scorched wing feathers kept falling out. His left hind leg had also been peppered with splinters of wood, scoring deep furrows across his once glossy flanks. Exhausted, Quenelda had no healing power left to treat the battlegriff before they had left the sanctuary of the combs. Root and I've Already Eaten were on their own!

Root had been plagued by doubts ever since they had taken off. What if they got lost? What if the battlegriff hit one of the pine trees whose tops they were barely clearing? What if he had misunderstood Quenelda's instructions? What if the Lord Protector's men intercepted him? Without map or compass, Root was no longer sure where he was; he only knew that the

Brimstones were slowly fading away behind him. But was he heading for the Sorcerers Glen?

'Oh, tooth and claw!' Root mumbled the litany over and over again. 'Earth guide us safely home. Please . . .'

A pearly dawn mist hugged the floor of the glen as he took out his telescope and anxiously searched the sky, dreading to see the red adder on black. A few clouds and a scattering of dragons, but nothing nearby – no sign of the SDS arrow formations.

'Come on, boy, we can make it!' Root encouraged I've Already Eaten, saying the words out loud to bolster his own confidence. But his voice sounded thin and weak in the silence, and only served to emphasize how alone he was.

Gnome and battlegriff had to put down almost every bell to drink and rest. I've Already Eaten caught a pigeon and an inattentive heron, and Root scavenged a handful of blackberries and some hazelnuts. The Dragonspine Mountains of the Sorcerers Glen loomed slate-blue in the far distance. As dark trees and white frothing rivers passed slowly below, Root knew that he might not reach sanctuary for many days, perhaps weeks, even if the weather held. Would Stormcracker survive that long?

The picture of Quenelda sobbing beside a dead dragon made him sick with worry as he urged his stricken mount up into the air once again.

Then a sudden gust of wind caught them and the battlegriff was blown sideways. The air warped, and a huge Imperial Black shimmered into view just above him, great talons curled barely strides above his head. Root almost fainted with relief.

Quenelda wept until exhaustion took her. Magic never worked out the way she intended. It was as if the harder she tried, the more elusive and uncontrolled her fledgling powers became. She simply did not yet have the strength or knowledge to heal her father's battledragon's many wounds. Bound by baleful spells these many moons, the dragon's own magic was exhausted. His injuries were too great and he was too weak. Nestling within the curve of Stormcracker's neck, she slept deeply on through the night and into the next day. She woke, bleary-eyed and dry-mouthed, to find a fading yellow sliver of daylight streaming in through the fissure on the far side of the cave. She ate some of the salmon and oatcakes donated by the miners, and drank water from the freezing lake.

Stormcracker hadn't moved, but his eyes were open. Quenelda fed him the last meagre meal of brimstone then sank down beside him.

She lost track of time. Daylight. The dark of night again. Sleeping, waking, sleeping . . .

Fading daylight seeped through the cavern. Torchlight flickered dimly on the cave walls behind her, growing with the sound of footsteps . . . and voices – Root's, and the deeper vowels of Tangnost, and a third Quenelda couldn't identify. Then she remembered, and the tears began again. She had found Storm, only to lose him again. They were coming to put him down. She stood, head pressed against the dragon's, listening to his shuddering heartbeats until Root ran over to her, enfolding her in a hug. His head was bandaged, but he was warm and had colour back in his cheeks.

'I did it!' Root was jubilant. 'Quenelda, I did it! Tangnost's here. The SDS are coming too! They let me fly ahead on a scout dragon by myself, just like my father! I've brought some field rations for Storm too – here.'

His joy was extinguished when he saw Quenelda's pallor.

'It's all right! They're not going to kill him! They are

going to take him back to Dragon Isle! They have a cradle . . .'

'A cradle?' Quenelda turned in confusion as Tangnost arrived. 'I don't understand.' She was ready to weep again.

Whatever Tangnost had been going to say died on his lips when he caught sight of the exhausted dragon, and even in the gloom of the cavern Quenelda could see the colour draining from his face. Instead, he only said, 'Yes, he will be carried in a cradle by four Imperials. They are outside, at the foot of the waterfall. Do you think he could manage to glide down to where they are? We have a surgeon with us.'

Quenelda nodded.

'Then we must cover his eyes. If he has spent ten moons in the mine, even the afternoon light will blind him.'

His companion, a young dwarf scout, beads braided in her dark hair, held up a heavy canvas hood with leather straps, as if asking Quenelda's permission.

'You will have to guide him.' Tangnost added.

They will cover your eyes, Storm. To protect them from the light . . .

But I do not want darkness . . .

One-Eye says you may damage your eyes if you do not cover them, and then it will always be dark. This is only until we reach the combs of Dragon Isle . . . We must go through the water one more time, but I will guide you . . . Can you open your wings one last time so that we may glide down to where they await us?

The great dragon raised his head wearily. *I will try, Dancing with Dragons . . .*

Root watched in horror as the injured dragon burst through the waterfall. Quenelda was struggling to raise Stormcracker's head to prevent a headlong rush to destruction upon the boulders below. He knew she would be using her growing powers, but they were not yet strong enough to come to the battledragon's rescue; he tumbled down as awkwardly as a new-born fledgling, before landing heavily on the ground.

Exhausted, Quenelda looked around the wide glen; at the grey slabs of craggy rock that jutted out from the base of the mountains, and the scree-covered lower slopes. Yellow gorse hedged the margins with a splash of colour.

With a chirrup of greeting and two swift bounds, a smaller Imperial darted forward to wrap Stormcracker's lacerated body in her own. Crooning softly, Soft Footfalls in the Air entwined her neck around his, raising his ruined head from the ground. The suppurating sores that marred his dull hide looked hideous compared to the brilliance of her scales; a sight that moved even the battle-hardened SDS troopers to tears of outrage.

Tangnost looked at the dragon with horror and doubt as they struggled to get him to his feet and furl his crumpled wings, wondering if he would ever grow strong enough to shed his old skin. If he couldn't, he would never fly again.

'Here . . .' The dwarf wrapped Quenelda in a warm cloak. 'Come and look.' He led her over to where a dozen engineers were unloading heavy equipment.

An SDS Major strode over, his armour blending into the growing shadows. 'Major DeMontfort.' He saluted Quenelda. 'Third Battalion Queen's Armourers. If you'll accompany me, Lady, I'll show you what we're going to do.'

Seeing her quizzical look as his crew rolled out a huge net and clipped it to four heavy chains, the major explained that it was a spider dragon net. Quenelda was still confused, and shook her head, trying to shed her own cobwebs. 'I don't understand. What are you doing with it?'

'We call it a field cradle,' the major went on. 'It's an idea your father came up with for returning injured dragons who could not fly from the battlefield, making use of your idea for critical-care cradles. It will be clipped onto a special harness on the escort Imperials.'

He led them over to the four dragons resting on the ground, pointing out the unusual harnesses and traces. 'I suggest you just rest with Stormcracker until we're ready for him.'

Quenelda nodded, and returned to the dragon's side: the surgeon was feeding him some field rations from a nosebag. Chirruping softly, Soft Footfalls in the Air urged him to eat more, cleaning his wounds with her rasping tongue.

The surgeon smiled at Quenelda. 'He's as ready as we can make him. Can you command him forward?'

Stormcracker followed Quenelda blindly into the padded centre of the net, his lowered nostrils almost tickling her head.

'I'll stay with him, keep him calm,' she said. Dusk was not far off now – she could hear the blackbirds calling in the thickets, and the cry of hunting wolves further down the glen.

Curl up, Stormcracker . . . Sleep if you can . . . Soon we'll be home, soon you'll be safe . . .

Home . . . home . . . The dragon obediently settled down, Quenelda coiled within his tail. Tangnost also chose to stay with him to monitor his progress. The web was clipped into place. It was all done quickly, efficiently.

The four Imperials rose up and spread their wings, their pilots checking that they were in no danger of getting entangled in the traces. Root took off beside them on his scouting Thistle dragon; he waved to Quenelda.

A horn rang out, short, long, short, long. As dark fell across the Western Highlands once again, tussocks of grass and heather were flattened as the Imperial Blacks took off from the floor of the glen to hold a hover at fifty strides. Abseiling down the bellies of their mounts, dwarf engineers checked the loading of the cradle straps. Quenelda signalled that everything was comfortable.

Within moments, the dragons were skyborne and heading southwest towards Dragon Isle.

* * *

It had been a long, tiring ordeal. Quenelda had slept fitfully, the rising and falling of the cradle lulling her and Stormcracker to sleep, only for the traumatized dragon to shake her awake with his restless nightmares. Flying for three days barely pausing for rest, they finally swept round the Dragonspine Mountains and into the Sorcerers Glen at dawn. Skilfully piloted, the dragons skimmed low across the loch, their cargo almost brushing the caps of the waves. Closer and closer the dragons sped towards the sheer, thousand-foot cliffs of Dragon Isle, and still they didn't slow. And then they were gone, as if the island had swallowed them whole.

CHAPTER FORTY-FOUR

An Unexpected Visitor

'Root Barkley to hangar deck three. Root Barkley to hangar deck three.'

'Wh-why do they want me?' Root stuttered when Tangnost roused him and told him to get dressed. 'It must be a mistake.'

The dwarf raised his eyebrows and remained silent, but his eye twinkled and a smile tugged at the corner of his mouth as he led Root to a porting stone. The world blurred, and Root wobbled as he stepped off – he was still half asleep. Tangnost led him out onto a small flight hangar. A figure was coming down from the pad, his back to them. He lowered his hood as he turned.

'Quester!' Root shouted with joy.

The two friends hugged each other. Quester seemed his usual cheery self, although he looked weary and there were dark shadows under his eyes. Root's heart suddenly thumped and his mouth went dry. *Chasing the Stars! Had something happened to Chasing the Stars?*

He could barely bring himself to ask when the hangar

crew parted to reveal a Widdershanks being unsaddled.

'Chasing the Stars!' Root stumbled and almost fell in his haste to climb onto the pad. Hearing his call, the mare leaped across, scattering the deck crew. Root flung himself at his beloved dragon, hugging her neck fiercely. She bugled softly, her tongue flicking out to wipe away the hot tears that tracked down the young gnome's cheeks. Deck and hangar crew stopped their work to smile at the noisy reunion. During these terrible times, good news like this was rare.

Root stood back to look at his dragon as she nuzzled him affectionately. A groom stepped forward with a feeding bag of honey tablets. Like Quester, the dragon looked well enough, although much thinner than Root remembered.

'Come on, girl.' He led her to an empty stall. 'Let's get you rubbed down.'

Quester was gulping down a second bowl of steaming porridge when Quenelda arrived. He was still trembling from his midnight flight to Dragon Isle. Tangnost had lit a pipe and was sitting quietly, letting the boy take his time. Root, who had just returned from bedding down Chasing the Stars, was not so patient.

'What has happened?' he prompted his friend. 'Why have you left Dragonsdome?'

'It's dreadful . . .' Quester's voice faltered. 'Felix DeLancy and his cronies are in charge. When you left' – he looked at Tangnost – 'the Earl appointed Felix Dragonmaster.'

'*Felix* is Dragonmaster?' Root could barely believe his ears.

'Yes! Even the roost masters and mistresses have to answer to him. He doesn't know what he is doing. The Lord Protector's men came to collect the remaining battledragons – an Imperial went on the rampage after they failed to put a dragon collar on properly. Two apprentices died – it was horrible!'

'*Died?*' Quenelda was aghast.

Quester nodded. 'Yes, Lady. They were torn to bits in the chaos. That's why I had to leave. Dragonsdome looks like a battlefield.'

'Which dragon were they trying to take?'

'Dangerous and Deadly.'

What the esquire had said suddenly sank in. 'But,' Quenelda said, frowning, 'Dangerous and Deadly is an

Imperial. They can't take them. Only the SDS is allowed to fly Imperials.'

Quester looked anxiously at Tangnost, who put a hand on Quenelda's knee, nodding at the boy to continue.

'Not any more, Lady. The Guild has changed the law. The Lord Protector may now breed and own Imperials.'

There was a stunned silence.

Quester suddenly remembered his task.

'A royal man-at-arms came secretly to Dragonsdome. He gave me this, Sir, from the Queen's Constable, to give to you by hand.'

Tangnost took the proffered scroll. Examining the wax seal, he broke it and his rugged face paled.

'What is it? Tangnost, what's wrong?' Quenelda's heart suddenly thumped. Was it bad news of her father?

The dwarf shook his head in disbelief. 'The Queen is betrothed to the Lord Protector. Once they are married, he will rule the Seven Sea Kingdoms through her! Then no one, not even the SDS, will be able to stop him!'

Chapter Forty-Five

Dragon Lord Down

Quenelda was sleeping under a blanket within Stormcracker's coils. Once again she was dreaming; he was dreaming. Four hearts merged until they beat as two, until the two were one dragon – one battledragon fighting for survival, fighting to protect his Dragon Lord, fighting and failing . . .

Boom . . . boom . . . Boom . . . boom . . . Boom . . . boom . . .

It was a familiar nightmare journey – a dream journey that had begun with the flight from the battlefield of the Westering Isles and would end here on Dragon Isle.

Dragonskull drums sounded. Up . . . Stormcracker was desperately trying to fill his damaged wings with air; trying to escape the carnage below. The blizzard was becoming worse, the wind howling.

Up he sprang into the sorcerous darkness. With every movement the grating bones in his injured hind leg flared white-hot with agony. Tendons burning, muscles aching, hearts pounding. A battlespell streaking through the air in front of him vented its power harmlessly in the sea. Another off to starboard struck one of the Razorbacks, which imploded. The splayed talons of Stormcracker's hind legs were caught by a Razorback rearing up from the frothy caps of the waves. He tasted salt in his mouth, stinging his eyes, raw on his injuries. The hull of an upturned transport rose beneath him, then dipped away into the trough of the swell.

He must leave this battlefield, bearing his wounded Dragon Lord away from the Dark Magic that was devouring everything in its path. He had never fled from a battle before, and anger burned hot inside as he turned eastward. He had but one task now: to take his Dragon Lord home.

The Earl swam into consciousness, the threads of his mind brushing those of Stormcracker. His wounds made him cry out. Quenelda gasped in her sleep as she saw her father through the night eyes of his battledragon; saw the terrible burns down his right face and side – the melted armour that welded him to his pilot's chair, the smoking ruin of his staff where corrosive Maelstrom Magic had eaten through his nexus.

He tried to turn his head, to call out, but his navigator

was clearly dead, his Bonecrackers also badly wounded. None could come to the Earl's aid. With his helmet gone and his staff burned beyond use, he could not reach his own Air Wing, let alone his Battlegroup – assuming there were other survivors in this white-out. Then the darkness swam and he lost consciousness.

The thread snapped, leaving Stormcracker alone again.

Kkkkkaaaaaaaaaaaarrrrrrrrrrkkkkkkkkkk!

The battledragon roared his loss into the night and Quenelda wept in her sleep, but the dragon's nightmare would not release them from its grip. The battledragon could feel movement on his back, but with every passing bell it lessened as more Bonecrackers and Marines died and slipped off him. He called throughout the long night, dragonsong vibrating through the night air.

No answer came.

Pain washed over Stormcracker in waves now, making it hard to focus, harder to fly. The cold was biting into his talons and wings, the weight of snow pushing him perilously close to the waves. Weakened scales had fractured. But two Imperials had joined his flight for sanctuary, both as badly injured as he.

Quenelda turned restlessly, caught within the coils of a familiar nightmare, and as she turned, the dream fragmented and broke. She reached out in her sleep, trying to hold the pieces together, for it always ended here. But this time the dream continued.

The deep green sea swell frothed below. It was littered with wreckage: the flat hulls of overturned ships; broken spars and rigging; frozen bodies, all deathly white, hard as ice. A riderless Frost dragon flew frantically past, heading for the open sea. A second followed, its pilot slumped around its neck. Up ahead, the ice shelf rose sheer to the horizon, and upon it stood a fortress of ice, ramparts glittering in the cold light.

The Earl came to. It was day. They were nearing the Ice Fortress and sanctuary. He could see dragons circling, and galleons at anchor rode the deep swell. Healers . . . warmth . . . revenge . . .

'Thank the Gods!' His voice was barely audible, unrecognizable even to himself as Stormcracker swept towards the fortress. He frowned through the pain. Something was wrong. No patrols had come out to escort him. Scouts should have found him bells before. Several galleons were on fire. There was fighting on the ramparts.

Had the hobgoblins attacked the garrison while the SDS were gone? Then he saw it: the banners that flew – the red adder on black!

'Cloak,' the Earl croaked. 'Cloak, Storm.' Combining what was left of their strength, they disappeared.

Treason!

A badly wounded Imperial was already putting down on the ice close to the fortress. Friendly faces below were encouraging the exhausted crew to dismount and then they were ruthlessly cut down by men bearing the badge of the Grand Master! There was a flash of sorcery, and the unwary dragon was despatched

Frantically banking Stormcracker to starboard as spells streaked out to where his position had been barely moments before, battledragon and Commander sought to put as much distance as possible between them and their forward base. Cursing, raging bitterly, the Earl turned Stormcracker south east, towards the distant Inner Isles and the mainland.

Quenelda cried out in her sleep as the images began to fade like smoke in the wind, then sank deeper into Stormcracker's nightmare. The blizzard raged. They were flying now, scant feet above the waves, hearts pumping weakly, weaving between huge icebergs that rose and fell on the deep sea swell.

Dark was falling winter-fast. There was a break in the snow-storm, but no land in sight. In the rapidly failing light the Earl had Stormcracker put down on one of the rolling icebergs, a dangerous, desperate manoeuvre. They woke to daylight. Freezing sea water encased the dragon's wings and armour, and many more of the critically injured had died in the night.

'Up, Storm!' The Earl urged his exhausted battle-dragon up, else they would all die. Stormcracker struggled weakly into the air, frost biting into his wings. Day followed endless night as they landed time after time, no longer knowing where they were in the endless blizzard. They must be flying in circles. And as each day passed, Stormcracker sensed the Earl slipping away, and the last of his own hope and strength fading.

Then the curtain of snow parted momentarily.

There! There were island cliffs directly up ahead, heron-grey, rising up to stark mountains. But they could not gain height – too injured, too tired. They would die at the foot of the cliffs, broken and freezing on the rocks.

Wait! There was a small sandy cove. The Earl turned

his dragon towards it. Now they were landing clumsily, tumbling, collapsing on the shale, as Stormcracker's wounded leg and wings gave way. Hot pain . . . oblivion took them all . . .

Voices drew them back – the familiar guttural language of the dwarfs. Longships were drawn up high on the beach, bright shields and sails the only colour in the rising storm. Clansmen were picking their way amongst the dead and wounded, careful of the dragon's dreadful injuries. Urgent voices called as they found the Earl. He was rambling, in a high fever, as they gently lifted him down a wing; then exhaustion and pain pulled the dragon down into darkness.

Stormcracker became aware that Thunder Rolling over the Mountains had gone; no sense of his bonded master existed. He roared his distress – roared until his strength left him.

Lost . . . So alone . . .

Tears rolled down Quenelda's cheeks. Dark days followed in the freezing cold, as winter storms lashed the coast. The dragon floated in and out of consciousness, alone with the dead and dying. And then, on a calm night, as the snow fell silently, the hobgoblins came. Swarming

. . . swarming up out of the sea. Dragons and ships and men arrived. The few Wingless Ones who had survived were questioned and killed by a tall scar-faced man dressed in black – the Lord Protector's Dragonmaster. Then another sorcerer's face, malevolent and pale, floated into the dream . . .

At the sight of that face, Stormcracker roared in his sleep. Panic flooded the sleeping dragon and girl.

'His Imperial is barely alive, my Lord.' Knuckle Quarnack watched the hobgoblins devour the dead with disgust.

'Where is the Earl?'

'There is no sign of him. We have searched the island. His seat is badly buckled and damaged and his navigator dead. We have found scores of dead Bonecrackers, but no trace of their master. Those few who were still alive knew nothing.'

'Impressive, the voice said thoughtfully, 'that they made it this far. Very well. I will break this dragon and make it mine – how the mighty SDS have fallen!'

With that, the Grand Master lifted his staff. A tear ripped through the air revealing a whirling darkness beyond that engulfed the mighty battledragon in its fearful embrace. Everything splintered into razor-edged shards and fragmented memories of cruelty and servitude, of cold iron and pain, and a never-ending darkness.

Lonely . . . so lonely . . .

Chapter Forty-Six

Dragon Quest

'Quenelda? Quenelda?' One of Tangnost's strong hands was gently shaking her; his voice was gruff with concern.

Quenelda woke with a start, shivering despite the heat in the roosts. Two Gulps Too Many's long tongue was washing her, the small dragon trilling anxiously at her distress.

'What is it, lass?' Tangnost's dark eye was troubled as he helped her free herself from the twisted blanket's grip. 'You're white as a ghost. You were shouting. Stormcracker was trying to flame . . .'

Quenelda swung round to look at the smoke still pouring from the battledragon's nostrils. He was still rumbling in his sleep. She turned her tawny eyes to the Dragonmaster.

'H-he *did* s-survive the battle. He and Storm, they landed on an island . . . And it *was* the Lord Protector,' she spat, 'who betrayed them.'

Tangnost helped her out from Stormcracker's coils, then quietly guided her to the officers' mess. Dragging a chair close to the fire, he motioned for her to sit, first dipping into the pan of hot milk on the range and giving her a steaming cup. Drawing deeply on his long curved pipe, he pulled up a stool and sat down in front of her.

'Lass' – he put a weathered hand on her knee – 'what makes you so sure your father survived?'

'S-Storm' – her hearts were beginning to slow as Two Gulps Too Many rested his little head on her knees – 'he knows. He remembers in his dreams.'

'Does he, now?' said Tangnost, leaning forward.

'The nightmares have always ended as I . . . as Storm's trying to get away over the battlefield. But this time there was more.'

'Go on,' he encouraged her.

'After escaping the battle, they flew through the night to high cliffs of ice with a great fortress. But the garrison was destroyed, and there were dead dragons everywhere on the ice. There were galleons flying . . . flying the . . .'

'Red adder on a black background?' Tangnost guessed.

Quenelda nodded. 'The Grand Master's men,' she whispered. 'He killed the survivors . . .'

'He betrayed the SDS; they flew into a trap.'

Tangnost's eye blazed. 'I knew it, in here.' He clenched his fist over his heart. 'Razorbacks – they are doubtless of his conjuring. And now he builds an army in the north greater than any in the Seven Sea Kingdoms, and all in the name of the Queen, soon to be his wife.' He shook his head. 'How very clever. The populace believe him to be a hero. He held the line in the north, relieved the besieged fortress of the Howling Glen. He alone kept the hobgoblins at bay, because they are his to command. The Guild give him whatever he asks for. They are blind to his ambition.'

'Papa then guided Stormcracker east towards the Inner or Northern Isles. He flew for days – putting down on icebergs till they reached land!'

'What?' Tangnost felt his heart leap. It was an exercise practised by the SDS for this campaign, but only for extreme emergencies. It was very dangerous, only the best pilots and highly trained dragons could do it. There was no way Quenelda could have known about it. 'I – I don't know where,' Quenelda continued. 'It never stopped snowing. But finally they put down on a tiny beach below high cliffs, and then longships came, and they found and rescued Papa . . .' Quenelda's voice cracked, anger sparked. 'Though they left Storm and the others. Left them to be killed by the hobgoblins!'

'Quenelda, don't be angry with my people. They could not have done otherwise. You need a battlegalleon to transport a single Imperial. The clans have no such ships. And even if they did, where would they have taken him? How do you hide an Imperial? Had they done so, all would know him for the Earl's dragon. It would have led them straight to your father. And as for leaving wounded men, they must have had good reason. We do not abandon our wounded to the hobgoblins. No, there was a purpose to it, ghastly though it seems.'

'Soon after,' Quenelda resumed. 'Soon after the hob-goblins and men came – the Lord Protector himself took Storm . . .' She trailed off, shuddering as she remembered that ugly rent in the sky that had devoured an Imperial. He . . . I don't know how, was taken . . . a dark castle . . . but Storm fought . . . despite his wounds, he fought . . . the Protector could not defeat his Elder magic, could not break his bond with Papa. So he was collared and sold into servitude in the mines. But, Tangnost' – Quenelda looked up at the dwarf, her eyes bright with hope – 'he's alive! We know Papa is alive! We know that he got away from the Westering Isles! We must find him – bring him home before the Queen is forced to marry! Papa will be able to stop the Lord Protector. He'll be—'

Tangnost put a hand out to gently touch hers. Quenelda looked quizzically at him. 'Quenelda,' he said gently. 'He may have long since died of his injuries. Or he may be too ill to challenge the Lord Hugo.'

'No!'

'Hush, lass.' The dwarf calmed her. 'If your father *is* alive, Quenelda, why hasn't he come home? We have to consider that question.'

For the first time since her father's disappearance, doubt crept into Quenelda's mind. 'Do you think he's dead?'

'No,' Tangnost said, shaking his head. 'I, too, believe your father is alive. Perhaps it is wishful thinking, but we have nothing to lose by trying to find him. We all loved him, and have suffered for it. Two Gulps,' he swallowed, 'died by my hand and you have been disinherited. Root, Quester and I are banished from Dragonsdome. Stormcracker has been badly wounded and is unlikely ever to be able to fly for the SDS again.' He smiled, crooked teeth catching the firelight.

'We will go and search for your father, who is at the

heart of all our worlds. But do not get your hopes up too high.' He gripped her hand, held it to his chest. 'I would not see you hurt again.'

But already he too was planning ahead. It was a huge responsibility he was taking on, and would require detailed planning.

'Autumn will soon be upon us,' he mused out loud. 'Stormcracker is still too weak for such an arduous quest. By the time he is fully recovered, flying conditions will be treacherous.'

'But Storm and you . . .' Quenelda protested. 'You've both flown and fought all over the Highlands and Islands, *and* you've trained to fly in winter.'

'I know, lass, but it's very dangerous – madness, many would say, to go on such a mission, especially at this time of year. And there are thousands of islands and inlets in the Inner and Northern Isles, and nigh on fifty dwarf clans live there, half of whom are seafaring. It's a vast area to search.'

He looked at Quenelda. 'Even if we do find your father,' he warned her, 'we may not be in time to prevent the Queen's marriage at the Midwinter Festival.'

But he, too, now held hope in his heart.

Chapter Forty-Seven
Broken Hearts

Physically, the dragon was slowly recovering. The best surgeons and dragonsmiths had worked their magic and the dragon's own strength and powers began to return. Two Gulps Too Many and Quenelda were rarely from his side, yet the dragon remained listless. Over the last moon, the ulcerated sores that covered his body had begun to crust over, and then close. Under Quenelda's guidance, several bones had been re-broken and reset, a tricky procedure, only made possible by her new-found assurance and skill in healing. Beneath the dulled tattered hide, hints of new-grown pebbled armour could be seen; and where it failed, the dragonsmiths had been grafting skilfully. But spiritually, the big dragon was dying, and everyone knew it – everyone except Quenelda.

'I'm more than satisfied with his progress, and yet there is no sign of him shedding his skin.' Tugging his long, luxuriant beard, Professor Rumspell, Dragon Isle's senior surgeon, hesitated, watching Quenelda assist a dragonsmith with the careful grafting of new skin onto

Stormcracker's tail. 'I'm guessing here, Dragonmaster, but I don't think his physical injuries are the problem any more, terrible though they are. Of course, he will never be operationally fit enough to fly with the SDS; his injuries are too severe to cope with battle manoeuvres. But he should be able to shed his skin, to fly once again – and yet he cannot.'

The surgeon sighed. 'I think it is guilt and grief combined. His spirit is broken. Without Quenelda he would already have died. He cares enough to respond to her, but it is not sufficient. He's slowly fading. A dragon raised by a Dragon Lord has an unbreakable bond – an echo of the Dragon Whisperers' bond. Without the Earl and the SDS, he's lost. It would be better had they both died rather than have him suffer this living death.'

Tangnost had a sudden thought. Thanking the surgeon, he strode over to Quenelda and Root, who were miserably watching the battledragon as he half-heartedly ate a small cauldron of brimstone offered by Quester. The youth had spent countless days waxing the huge dragon's pebbled hide and oiling his talons under Tangnost's guidance.

'We're approaching this the wrong way,' the dwarf announced.

'What do you mean?' Quenelda was instantly alert to the change in Tangnost's bearing.

'We're trying to get Stormcracker to shed his skin. Professor Rumspell says that physically he's mending, gaining in strength every day; that there's nothing stopping him trying to fly. But he'll never be a battle-dragon again, never fight with the SDS; his whole purpose in life is gone. It's a sickness of the spirit that is holding him back. He—'

'He's pining,' Quenelda finished for him. 'He's *pining*!' Hands on head, she shouted, suddenly alive, suddenly laughing, hugging Tangnost. 'Of course!' *How could I have missed something so obvious?*

'What?' Root looked baffled.

Tangnost nodded, knowing that Quenelda had understood. 'He's consumed by guilt,' he explained to Root. 'He sees no point in living because he believes he abandoned the Earl.'

'Tell him what we're planning, Quenelda.' He watched the battledragon. 'Tell him that if he gets fit enough, we're going to search for your father. Maybe that will make a difference, if he has something left to fight for.'

'Yes!' With a hopeful smile and a bounce in her step,

Quenelda went over, Root following behind. Stormcracker was yearning for her father – just like her! Why hadn't she realized that?

We are going to find Thunder Rolling over the Mountains? The battledragon's golden eyes lit up with sudden hope, and Quenelda knew with a rush of adrenaline that he was going to be alright.

Yes. One-Eye will help us . . .

Stormcracker shuddered, and let out a long soft breath, his muzzle lipping at Quenelda's shoulder. The glint in his eye grew stronger. He raised his massive head towards the sky and bellowed, an earth-shaking challenge that rattled the combs of Dragon Isle. A challenge had been thrown down to those who had betrayed the SDS.

But you must be strong. The path is treacherous. The No Wings who betrayed us will try and stop us, will try and kill us before we find him.

The dragon creatures from the Abyss . . . they will fight us?

Quenelda nodded. *You must be strong to defend us, to hide us. We have to find the path you took, find Thunder Rolling over the Mountains and then bring him home safely to roost here on Dragon Isle. We are going on a quest . . .*

I will be strong, Dancing with Dragons . . . the battle-dragon promised, smoke pouring from his nostrils. *I will build up my strength so that we can face the dark together.*

Stormcracker's eyes locked with Quenelda's, before he turned back to his food – only to find it gone. Curled up in the empty cauldron, Two Gulps Too Many burped happily in his sleep.

Chapter Forty-Eight

Rising from the Ashes

'Look.' Quenelda grinned as the first frosts turned the gantries and landing pads of Dragon Isle white.

Root followed her gaze. Stormcracker was crunching his way through a Highland cow with obvious relish. The gnome couldn't see anything unusual, and now it barely made him queasy to watch. For the last two weeks, the dragon had barely raised his muzzle from the feeding troughs. Despite that, he was looking in even worse condition: whole sections of his skin had sloughed off and were hanging in tatters, but he didn't want to upset her by mentioning that.

He shrugged casually. 'I can't see anything . . .'

'Wait – wait and watch,' Quenelda said mysteriously.

Head raised, Stormcracker gulped down the last chunk of still-warm meat with a satisfied crunch. Then he leaned against a roost pole so hard that bits of his skin peeled away. Walking over, with Root at her heels, Quenelda reached down and picked up a piece of skin that had fallen off and gave it to her esquire, who looked at it blankly then returned it to Quenelda.

'He's shedding his skin, silly!' She was grinning from ear to ear. 'He's shedding his skin! He's going to be all right. He's going to be able to fly again!' She clasped Root in a hug. 'We're going to search for Papa!'

'Can we do it?' Quenelda was exhausted after a long week of exercises with Stormcracker, strengthening the battledragon's wing tendons and muscles. She watched Tangnost, followed by Quester, complete his careful inspection, Two Gulps Too Many waddling solemnly behind. On his unconventional diet, the little dragon was growing so fast that he kept tripping up the Dragonmaster with his huge feet; Tangnost was resisting a growing urge to kick the fledgling.

Quenelda knew that getting the big dragon fit to fly to the frozen north was the least of the challenges facing them if they were to find her father. Doubts were beginning to assail her.

'We've only been as far as the Brimstones. I don't know how long this journey will take, or where it will lead us. I don't know' – Quenelda bit her lip: she didn't have the right to ask Root to give up everything for her –

for her quest; he'd already given so much – 'whether we'll . . .'

'Whether we'll ever come back?' Root finished for her as he slid down to sit at her side, resting his head against one of Stormcracker's huge talons. 'I know that it will be very dangerous; that we'll be hunted by hobgoblins and the Lord Protector.' He smiled crookedly. Once he would have been petrified. He *was* petrified! 'But think what the bards will have to sing about us in the future!'

Root grinned as Stormcracker's head swung round to consider them both through grave, golden eyes. As he gave the huge battledragon a pat on the nose, Quenelda realized how much he had changed; how much they had all changed.

'Think about it!' Root said. 'A quest to find a lost Dragon Lord; led by a legendary Bonecracker – the Earl's shield – a Dragon Whisperer, and an apprentice made esquire, all flying on an injured battledragon brought back from the dead! How can we possibly fail?'

Waddling over to nestle against Stormcracker, Two Gulps Too Many hiccupped happily. Root ducked. Quenelda laughed as the noxious yellow flame licked about her. 'Don't worry – we won't leave you behind!'

Quenelda and Root's first thrilling adventure:

Imagine you could talk to dragons . . .

Quenelda has always had a magical bond with dragons, and her greatest wish is to fly one and fight alongside her father in the brutal war against the hobgoblins.

Root's greatest wish is to avoid fearsome, fire-breathing dragons at all costs, so when he is made Quenelda's esquire, sparks start to fly.

But an unexpected friendship is forged, and when Dragonsdome is threatened by a deadly plot, this unlikely duo must find a way to defeat the dark forces.

Epic battles, whispered legends and soaring magic weave together in this breathtaking debut fantasy.

'Captivating' *Sunday Times*

Also available from Random House Children's Books:

'The sleeping dragon awakes!'

Aeons ago, winged dragons spread terror across the Chinese empire. Their descendants, magnificent horses bred and ridden by the Wild Horsemen, are known as dragon horses.

But now an ancient evil is stirring – and two brothers are about to be drawn into battle. Rokshan must travel to the Valleys of the Horsemen - and onto the Plain of the Dead, where the great stallion Stargazer, lord of the horses, is waiting for him. While his brother, An Lushan, chooses a different path entirely . . .

'Intensely colourful . . . an epic adventure' *Telegraph*

'Dangerous journeys and desperate battles, treacherous enemies and loyal friends' *Books for Keeps*

Two swords, angled for slicing, came whirring towards my chest. My block was simple: a step of the back leg, a shift of weight, my right sword joining the left in front of me, cutting side slanted down. His blades hit mine. The impact resonated through my arm bones.

Does young Eon have the power to become a Dragoneye? Now the years of gruelling training, under a ruthlessly ambitious master, will be put to the test: it's time for the terrifying Rat Dragon to choose his next apprentice.

Halli loves the old stories from when the valley was a wild and dangerous place – when the twelve legendary heroes stood together to defeat the ancient enemy, the bloodthirsty Trows.

Longing for adventure, he tries to liven things up by playing practical jokes. But when one goes too far, he reawakens an old blood feud and finds himself on a hero's quest after all. Along the way he meets a ruthless thief, a murderous rival, and a girl who may just be as fearless as he is . . .

An epic saga with a funny, unique spin, and an unforgettable anti-hero.

'Quite simply stunning' *The Guardian*